# VENGEANCE

# VENGEANCE

A NOVEL

CLAIR M. POULSON

Covenant Communications, Inc.

Cover image *Handcuffed* © Images by Trista courtesy of iStockphtography.com

Cover design copyright © 2011 by Covenant Communications, Inc.

Published by Covenant Communications, Inc.
American Fork, Utah

Printed in Canada
First Printing: March 2011

17 16 15 14 13 12 11     10 9 8 7 6 5 4 3 2 1

ISBN-13: 978-1-60861-193-5

To my twenty-one grandchildren. They keep me young and inspired.

# ACKNOWLEDGMENTS

Thanks to the wonderful staff of the *Eurodam*. They provided much of the inspiration for this story.

And special thanks to Kirk Shaw, with whom I have worked on several books now. Kirk is a great editor, and I feel fortunate to work closely with him.

# PROLOGUE

Aubree shrank in the witness chair under the withering gaze of George Sedwig, one of the most successful defense attorneys in the state of California. Of course, being only eight, Aubree knew nothing of his fame, but she was keenly aware of his irritation with her. With an effort, she drew her eyes from him and cast a furtive glance at her father, who was seated beside the attorney's partner. Stone Lansing's hair was ebony like hers, and his dark brown eyes matched her own in both their intensity and their chocolate brown color. But his eyes were closed now, as they had been for most of the time since she'd taken the stand.

The attorney was saying something, but the words slipped Aubree's grasp as at that moment Stone's eyes snapped open and met her own. His gaze burned with anger and something else she couldn't identify, and she drew in a sharp gasp as the attorney rapped his pen on the side of the stand nearest her. Yes, the attorney frightened her. But she feared her own father even more.

"Aubree, answer my question," George Sedwig said sternly. He hooked his thumbs through the belt loops at his ample waistline and adopted an impatient stance. His small mouth was screwed up tightly as he waited for her response, and his dark, close-set eyes scrutinized her closely.

She tried to speak, but her voice broke as the tenuous courage she'd gathered in preparation for this day collapsed. "I . . . don't remember what you asked," she finally managed to stammer in a tiny voice.

"Speak up so you can be heard!" the attorney said so loudly that Aubree winced as if she had been slapped. She wanted nothing more than to be off this stand and out the door. Her father closed his eyes once more, but the furrow between his brows grew deeper.

The prosecutor was on her feet in an instant. "Your Honor," she said furiously, "this witness is just a little girl." She cast a sharp glance toward George Sedwig. "Please instruct counsel to be gentle with her. This isn't exactly easy for her."

The Honorable Edwin Edwards nodded and instructed, "Counsel, approach the bench." When both attorneys stood before him, he said, "Mr. Sedwig, calm down. You are getting nowhere by badgering this young witness." Then, before the lawyer could respond, he turned his head to the veteran prosecutor and said, "You called her, Ms. Kellerman, and she must answer Mr. Sedwig's questions. Would you like a moment to speak with her and instruct her accordingly?"

"Yes, thank you, Your Honor," Danielle Kellerman responded.

"Have her ready when you get back." The judge rapped his gavel briskly and announced, "We are adjourned for ten minutes."

Relieved, Aubree left the stand and hurried straight to Danielle Kellerman, who led her out of the courtroom. As they left, she couldn't help but notice that her father was talking with his attorney, his expression furious. Aubree fought the urge to cry, and she put her head down, focusing on putting one foot in front of the other until the door shut behind them.

Ten minutes later, after a reassuring talk with the prosecutor and the victim's advocate, Aubree reentered the courtroom and, trembling only slightly, retook the stand. Following Danielle's advice, she stifled the urge to look at her father—who was on trial for murder.

George Sedwig approached the stand again, but Aubree remained composed this time, determined to answer his questions the very best she could without becoming frightened. She held her head high, kept her hands folded neatly in her lap, and looked straight at the attorney. Over and over in her mind, she repeated the words she'd been told in the recess: *you have friends in this courtroom.*

"I'm sorry if I upset you," Mr. Sedwig began, glancing toward the judge, his voice soft and restrained. "I like children. I raised three of my own and I have several grandchildren. But what we are doing here today is very important. So please think very carefully about what I am about to ask you."

Aubree nodded her head, causing her thick black hair to fall into her eyes. She brushed it back with one hand and attempted to sit up straighter. She remembered Danielle Kellerman's advice. All she had to do was tell what she saw and what she remembered. *They can't make me answer a question I don't know the answer to,* she reminded herself.

George Sedwig cleared his throat and asked, "Did you see your father kill the man whose body you saw on the floor in your house?"

Aubree thought a moment. "No," she said slowly.

"So you don't *know* that he actually killed the victim then, do you, Aubree?"

Aubree folded her hands in her lap in an effort to stop them from shaking. Then she said softly, "Daddy had blood on his hands. I saw it."

"That wasn't my question!" George Sedwig's voice wasn't soft anymore. "Please just say yes or no. I know you can do that. Did you see your father shoot Olin Gentry?"

Though Aubree was certain of her father's guilt, she answered truthfully when she ducked her head and said, "No."

"Now, let's review for a moment what you *did* see so that the jury can understand exactly what the truth is." He nodded at the twelve men and women who were all watching Aubree like circling vultures. "You were hiding in the closet of your parents' bedroom—is that what you said?"

"Yes."

"And why were you in that closet?"

"I was playing with my dolls," Aubree answered. "I like to play in there."

"Weren't you actually hiding from your nanny, Bridget Summer?" he asked, leaning toward her, his eyes narrow, his lips so tight that they had turned white at the edges.

Aubree thought about the question for a moment. It had all happened months ago. She couldn't remember everything as clearly anymore. But suddenly she did remember the answer to this question. Bridget had been her new nanny, and she hadn't seemed to like children much. That morning, Bridget had scolded Aubree for not eating every last bite of her cereal. She had even threatened to not give Aubree any lunch. So Aubree had licked her bowl clean then left the kitchen in tears and headed for her favorite hiding place, the huge closet off the master bedroom. She kept dolls hidden there behind the rows and rows of shoes her mother seldom wore.

"We're waiting," Mr. Sedwig said.

"Yes, I was hiding from her, but I play there a lot," Aubree said, her chin quivering. "It's my favorite place to be alone."

"Was Miss Summer having a fight with her boyfriend that morning?" he asked.

Aubree tried hard to remember, furrowing her brow in thought. The man who had died in her parents' bedroom was Miss Summer's boyfriend. But Aubree had no idea if she had been fighting with him that morning. But maybe that was why she had been so mean at breakfast, Aubree reasoned to herself.

"We're waiting," Mr. Sedwig said again.

"I'm trying to remember," Aubree said, shifting nervously in the big witness chair. "I don't know if they were or not. I didn't see them fighting."

"But they fought a lot, didn't they?"

"I don't know," Aubree said honestly. "Miss Summer's boyfriend didn't come to the house very much."

George Sedwig nodded. "But he was there that day because someone killed him right there in the bedroom," the attorney said. "Why don't you tell us what else you saw and heard that morning while you were hiding from Miss Summer."

The attorney helped Aubree remember and testify about the rest of the morning—especially the heated argument she'd heard while playing in the big closet full of clothes and shoes. One of the voices had been her father's. Mr. Sedwig pressed her, trying to get her to tell the court that one of the voices had been Miss Summer's. But Aubree honestly didn't remember; she guessed that it could have been. She was sure, however, that one voice belonged to Olin Gentry, because he had been especially loud. Aubree also told the attorney that there had been at least one more voice that she didn't recognize at some point during the argument, a man's voice.

When Aubree heard a loud bang, she had become frightened and forgotten her dolls. She had fearfully worked her way through the closet to the door. After a few minutes she had gathered her courage and quietly pushed the door slightly open and peeked through the crack. What she saw frightened her more than anything she'd ever experienced.

Aubree had seen her father standing over Olin Gentry's body, his hands dripping with blood and holding a gun. He'd stood there for a moment, his expression contorted and his hand shaking. Then he had glanced at the closet door. She didn't know if he had seen her, but she was afraid that he might have. She moved back from the door, trembling with fear. A moment later, she heard something drop to the floor and footsteps recede across the room. She listened as the bedroom door shut. Trembling fiercely, she had peeked once more. The gun was lying beside the body and her father was gone. She pulled the closet door shut, and, hugging herself in the darkest corner of the closet, she'd stayed there for hours. It was only when police officers entered the bedroom that she'd finally revealed herself. Today in court was the first time she'd seen her father since that devastating day.

Try as he might, George Sedwig could not get her to change her testimony in any way. She knew what she'd seen, and the image of her father with blood on his hands and holding a gun was burned permanently into her brain.

When Aubree's turn on the stand was finally over, others were called to testify, helping Danielle Kellerman build a strong circumstantial case against Stone. It was established that he had argued with the dead man, Olin Gentry, at a local bar just two evenings before the murder. And on several occasions he'd been overheard telling Miss Summer not to allow the man in his house or they'd both regret it. The murder weapon was entered as evidence—a pistol belonging to Stone with his fingerprints on it. It had been found lying beside the body.

A few days later, Stone Lansing was found guilty of second-degree murder. Members of the jury told the press that they were convinced the killing had not been premeditated but had occurred in the heat of an intense argument, which Aubree had overheard. They also stated that they had been swayed heavily toward Stone's guilt by the testimony of his young daughter.

Stone went to prison proclaiming his innocence. But no one, not even his wife or daughter, believed him. He entered prison an angry, defeated man.

# CHAPTER ONE

*Ten Years Later*

Sunlight streamed through the small jail cell window, causing Stone Lansing to smile to himself. It seemed much brighter to him now than it had each morning for the past ten years. Before, it had been only a cruel reminder of the outside world and the freedom that had been denied him. But all that was about to change. Within a few hours he would feel the rays of the sun on his back as he left the prison gates a free man.

His smile faded as a cloud passed beneath the sun. He thought of the daughter whose testimony had helped to seal his fate. Though she'd been only eight at the time, the jury had believed every word she'd said. Her testimony, combined with that of the other witnesses who had lined up to get their shot at him in court, had been enough to send him to this miserable place for almost a decade.

Aubree was eighteen now, old enough to recognize that what she had done had cost him a lot of good years, a lucrative advertising business, and his marriage to her mother. Stone sighed and turned to the small mirror in the cell and examined his face. In the subdued light of the jail cell, his brown eyes looked almost black. His curly black hair had been recently cut, and even at this hour of the morning every strand was in place. However, there were now gray hairs scattered through the black. Though he hadn't seen Aubree in person since that day in court, he'd seen pictures of her with her mother on TV and in magazines and knew that she looked as much like him as ever. *She's her father's child,* he thought as a wave of bitter irony overtook him.

As the minutes ticked by, Stone continued to stand at the window, drumming his fingers against the edge. As always, his thoughts turned eventually to his wife—his ex-wife, now. Though Aubree had testified, Vanessa had respectfully kept her mouth shut. He'd been grateful at the time, even though it hadn't been enough to save him. But the gratitude had withered when, only a few months after he'd been sent to prison, he'd learned of her own painful betrayal. She had divorced him, sold his business, and kept most of the profits. His attorney had been successful in convincing the judge who presided over the divorce to place fifty thousand dollars in a bank account that Stone could access following his release from prison, but it was a pittance compared with what had been lost. In more ways than one, Vanessa had left him a poor man. Stone gritted his teeth as he thought of her new husband, Reginald Kern, a law partner of George Sedwig. It was only one of a long list of ironies that they had been brought together through the very events that had torn the Lansings' marriage apart. So, for obvious reasons, when George Sedwig had died of a heart attack about the time that the appeal process had begun to move forward, Stone had dismissed Reginald and retained new counsel to handle the appeal.

Stone forced his clenched jaw to relax and sat down, facing away from the light of the window. There was nothing he could do about Vanessa's marriage. But he did intend to lobby for a return of the money that had been taken from him. If it was only Vanessa who had it, he might walk away. But the thought of his wealth being enjoyed by Reginald Kern . . . that he couldn't stand.

He flinched as his cellmate, Andy, a large man with a missing front tooth, rolled over in the top bunk and looked down at where Stone sat. "It's your big day, eh?" Then his face fell slightly and he added, "Wish I was going with you."

"You turn will be here before you know it," Stone said, though he knew the words sounded hollow. Time spent in prison went by anything but quick.

"I wish," Andy responded with suddenly moist eyes. "I miss my kids more than anything. When I get out, you can bet it'll be for good."

Stone nodded in agreement, hoping for Andy's sake that it was true. He'd heard a lot of men say those words—and had seen a lot of them come and go more than once. And though Stone likewise had no intention of ever seeing the inside of a prison again, he knew he couldn't guarantee it.

Stone stared at the wall a moment in silence. Then, his face still turned away from his bunkmate, he said in a low voice, "I look forward to seeing my kid too."

Andy's expression tightened, and he sat up in the bunk. "Now, come on, Stone. She was just a kid when she testified," he said.

Stone ignored Andy's comment. He'd dreamed of this day for the past ten years, and he had no intention of changing his plans. He hoped fervently that what he planned to do would help make up for all the time he had lost.

Andy shook his head and muttered something unintelligible as he lay back down and pulled his blanket over his head.

A few hours later, with his release money in his pocket, Stone walked out of the prison a free man. He took a deep breath and looked around him. The sun was still shining brightly, the air was fresh and clean, and his mind was clear. It was time to make things right, and he knew what he had to do.

\* \* \*

IT WAS LATE AFTERNOON AS Aubree sprinted to the far end of the tennis court to retrieve a ball for Brandi, laughing as she ran. It had been a beautiful day, and Aubree and her adopted twin siblings, Brandi and Ryan, had spent most of it playing in the huge backyard of their sprawling Malibu estate. "Great serve, Brandi!" Aubree called, and was rewarded by a sunny smile from the blonde-haired, blue-eyed eight-year-old standing on the other side of the net.

"Do you think they'll have tennis courts on the ship?" Ryan asked, coming to stand beside his sister.

Aubree smiled. The three of them had been discussing their upcoming cruise on the Baltic Sea for weeks now, and as the trip grew closer it was all the twins could talk about. "Who knows?" she replied. "There's a pool on board. Why not a tennis court?"

"Are you sure that Mommy *and* Daddy are going to be able to come on the cruise with us?" Ryan asked as he swatted at a bee with his racket, his lips turned down in the beginnings of a pout.

Aubree hesitated, wanting to reassure her little brother but not wanting to give him false hope. She loved her mother, Vanessa, dearly, but despite what Vanessa spent on her children in money, she was skimpy with them in time. It was almost expected that the glamorous model would have an urgent client meeting come up or that a last-minute photo shoot would intervene with plans, no matter how carefully laid. Aubree understood that her mother was busy—after all, Vanessa was very much in demand. She appeared on the cover of magazines on a regular basis, and she even owned her own studio. But Aubree sometimes secretly wished that she had a little more time and a little less money.

Reginald Kern, the man Aubree's mother had married after her husband went to prison, had a demanding career as well, and his work as an attorney seemed to dominate his life. Aubree's brow furrowed as she thought of her stepfather. At first, Aubree had struggled in overcoming her fear of Reginald simply because he'd been the law partner of Stone's defense attorney, George Sedwig, and had sat beside Stone during the trial. But her fear had subsided as he treated her and Vanessa with respect. Though at fifty-eight, Reginald was sixteen years Vanessa's senior, her beauty regimen made her look even younger than she was, and people often mistook her for Reginald's daughter—something Vanessa took pride in. Aubree didn't know what to think about that. Reginald was not home much, but when he was, he spent part of his time with his wife and the kids. For the twins' sake, Aubree hoped that this time everything would work out so that the family could spend a much-needed vacation all together. "I think they'll both be able to come, Ryan," she said finally then changed the subject quickly before he saw the doubt in her face. "Come on, you two. Let's practice serving some more." As the three turned back to their game, Aubree was startled to see Vanessa emerge from the house and begin running down the long brick path to the tennis court. Aubree hadn't even known she was home, and she was not remotely prepared for what Vanessa said when she reached them, her pale green eyes filled with concern.

Out of breath, Vanessa smoothed her gray silk skirt and attempted to regain her composure. Glancing at the twins, she said in a falsely cheery voice, "All right, you two, why don't you get a drink of water while I talk to Aubree for a second."

Ryan and Brandi exchanged a concerned look but obediently shuffled toward the drinking fountain. When they were out of earshot,

Vanessa put her hand on her daughter's arm and began to speak in a low voice, her expression darkening. "None of this should have happened. I can't believe they didn't give us more notice than this . . ." She twisted a strand of red hair nervously around her finger.

"More notice for what, Mom? You're worrying me."

Vanessa sighed and then leveled her gaze with Aubree's. "Honey, your father is out of prison."

"What!" Aubree recoiled at the words, her head spinning.

"Reginald just found out and called me at the studio," Vanessa continued. "He couldn't get out of court, so he asked me to come home to tell you." Her face was lined with fear.

"But, Mom, he can't be getting out already!"

"That's what I thought, but apparently he became eligible for early parole . . ." Vanessa trailed off, glancing toward the twins, who were now playfully splashing one another at the water fountain. Turning back to her daughter, she drew in a deep breath. "Aubree, I don't want to frighten you any more than you already are, but I need to tell you a few things—for your own safety."

"Okay," Aubree said weakly, feeling as if she were about to collapse.

Vanessa closed her eyes. "After Reginald and I got married, he told me about a conversation he'd had with George Sedwig before he died. He was . . . very disturbed by it." Tears formed in Vanessa's eyes, but she continued. "George told Reginald that before Stone went to prison, he vowed he would get revenge on you for testifying in court. Reginald said that Stone blames you that he went to prison." She shook her head as the tears fell. "But it was my fault. I should never have allowed you to testify."

"I was just a little girl," Aubree said desperately, her fists clenched tightly against her chest. "All I did was tell the judge and jury what I knew. So did a lot of other people. If we hadn't, Dad would have gotten away with what he did."

"I know that, Aubree, but that's not how Stone sees things. Reginald is afraid that he might also harm the twins. And me as well, for marrying someone else." Vanessa began to tremble. "Apparently he said that after he was through with me, nobody would be interested in putting my face on their magazines."

Aubree shuddered. "Can't we get a restraining order, or . . . or something?" she asked weakly.

"Reginald is working on that. But a restraining order is just a piece of paper. I worry whether it's enough."

"Mom, I'm scared. What can we do?" Aubree cried as her contented life came crashing down around her.

A determined look crossed Vanessa's face. "First I need to explain to the twins a little of what's happening. I don't want to scare them, but I need them to understand that this is a very serious situation." When Aubree nodded, she continued. "Then I'd like to call a friend of mine—Kevin Jensen. You might remember him, actually. He's a police officer who's worked security on some of his days off for several of my higher profile modeling jobs. I want to get his advice. Then, when Reginald gets home, we'll figure out a plan to keep you safe."

Aubree nodded once more, finding some comfort in her mother's words.

"I'll keep you safe, Aubree. I promise. Reginald and I will see to it." She seemed thoughtful for a moment. "Brandi? Ryan? I need to talk to you for a minute."

When the twins had rejoined them, Vanessa knelt in front of them and related, in less specific terms, the conversation she and Aubree had just had. However, this time her expression was calm and her green eyes were comforting. Yet when she finished, Brandi and Ryan edged closer to their mother until they were in her arms.

"Will the bad man find us?" Brandi whimpered, clutching her brother's hand and her mother's shoulder.

"No, darling. You don't need to worry," Vanessa soothed. But beneath the comforting words, Aubree could hear the unmistakable pitch of fear.

* * *

That evening as Aubree sat curled on the sofa in the large family room, she put an arm around the twins' shoulders and attempted to smile for their benefit. Though the servants had been warned and the mansion's expensive alarm system had been armed, she felt more vulnerable than ever before. Vanessa and Reginald had been in the next room for more than an hour now, discussing what they would do. But they kept their voices low, and Aubree had been unable to decipher anything of what they were saying.

Earlier in the evening, Vanessa had spoken with Kevin Jensen, who had advised her to press forward with the restraining order and to keep him apprised of their plans. He had also volunteered to assign one of his men to monitor Stone's activities until further notice. When Aubree heard this, she had felt a little better, but as darkness fell over the estate, she imagined her father in every shadow.

A few minutes later, Reginald entered the family room followed by Vanessa. Brandi and Ryan bolted from the couch toward their father, who scooped them up in a bear hug and carried them, one in each arm, giggling toward the sofa. Vanessa sat beside him, and when the twins' laughter had subsided, Reginald spoke. "Your mother and I have gone back and forth about this." He looked toward Vanessa, who nodded. "And although we're not wild about the idea, we believe you'll be safest here. The mansion is protected by a top-of-the-line security system, and the servants have been warned not to let anyone in and to call the police at the slightest sign that something isn't right. Aubree, tomorrow you'll skip your violin lessons and your riding class. Brandi and Ryan, I've called and excused you from your summer day camp. Francesca and Aubree will look after you."

Vanessa spoke up. "I talked to Kevin Jensen earlier this evening, and he seemed to agree that this is the best idea, given the situation." Her eyes flitted down and she added, "I'm sorry one of us can't take off work to be here, but Daddy and I both have jam-packed days tomorrow. Kevin gave me the number for his cell phone, and if anything at all should happen, you can call him. He told me he could have an officer here in as little as five minutes."

Aubree nodded slowly. "That sounds okay. I guess it's only really one more day until we leave for the cruise."

Reginald cleared his throat and Vanessa sighed, quietly saying, "Most of us will be. I'm sorry, kids, but the trial setting on one of Reginald's cases has been moved up and will prevent him from coming."

"I also want to make sure that everything possible is being done here with the restraining order," Reginald interjected with a slight frown.

Aubree winced at the look of disappointment on Brandi's and Ryan's faces. "You're not coming, Daddy?" Ryan asked as his chin began to quiver.

"I know you're disappointed, champ. I wanted to come so much. I told the superior court judge about our trip—that we've had it planned for months—but he doesn't seem to care. I even asked if another attorney could cover for me, but the judge says I have to be here for the trial because the defendant is my client." He paused, looking sadly at the twins. "I'm sorry, but this is beyond my control."

Brandi jumped to her feet. "Daddy, that's not fair," she cried, balling her little hands into fists at her sides.

"I know, Brandi, but there's nothing I can do about it. Believe me, I would if I could. You guys and your mom and Aubree will still be able to go, and I promise I'll make it up to you somehow."

Brandi refused to look at him and simply shook her head.

His patience clearly wearing thin, Reginald reached out to take Brandi's hand in his. Then he said in a low voice, "Do you understand what Mommy has told you about the bad man? That this man wants to hurt or even kill Aubree and possibly you two as well?"

Brandi nodded fearfully as the color drained from her face. Reginald's expression turned thoughtful, and he looked at Aubree. "Before George died, he told me everything Stone had said about you and your mother—every threat and every evil intention. I won't repeat it now, because I don't want to scare you any more than you already are. But I do want you to understand that I'm taking this situation very seriously."

Running to her mother and burying her face in Vanessa's shoulder, Brandi began to cry. Ryan glanced from Reginald to Vanessa, then followed his sister. Vanessa stroked Brandi's hair for a moment, then stood and took the twins by the hand. "We're all tired and very worried," she said to Reginald with a frown. "Aubree, will you tell Francesca that Ryan and Brandi are ready for their baths? I think we'll all feel better after a night's rest."

A few hours later, Aubree stood in the darkness of the twins' bedroom door and watched her siblings for a moment before making her way to her own bedroom. They looked so peaceful in their beds. They had no real idea of the danger that they were all in—a lucky thing for them. Brandi's long blonde hair was strung over her pillow, almost like a halo. Her pretty face was relaxed as she slept, her lips curved in a half smile. Ryan's blond curls covered his ears and crept over the collar of his pajamas. He moaned in his sleep and turned, one arm reaching out to pull his stuffed dog closer. Aubree felt a catch in her throat as she remembered Reginald's words. *This man wants to hurt or even kill Aubree and possibly you two as well.* How could anyone want to hurt her or these children?

Tears filled her eyes, and she rubbed at them as she quietly left the room, closing the door behind her. Once again, the image of her father's bloody hands came into her mind, along with a horrible thought. Maybe next time it would be her blood that stained them.

# CHAPTER TWO

STONE LANSING WAS WELL AWARE that he wasn't exactly up to speed on the goings-on of the outside world. In all, he had been on the inside for a total of almost eleven years: nearly one year in jail awaiting his trial, and then ten years in prison. The most pressing example lay with his estranged family. Though he had seen their pictures from time to time in various newspapers that had been allowed in the prison, he had no idea where his ex-wife and daughter now lived. As he walked, he mulled over the possible ways of locating them. But even as he considered them, he knew that finding his ex-wife and daughter would be the least of his difficulties.

*First things first,* he thought with a sigh, patting his nearly empty pockets. Although he had the money he'd been given when he walked out of the prison—money every parolee received—he'd spent much of that on a hotel room and food the previous night. Until he could access his bank account, he wouldn't be able to purchase new clothes, transportation, or anything else he needed to begin a new life on the outside. He knew that there should be well over fifty thousand dollars in his account—unless Vanessa had somehow gotten ahold of that as well.

Looking at the clock and seeing it was nearly nine, Stone prepared to leave the hotel room, intending to visit the bank as soon as it opened. Then, at long last, he would be prepared to set in motion the plan that had consumed him for the last ten years.

\* \* \*

"I'm bored, Aubree!"

Aubree smiled and put down her hairbrush as she turned to face Brandi. "I'm sorry you have to stay in all day, pumpkin." As Ryan appeared at the doorway as well, she reached out to tousle his golden curls. "Have you two already eaten breakfast?"

"Yeah, Francesca made eggs. The runny kind," Ryan said grumpily.

"Uh-oh. Well, I'll tell you what. After I'm finished getting ready, we'll play a board game. Sound good?"

The twins' expressions brightened, and they nodded eagerly.

"Okay, then, you two pick one out and get it set up. I'll be down in a minute."

As her siblings hurried down the long hallway, Aubree turned back to the mirror, running the brush through her long black hair a few more times. When she was finished, she studied herself for a moment with a critical eye. Vanessa often told her that she would one day be a model like her—that she had the looks, the slender build, the grace, and the smile that would take her to the top of the profession. In fact, Aubree had already been photographed with her mother a number of times, and her own picture had appeared in several magazines. However, though she was glad that her small ventures into the world of modeling pleased her mother, her heart simply wasn't in it. She was enrolled to begin college in the fall at UCLA, and she was much more interested in studying business management—something Francesca Bruno, the Kernses' cook, who also looked after the children, encouraged. She smiled as she thought of the short, stout Italian woman. Francesca had been with the Lansing/Kern family for as long as Aubree could remember, and she and Aubree had developed a close friendship—even if she did make runny eggs.

With one last glance in the mirror, Aubree turned and headed downstairs to play with the twins. She glanced at the clock and, seeing it was only nine forty-five, sighed. It was going to be a long day. Though she felt much calmer after a good night's sleep, she was certain that the hours until her parents came home weren't exactly going to fly by.

* * *

Stone Lansing had plenty of money in his pocket now. With a relieved sigh, grateful that at least his pittance of an account had been preserved, he stepped back out into the street and headed toward the nearest pay phone with a determined step. Digging in his pocket for some change, he slipped the coins into the slot and then thumbed through the phone book. When he had located the number he wanted, he leaned back against the booth and waited as the rings sounded in his ear. He knew it was a long shot, but it was somewhere to start.

"Pinnacle Studios, this is Russ," a young male voice answered brightly.

"Hello, I'm trying to reach Vanessa L—" Stone coughed to cover up his mistake and finished, "Kern."

The young man's voice took on a note of irritation. "I'm sorry, but Vanessa is unavailable."

Stone waited a moment, but when Russ didn't ask him to leave a message, he pressed. "Do you know when I might be able to reach her?"

"I'm sorry, but no. Who did you say you were? Vanessa is a very busy, very in-demand model, and anybody who actually has a valid need to talk to her has her cell phone number."

Stone bristled but forced himself to keep his cool. Thinking quickly, he replied, "My name is James Patton, and Vanessa left this number in an e-mail inquiring about cello lessons for her daughter." Stone had no idea if this was plausible or not, but he continued. "Slots are filling quickly, and lessons begin next week, so if you could put me in contact with her it would be much appreciated."

"Next week?"

"That's right. So if you wouldn't mind giving me her cell phone number—"

"Sorry, pal. I don't know who you are or what you want with Vanessa, but she'll be out of the country with her family next week," Russ replied icily. And with that, the line went dead.

Stone hung up the receiver, his face drawn in a grimace. Then he slowly began to thumb through the pages of the phone book once more, unwavering in his determination.

"Kern and Stanton Law Office," a reedy female voice answered a few moments later.

"I'm returning a call from Reginald Kern." The man's very name left a bitter taste in Stone's mouth, and he felt the need to spit.

When the receptionist replied, "I'm sorry, but he's with a client. May I take a message?" he sighed in relief and declined, then hung up. He'd learned what he needed to know. Reginald wasn't at home.

\* \* \*

By the second time through Candy Land, it was clear that the game had run its course in keeping the twins occupied. Aubree looked longingly out the window at the beautifully manicured lawns lined by tall palms. A gardener worked in the expansive flowerbeds that lined the walkway, and the sun glinted off the pond near the tennis court. And although her mother and stepfather hadn't forbidden it, she couldn't bring herself to leave the safety of the house.

Glancing at the clock and seeing it was eleven thirty, she announced, "Let's go see what Francesca's cooking for lunch." Smiling teasingly, she nudged Ryan and added, "Or maybe she's got leftovers from breakfast saved for us."

"Ew." Ryan giggled as he and Brandi jumped up and headed toward the kitchen.

Poking their heads through the large kitchen entryway, Aubree smiled when she heard Francesca softly singing to herself as she sliced fruit for the large platter on the granite countertop nearby. Turning around, her face lit up. "Ah, my hungry little ones, I am making you something special for your lunch today. Come, sit at the table."

"It smells delicious," Aubree said appreciatively, her stomach rumbling as the three siblings sat at the table.

"I know it is a difficult day for you," Francesca said, her dark brown eyes filled with concern. "So I try to help." She placed the platter of fruit on the table in front of them, then turned back to the stovetop and the steaming pot of clam chowder—Aubree's favorite.

As Francesca began ladling the thick soup into serving bowls, a sharp rap on the door caused her to pause mid-ladle. Waiting a moment to see if another servant would answer, she finally looked at Aubree and said, "I will be right back."

Aubree listened anxiously as Francesca opened the door. A few tense seconds later, she breathed out a sigh of relief as she heard Francesca tell the delivery man that Reginald had been waiting for this package. Aubree picked up a saltshaker from the center of the table and turned it over in her hands while Brandi and Ryan continued to eat slices of watermelon.

At that moment, Aubree heard Francesca inhale sharply, then direct the deliveryman in first Italian and then English that she had to shut the door.

"But you haven't signed—"

"I'm sorry. Good-bye!" Francesca cried as the door slammed shut.

Aubree jumped to her feet as the twins watched, wide-eyed, then she ran to the door, where she found Francesca standing with her back against the door, her face pale and her body trembling. "Children, please go back into the other room," Francesca directed.

Aubree remained rooted to the ground, however, staring out the glass panes adjoining the doorway. She saw the deliveryman standing a few feet from the doorway, a confused look on his face. Then she looked beyond him down the walkway where another man was standing at the end of the driveway.

The man had jet-black hair and was wearing tan slacks and a blue sports shirt. He stood where he was for a few more seconds then began striding toward the house. Though it had been ten years, Aubree recognized her father instantly. And he appeared to be looking directly at her. Even from this distance, his black eyes looked cold and determined. Aubree's heart began to pound so fiercely she almost wondered if it would burst.

"Francesca," Aubree whispered frantically.

"Take the twins upstairs, dear. You'll be safe here in the house. Call the number your mother gave you—you remember where it is?"

Aubree nodded then turned and rushed back to the kitchen, where Brandi and Ryan still sat. "Come on, you guys," she said quickly, grabbing their hands and trying to remain calm. "We need to go upstairs right now."

"Is the bad man here?" Brandi asked fearfully.

"Yes, but we'll be safe inside," Aubree told her, hoping she sounded convincing.

Grabbing her cell phone from her pocket, Aubree and the twins left the kitchen through the back entrance and hurried upstairs where they huddled together on Aubree's bed. Downstairs, Aubree heard a sharp knock on the door.

Frozen with fear, Aubree held the cell phone in front of her for a moment without so much as breathing. When, after a few moments of silence, the knock came again, harder this time, she sprang into action and with shaking hands dialed the number she had saved in her phone the previous evening.

As the line rang, all she could think of was that her father—the man she feared more than anyone else—was mere feet away.

# CHAPTER THREE

"LIEUTENANT JENSEN."

Aubree gulped in a breath so she could respond. "I-I, you know my mom, Vanessa? She talked to you yesterday and—" Downstairs she could hear Francesca yelling something in Italian. Forcing herself to stay focused on the phone call, Aubree continued. "It's my dad. He's here."

"He's at your house?" Kevin responded, clearly alarmed.

"He's at the door now. Francesca, one of our servants, is down there now, but she didn't let him in."

"Good. Are the twins with you?" he asked quickly.

"They're right here with me." Aubree protectively tightened her grip around Ryan's and Brandi's shoulders.

"I can have my men there in five minutes. And in the meantime, I'll stay on the phone with you," he told her reassuringly.

The next five minutes ticked by slowly as Aubree remained on the line with Kevin Jensen. Although the lieutenant was clearly doing his best to keep her distracted from the tense situation at hand, Aubree couldn't help but strain her ears to hear the conversation going on downstairs—Francesca's side at least.

"I tell you, I cannot let you in, Mr. Lansing!" A pause. "She does not want to see you. You must go now."

Ryan whimpered softly, and Aubree stroked his hair as the three waited. When sirens wailed in the distance a moment later, Aubree took a deep breath and let it out slowly.

"Are those the police officers?" Brandi asked.

"They sure are, pumpkin," Aubree replied with relief. It was going to be okay.

"Aubree?" She heard Kevin Jensen speaking and returned her attention to the phone. "I'm going to hang up now. Our officers are on the scene, and they have a visual on your father. We've been trying to contact your mother and stepfather, but so far we've been unable to do so. I'll be there as soon as I can, but until then, the officers will take care of you."

When she had hung up the phone, Aubree and the twins moved cautiously to the window. Red-and-blue flashing lights reflected off the façade of the mansion, and she saw her father being escorted off the grounds by two armed officers, his head down and his shoulders slumped.

Aubree shuddered and looked away, pulling the twins back with her. If they had gone outside earlier . . . She shrugged away the unpleasant thought and, despite the fact that Lieutenant Jensen had told her he'd been unable to contact her mother, dialed Vanessa's cell phone. Getting no answer, Aubree struggled to hold back her tears. She needed to hear her mother's reassuring voice right now.

A knock came at the bedroom door, and the three children jumped. However, they quickly relaxed when a young officer in uniform entered the room to escort them downstairs. When Francesca saw the children, she ran to them and gave each a tight hug, murmuring something in Italian.

"He said he only want to talk to you and to your mother," Francesca said a moment later, frowning, a confused look on her face. "He seemed so . . . so desperate when I refused to let him in."

The front door opened, and a man about forty years old wearing slacks, a collared shirt, and a badge walked through the door. Seeing the children, he walked toward them and extended his hand. "Aubree? I'm Lieutenant Kevin Jensen. I'd like you and the twins to talk with me."

* * *

"I swear I only wanted to talk to her," Stone said to the officer, his eyes downcast.

The officer who'd been questioning him for the past half hour sighed and shook his head. "Sure you did. Can't say I believe you, but unfortunately, since you didn't actually harm anybody, and since the restraining order wasn't in effect yet, we can't do much about it." The officer's piercing blue eyes narrowed, and he leaned across the table toward

Stone. "But it is now. If you go an inch closer than one thousand feet to Aubree, Brandi, Ryan, or Vanessa Kern, you will be arrested. Understand?"

Stone nodded, his lips tightly pursed. When he was escorted from the building and released, he slumped down on a nearby bus bench, disappointed—but not surprised—that his attempt had failed so miserably. He had tried to contact his wife and daughter several times during the course of his imprisonment through letters, but all had gone unanswered.

Gritting his teeth, he stood as a bus approached, a destination fixed in his mind. Reginald Kern hadn't been on the officer's list.

\* \* \*

"Vanessa? No, no, everything is all right. I'm just glad to finally be talking to you." Kevin Jensen flashed a thumbs-up in Aubree and the twins' direction and then walked a few steps away as he continued his phone conversation with Vanessa. It had been two hours since Stone had been taken away, and everyone but Lieutenant Jensen had long since left the scene. The other officers had asked Francesca, Aubree, and the twins a few questions, but when it had been determined that no one was hurt and that Stone hadn't damaged anything, there was nothing else they could do. However, Kevin had been unable to contact either Reginald or Vanessa, and he promised to stay with the children until he was able to do so.

Aubree was grateful to have another adult around—especially a police officer. He put her at ease by asking about her riding lessons and her plans for the fall at UCLA, and he kept the twins entertained by answering their many questions about his job as a police officer.

Kevin reentered the room. "Aubree, your mother would like to talk to you."

"Mom?" Aubree began, the day's emotion catching in her throat.

"Oh, Aubree, I'm so sorry!" Vanessa exclaimed. "You must have been so frightened."

"It's okay, Mom. It was really scary . . . but the twins were both brave." Aubree tried to smile as she reached down to squeeze Brandi's hand. "I'm just glad the police got here so quickly . . ." She trailed off. "Will you be home soon?"

There was a pause on the other end of the line, and Aubree's heart sank. "You can't make it home?" she asked, unable to hide the disappointment in her voice.

"I wish I could, Aubree. But I'm hours away at a photo shoot for one of my biggest clients. Even if we skip the last photo set, by the time I finish here and make it home, it'll be nearly nine. Our flight for the cruise leaves tomorrow, and I have to finish by then."

"What about Reginald?"

"He's in back-to-back meetings." Vanessa paused again and said, "Now, I know it's not ideal, but I think I have a solution. Lieutenant Jensen has assured me that the restraining order is in place, but I still don't feel comfortable having you stay at the house until Reginald gets home. In fact I'd prefer that you stayed somewhere Stone doesn't know about until the cruise leaves tomorrow. When Lieutenant Jensen and I talked a few minutes ago, he very generously offered to let you and the twins stay the night with his family as a personal favor to me. I'll pick you up in the morning and we'll go to the airport together. I've met Kevin's wife, Rosanne, and their children; they're wonderful people."

"I . . . I guess that would be all right," Aubree agreed, disappointed but realizing she didn't have much of an alternative.

"Thank you for understanding, Aubree. I really must go, but please give the twins a hug for me, and I'll come to the Jensens' house as early in the morning as I can."

A moment later, Aubree handed the cell phone back to Kevin and explained what was happening to the twins. To her surprise, the twins didn't seem the least bit unhappy about this turn in events.

"We get to stay the night at a real police officer's house?" Ryan asked, hardly believing his luck.

Kevin chuckled, though his green eyes cast Aubree a sympathetic glance. "You sure do. Now, come on, let's get your things. Your mom told me you've already got your bags mostly packed for the cruise, so I don't imagine it will take us too long."

Aubree smiled. "You're right. They've been packed for a full week now. I'll go get my things ready as well."

*Everything will be all right,* Aubree reassured herself as Kevin Jensen waited and she headed up to her room to finish packing. *Tomorrow morning we'll leave for the cruise with Mom and leave this mess behind.*

* * *

Stone stood outside the glass doors of the law office debating his next move. He'd gotten off at the wrong bus stop, and by the time he was able to reach his destination, the afternoon had all but slipped away. Frustrated and tired, he tried to relax, to appear cool and collected, as he entered the office building and took the elevator to the fourth floor. The last thing he needed was a run-in with security before he was able to do what he came to do.

"Hello, I'm here to see Reginald Kern," he began in what he hoped was a friendly manner as he approached the reception desk.

The red-haired woman at the front desk peered up at him over thick-rimmed glasses. "Do you have an appointment with him?" she asked in the same reedy voice he recognized from the phone.

"I don't," Stone said apologetically, "but I only need to speak with him for a few moments. I'm not in a hurry—I can wait."

The receptionist studied him for a moment and then sighed. "He hasn't come out of his office all day, and you're the second guy asking to see him without an appointment. I imagine he'll be surfacing to taking a lunch break sooner or later, though. You might be able to talk to him then. But don't blame me if he isn't real happy."

Stone nodded, pleased. "I'll just have a seat and take my chances, then." Turning, he selected a chair a few feet away from the hallway leading back to the attorneys' offices. He was determined to wait all day if he had to.

* * *

Aubree was grateful for the Jensens' generosity, but she felt ill at ease and a little lost as she entered the one-story brick home. As Kevin gave them the short tour, she realized she'd never been in such a small home. The kitchen was about the size of the closet she'd been playing in the day of the murder—and that closet was small compared to those in the new mansion.

There was a yard outside, but it was tiny in comparison with the yards at the Kern home. In fact, the Jensens' entire neighborhood could probably fit inside the Kern estate with room to spare.

As Kevin introduced Aubree and the twins to his wife, Rosanne, who was cooking lunch, Aubree realized that there was something else quite different about the Jensen home. Mrs. Jensen appeared to be the cook, the housekeeper, the dishwasher, and so forth. There were no servants, no gardeners, and no chauffeurs. However, Rosanne—a short, slightly plump woman with short brown hair and brown eyes—looked quite happy. The kitchen was messy, but the smells coming from the stovetop were every bit as good as when Francesca cooked. The refrigerator was covered with drawings and photographs of children. Kevin explained that they had a daughter of twelve, a son who was fourteen, and another daughter who was seven.

"I hope you like spaghetti," Rosanne told them. "I bet you're all starving."

"We didn't eat much of our breakfast," Brandi admitted. "And we love spaghetti!"

Rosanne beamed. "I'm glad to hear that. Annie—our seven-year-old—is in the other room playing. I'll go get her and then we can pray."

That was something Aubree had never encountered. However, when the Jensens sat down, they all folded their arms and bowed their heads. Aubree did so as well, encouraging the twins to follow her example. Kevin Jensen explained that in their family they always prayed before meals. Annie offered the prayer, speaking to God as if He were in the room with them. She blessed the food, expressed thanks for their visitors, and asked that they all might be kept safe. Aubree felt a lump in her throat, and a comforting glow seemed to settle over her as she listened to the little girl pray. For the first time in her life, she seriously considered that there could really be a God in heaven.

\* \* \*

At three o'clock, Stone heard footsteps coming down the hall. He strained his ears, trying to catch the muted voices that accompanied them.

As the footsteps approached the reception area, Stone recognized one of the voices as Reginald's. Stone's hand clenched involuntarily, and the hair on the back of his neck stood on end. *You're lucky you're not alone,* he thought as he forced himself to relax.

Peering around the wall, Stone saw Reginald facing another man in the hallway. Though Stone was still unable to make out what he was saying, it was clear that Reginald wasn't happy. Then, suddenly, the second man spun around and began to march toward the door.

It was all Stone could do to hunch down in his chair with his head in his hands, hoping he hadn't been seen yet. However, after a moment it was clear enough that Reginald's attention was solidly focused elsewhere.

"I hope we've resolved everything," Reginald said, clearly trying to maintain a semblance of cordiality.

The other man snorted derisively. "We ain't resolved nothin'."

Stone lifted his head slightly as the man walked past the receptionist's desk. When he turned to look at Reginald once more before storming through the doorway, Stone caught a glimpse of the man's face and narrowed his eyes in confusion. *I know him,* he thought with surprise, though at the moment he wasn't sure where from. A few moments later, Reginald walked out the door as well, and Stone stood quickly to follow. Seeing the secretary's confused glance, he shrugged as he walked by. "He looked busy. Maybe I can catch him on the way out."

As Stone exited the lobby he saw Reginald entering the elevator— alone. Seizing his chance, Stone sprinted forward, catching the doors before they slid shut. At first Reginald's expression was merely startled. But as his eyes registered recognition, his features hardened into an angry scowl.

"So you're coming after me too now?" Reginald asked mockingly.

"Yes," Stone said simply and took a step closer to the lawyer.

Fear flickered on Reginald's face, and he backed up against the elevator wall. Then his eyes narrowed. "Do you want go back to prison, Stone? I'm sure the accommodations were lovely," he said. "Go ahead. Hit me. I'd love nothing more than to be rid of you for another ten years. Go ahead, split my lip. Vanessa will kiss it better," he said with a sneer.

Stone gripped the elevator railing tightly, conflicting emotions pulling at him. Oh, how he wanted to make Reginald Kern pay for the pain he had suffered for the past ten years. But the crushing truth was that the pompous lawyer was right. Anything Stone did to Reginald would send him back to prison. *It's not what you're here for now,* Stone reminded himself. He needed information. Justice could wait until later.

The elevator had come to a stop on the ground floor, but Stone stood near the doorway, pressing the button to keep the doors closed. "You moved in on Vanessa before I had been in prison but a few weeks."

"Clearly she didn't object," Reginald replied, meeting Stone's gaze.

"Where is she now? And where is Aubree?" Stone asked, ignoring Reginald's reply.

"Safe. I don't put much stock in the restraining order, but I figure that even you're smart enough not to break parole by leaving the country like they'll be doing."

"The cruise?"

Reginald's brow furrowed. "I don't know how you came by that information, but yes, they are going on a cruise." He smiled, and a glint appeared in his eye. "I've been detained by some court business, but I'm planning on surprising them at the next port. I can't stand to be away from my gorgeous wife and loving children for long. Aubree is looking more and more like her mother, don't you think?"

Every impulse in Stone's body screamed at him to punch Reginald in the mouth. But at that moment Reginald stepped forward, bumping roughly against Stone and causing his finger to slide from the elevator button. The doors slid open, and Reginald stepped out.

He glanced back at Stone, the confident sneer back on his face, and began to walk away. However, before he had gone more than a few steps, Stone called out, "The man you were talking to upstairs, who is he?"

Reginald froze, then spun around, his face a deep shade of red. "I don't know what you're talking about. And if you ever come near my office again, I'll be the one holding the elevator shut."

* * *

Vanessa flipped open her cell phone to look at the time. Shocked, she closed it again and turned to look for her manager, Miles. This was the first break she'd gotten since she had talked to Lieutenant Jensen and Aubree, and far more time had passed than she'd realized. It was now six o'clock. And even more frustrating, the photographer was demanding she stay to finish the their work there on Catalina Island in the morning. Spotting Miles, Vanessa hurried toward him. "I thought I told you that I had to leave here either late tonight or very early in the morning," she snapped as he turned to meet her.

"Sorry, baby, but they want some sunrise shots here on the island. And I'm afraid they want to redo some of the afternoon shots tomorrow as well. We must please our clients," Miles told her, taking her by the arm and guiding her away from the photographer he'd been speaking to.

"Miles, I promised my daughter I'd be home early enough tomorrow to pick her and the kids up from Lieutenant Jensen's place and catch our flight to Denmark on time. If we do more shooting tomorrow, I won't make our flight. I won't even be able to meet them in Copenhagen before the ship leaves port."

"Relax, darling. That's what you have me for. I'll arrange it so you can meet them at the next port. No big deal."

"It *is* a big deal, Miles. Were you listening to anything I said earlier?"

Miles frowned, his high forehead wrinkling in displeasure. "I was listening. But I don't know that *you* captured the significance of what I told you. This work is for your biggest client, and they're not so happy right now, if you haven't noticed. They decided that what we did this afternoon isn't quite what they want. I'm sorry, but there's nothing you can do about that now. What you *can* do is get back out there and finish this shoot, then get some sleep and do the one in the morning. You've got to keep those people happy. You're great, baby, but this is the kind of thing that can sorely disappoint very important people. You must keep your clients happy."

Fuming but well aware that she had few other options at this point, Vanessa turned without responding, dreading the phone call to let her children down for the second time that day.

\* \* \*

As the Jensen family gathered for dinner that night, Aubree felt as comfortable as if she had known them for much longer than just one day. Annie and the twins had spent the rest of the afternoon playing in the backyard together, and Rosanne had shown Aubree the scrapbook she was making for her son's upcoming birthday. Aubree had been impressed, and Rosanne had helped her make several pages for her family's upcoming vacation.

Jimmy and Elise, the Jensens' other children who had been at soccer camp and summer school during the day, joined the family, and were delighted to realize that company would be staying for the night. When it came time to pray, the family knelt beside the table. It seemed a little awkward that everyone would get down on their knees beside their chairs, but Aubree didn't want to seem rude, and so she knelt, signaling for the twins to do the same.

Kevin asked his wife to pray. When Rosanne had finished her prayer and everyone got off their knees and onto their chairs, Aubree asked curiously, "Where did you learn to talk to God like that?"

"Like what, dear?" Rosanne asked, smiling as she stood and helped Annie spoon some casserole onto her plate.

"Like . . . like, you know, to Him. The only prayers I've ever heard were prayers that everybody said together in church at Christmas and Easter. Or the prayers the priest says then."

"It's how we're taught to pray in our religion. We believe that God cares very much about our lives and wants to hear from us. I try to talk to Him as I would a dear friend."

Aubree nodded thoughtfully and began eating the steaming food Rosanne had dished onto her plate. Around her, the Jensen family laughed and talked and discussed what they had each been doing that day. Aubree and the twins were included in the conversation as if they were old friends. *This is a real family, a close family,* Aubree realized as she watched Ryan and Brandi giggle at Jimmy as he told them a silly joke. Her family seldom ate together, and family activities, when they happened, rarely included Reginald. From the frequent glances she received from the twins, she was quite sure they were also touched.

The meal was simple but both tasty and filling. Following dinner, Aubree received another shock—the entire family was required to pitch in and clean up the kitchen. Not wanting to seem ungrateful, she asked how she could help. For the first time in her life, she found herself washing dishes. But instead of being repulsed, she again felt a keen sense of loss at what she'd never experienced in her privileged life. There and then, she vowed within herself that someday, if she ever got married, she would try to create a family atmosphere like that which existed here in the humble home of the Jensen family.

When all the dishes had been washed and dried, Mrs. Jensen herded the children into their modest living room. "It's time for scripture reading," Lieutenant Jensen announced.

To Aubree's surprise, it wasn't the Bible that was brought out. Aubree had actually read a little in the Bible and had heard it preached from on those occasions when her mother took her to church on

Christmas and Easter. The book the Jensens opened that evening was the Book of Mormon. Aubree thought she might have heard of it, since she did know a little about Mormons, but when they began to read, the words were foreign to her. She couldn't help but be impressed with how each of the Jensens took turns reading a few verses. However, when they asked her if she'd like to read, she declined. So did the twins.

They had not yet finished reading when Lieutenant Jensen's cell phone rang. "Excuse me," he said apologetically. "I need to take this. It goes with the job."

He left the room but returned a moment later, his cell phone in hand. "It's your mother, Aubree."

Aubree took the phone from his hand with a smile, hopeful that Vanessa was calling to say the shoot on Catalina was going well and that she would be there first thing in the morning to pick them up to go to the airport. However, her expression fell as Vanessa explained that she would no longer be able to fly out with them in the morning.

"You want us to fly to Copenhagen by ourselves?" she asked angrily when Vanessa had finished.

"It's not what I had planned, sweetie," Vanessa said, sounding tired and out of sorts. " If there was any other way, I'd be there. I thought about canceling the cruise altogether, but I couldn't bring myself to do it. You'll be safe once you get on that airplane, and Kevin promised me he'd escort you himself until you are safely through security. I bet you'll be having so much fun on the cruise that it'll seem like no time until I can meet you."

"When will that be?" she asked, feeling very gloomy.

"My agent, Miles, says he can arrange it so I can meet you in Tallinn, Estonia, the first port you have after Copenhagen."

In the background, Aubree heard the doorbell ring, and a few moments later Rosanne welcomed Reginald into the house. Swallowing back her disappointment, Aubree finally said, "Okay, Mom. But please get there soon. We need you."

"I won't let you down again, Aubree," Vanessa promised resolutely. "I'd like to talk to Brandi and Ryan for a minute, and don't let them hang up without handing the phone back to Kevin so I can make sure that all the details are taken care of."

Aubree handed the phone to Brandi, then moved toward the entryway to meet Reginald, glad not to have to see the disappointment on the twins' faces for the second time that day as Vanessa explained she would not be joining them. Her mind whirled as she thought about traveling out of the country with the twins by herself. Any other time this would have seemed like a challenge, but given the current circumstances, she felt all the more apprehensive. Yes, there was a restraining order in place against her father. And yes, his parole did prohibit him from leaving the state, let alone the country, but she still felt vulnerable at the thought of being so far away from everything she knew.

Reginald stayed for only a short time since the twins' bedtime had arrived. He gave Kevin Jensen the children's passports as well as a phone, explaining that it was satellite operated and could be called from anywhere in the world. Reginald seemed distracted by something—work, Aubree assumed—and, after offering a few pats on the back and words of encouragement that "everything was just fine," he left. However, his brief visit seemed to cheer the twins up after their mother's disappointing news. By the time they were finished getting ready for bed, Brandi and Ryan were giggling as they climbed into bed.

"I'll wake you up in the morning," Aubree told them. "We'll have to be at the airport pretty early to make our flight on time."

"I know," Ryan said and yawned sleepily.

"And Mom will be there to meet us soon, right?"

"That's right," Aubree told him, certain there was no way Vanessa would disappoint them again. "Now go to sleep, you two. I love you, and I'll see you in the morning."

"Love you too, Aubree," the twins chorused as she shut the door.

* * *

Stone stood on the teeming sidewalk, unsure which direction to move. His encounter with Reginald had left him angry and frustrated, and he had spent the past hours in a small café, considering his plans. In some ways he felt he knew less now than he had that morning. And he wasn't at all certain what his next move would be. But sometime during his time at the café, something had clicked, leaving him with no doubt as to his objective.

Unfortunately, however, there were immediate concerns to be addressed first—such as where he would stay tonight. As the hour grew later and he walked back toward the bus stop, Reginald Kern's taunts turned over and over in his mind, adding further strength to his resolve that his time in prison would not have been spent in vain, even if it meant breaking his parole.

* * *

The next morning, after a hearty breakfast and good-byes from the Jensen family, Kevin, at the last minute, drove Aubree and the twins to the airport. Reginald, though he had promised to take them himself, had called Kevin saying he had an emergency meeting with a client and wouldn't be able to do so.

Aubree couldn't help but feel nervous, but she realized she was excited as well. She was eighteen years old—an adult, after all—and she could handle this. The twins were counting on her. They had money, they had tickets to Copenhagen, they had their passports and visas, and they had the passes they needed to catch the ship. If she could keep her wits about her, they'd be okay. Aubree had flown a lot, and so the airport didn't intimidate her. Finding her way around a foreign city worried her a bit, but Kevin assured her that Vanessa had arranged for someone from a car service to be waiting for her at the gate in Copenhagen to take her directly to a hotel where she and the twins could relax in privacy until it was time to board the ship.

A short while later, with Kevin's help, they had their bags checked and were on their way to security. They were due to depart in an hour for Chicago, where they would have a three-hour layover.

"Are you sure you can come with us to the gate?" Aubree asked Kevin as they approached security.

"Of course. I'm a police officer on official business." He winked and helped the twins lift their small carry-on bags onto the conveyor belt.

Although she was sure she was being paranoid, Aubree couldn't help scrutinizing the faces in the throng of people moving through the corridor as she and the twins left the security area and headed for their boarding gate. Surely her father couldn't know they were here— let alone make it past security. But still, Aubree worried. Lieutenant Jensen must have noticed, because when they arrived at the gate, he kindly asked, "Would you like me to wait with you until the flight leaves? I don't need to be in to my office for another hour."

Aubree considered but then shook her head, feeling slightly more confident now that they were sitting directly outside the gate. "You've done so much for us already. Thanks for the offer, but I think we'll be just fine now."

Kevin nodded. "Please call if you need anything—it's no bother at all."

"We will. And thank you again. We really enjoyed staying with your family, didn't we, guys?"

Brandi and Ryan nodded. "Tell Jimmy and Annie bye for us," Ryan said. "Maybe they can come over and play when we get home."

Kevin smiled. "I'm sure they'd love that." Then he turned back to Aubree. "I almost forgot. I brought you something for your trip." He handed her a plain blue book. "That's a copy of the book we were reading together last night—the Book of Mormon. Maybe you'll get a chance to do some reading while you're on your trip."

"Uh, sure. Thanks." Aubree took the book with a smile, unsure whether she would actually read it but also not wanting to offend Lieutenant Jensen after all the trouble he'd gone to for them.

"Well, I better get going," he said. And then, waving good-bye, he walked back toward security.

As Aubree watched the police officer walk away, she felt a sudden lump form in her throat. Then, pulling the twins closer, she offered a first, silent prayer. *Heavenly Father, if you're there, please keep us safe.*

# CHAPTER FOUR

MODERN TECHNOLOGY WAS INCREDIBLE. Though Nadif was halfway around the world, his voice was clear. This was a good thing, since his broken English coupled with a bad connection would have made it almost impossible for the American to understand him. And it was very important that the two men understand one another.

"They're on their way; they just left LAX," the American said. "They'll be aboard the *Stargazer* by ten o'clock the morning after tomorrow, Copenhagen time. Keep an eye on them."

"Just make sure you have things ready on your end," Nadif replied, sounding irritated.

"There's plenty of time."

"The timing is my business. Just have everything ready," the Somali man countered.

"You don't have to worry about it. I'll be sending you an account number in code later this afternoon. When the job is completed, I'll expect you to deposit my share of the profits within twenty-four hours."

Nadif scoffed. "I am a professional. The job will be finished quickly and discreetly, and you'll get your money."

"Likewise," the American replied coolly.

"I will receive the weapons as arranged and on time?" Nadif asked, his voice low. Weapons—automatic rifles, to be exact—were what mattered the most to him. Money was what mattered most to the American.

"You'll get them exactly as I outlined earlier," the American told him impatiently.

"I hope so. For both my sake and yours," Nadif warned.

"You have nothing to worry about," the American said and promptly disconnected.

\* \* \*

Stone was sound asleep when a series of sharp raps on his motel room door caused him to sit bolt upright in bed. Glancing around the room, his heart beating like a hammer in his chest, he tried to orient himself. The clock on the night table read 10:30 AM, though the room was still dark because of the shade over the window. He hadn't meant to sleep so late. Looking at the orange shag carpet and tacky wallpaper, he remembered checking into the rundown motel late the night before. Though the room was furnished with seventies décor and he didn't want to know what the faded stains on the floor were, the place had seemed like the Ritz compared to where he'd been staying for the past ten years.

The rap on the door came again, and this time Stone swung his legs out of bed and hurriedly put on his clothes from the night before. Moving cautiously toward the door so as not to make any noise that would reveal he was in the room, Stone peered through the peephole and saw a little man with bulging eyes and a thin face. Stone debated a moment longer, then finally opened the door a crack, keeping the security chain place.

"Can I help you?"

"Are you Stone Lansing?" the rat-faced man asked.

"Who wants to know?" he responded, his senses alert to the possibility of danger. He didn't have a weapon, and he felt suddenly vulnerable.

"I've got a message for you," the man said.

"Who are you?" Stone asked forcefully.

"Folks call me Rambler. That's all you need to know. This is about your ex-wife and daughter," the man said, gauging Stone's reaction. "Now let me in."

Stone frowned, caught off guard. He debated a moment longer, and finally the small, unkempt man said, "Look, I don't like being seen here." He smiled crookedly. "After all, *you* don't have a very good reputation."

Stone was certain he could say the same of Rambler, but he now felt confident that this man meant him no harm. If he had information for him . . . it was worth looking into. He unlatched the chain and stepped back, signaling for Rambler to enter.

Stone winced as the man entered. The smell he brought into the already musty room was almost overpowering. "What do you know about my family?"

"Aubree and the twins are on their way to Copenhagen, Denmark. They'll be getting on a cruise ship there. The name of the ship is *Stargazer,*" Rambler said.

"That's old news," Stone said, turning away. "Although I don't know how you came by that information."

Rambler grinned, showing several missing teeth. The ones that were left were yellow and misshapen. "Oh, you might say a little birdie told me," he said.

Stone did not smile. "Don't play games with me," he warned, suddenly battling the impulse to rid the man of the rest of his rotting teeth with a quick jab to his face.

"No games here," Rambler said without the smile. He shuffled backward a few steps, closer to the door he'd just come through. "I have my sources, but they're confidential. Anyway, I figured you'd do your research. But that's not why I'm here."

"Out with it, then," Stone said as he felt the heat continue to build within him.

"I don't want any more questions—just a small fee for my services. Rumor is you're out for revenge and that you've run into some roadblocks. That's where I come into the picture—again, for just a small fee. Be here tomorrow at this time, and I'll drop off a driver's license, passport, and visa," he said. "The name will be different, of course, but I'm sure you can appreciate that."

Stone was stunned now, and the anger drained away. This foul little man was offering him an unforeseen but golden opportunity—but at what cost? The whole situation reeked of a trap. And yet . . . perhaps it was worth it either way. He'd spent much of the night tossing and turning, mulling over what his next move would be. He would be taking a great risk, but if he didn't act now . . .

"How much," Stone asked gruffly.

"Eight thousand dollars," Rambler replied easily.

"Too much. And it'll trigger a red flag on my account."

Rambler considered for a moment. "I suppose you're right," he said finally. "Six, then. And that's mighty generous of me. You're not exactly in a position to barter, Stone."

Stone's jaw tightened, but at last he nodded. "All right. But I don't pay until you show up with everything as promised."

"Of course," Rambler said as he reached into his pocket and brought out a small camera. "You might want to put on something a little more presentable. I need a picture for the documents."

Still wary, Stone pulled on a clean shirt and combed through his dark, curly hair. Rambler snapped a couple of pictures, then he put the camera back in his pocket. "You'd better not be playing games with me," Stone said in a low voice. "You'll wish you'd never met me if you are."

Rambler backed up again and bumped the door. "Be here tonight," he said. "In fact, lay low until I get back with you."

With that, Rambler opened the door and rushed out. Slumping back down on the bed, he tried to think through what he had just done. Leaving the country would certainly violate his parole, but his contacts with his parole officer were only monthly. After the one scheduled on Wednesday, his next visit wasn't scheduled for another four weeks, and he would be back by then. Still, if he was caught, he would be sent back to prison. But some things were worth it.

\* \* \*

Nadif spoke rapidly but decisively as he gave instructions to a subordinate in Berlin, a German by the name of Cord. He spoke in German, a tongue they both knew well. "Board the next flight to Copenhagen. Three young Americans should be arriving there early tomorrow morning." The Somali man's voice acquired an edge to it. "I want you to make sure of one thing, Cord—one very simple thing: see that the three young Americans board the cruise liner *Stargazer*." He told him when they should be boarding and then proceeded to describe the three children. "The oldest girl's name is Aubree Lansing. The twins' names are Brandi and Ryan. You shouldn't have any trouble recognizing them when you see them. They will stand out."

"What do I do if they don't get on the ship?" Cord asked.

"Grab them and then call me," Nadif said coldly. "I don't trust my American contact much. He says the three young people will be boarding the ship at the appointed time. It is very important that they do. If they don't, it means we have been double-crossed. That would make me very angry. But if you do have to grab them, do it discreetly. We don't need the Danes making a fuss about missing American tourists."

"I can be discreet," Cord said simply. "Do you want me to try to find them as they leave the airport?"

"That's exactly what I want," Nadif agreed. "I don't know what flight they will be on, but my contact in Los Angeles should be calling me with that information soon. We must be very cautious. I don't want my American friend to know I don't fully trust him."

"You'll call with the information once you have it?"

"That's right. Now, once you find the children, keep track of them. I don't know who will be meeting them in Copenhagen or what they plan to do until they board the ship. But whatever they do, you are to follow them."

Two hours later, Cord made flight arrangements. He was anxious to get to Copenhagen. It had been a while since his last assignment, and he was eager to begin.

\* \* \*

Stone thought it would be wise to gain a slight upper hand before Rambler returned—in case he was indeed being set up. So when the room next door became vacant, Stone rented it as well and moved his belongings to it. The attendant didn't ask why, but Stone was sure he'd had stranger requests.

Though he had several hours to wait until night fell, Stone hunkered down in the new room, making only a brief visit to the bank to withdraw the money for Rambler as well as some for the trip he would be taking. He left the light burning in his first room with the TV going but kept the lights off where he sat. The minutes dragged on, but if there was one thing Stone had learned to do in prison, it was to sit and do nothing for hours at a time. When at last dusk fell, he parted the heavy blinds just enough to be able to see if anyone approached.

At eight o'clock, he watched as a figure emerged from the darkness and approached Stone's first room. It was Rambler. Stone waited while Rambler knocked at the door. Stone wanted to be sure that he was alone. When Rambler knocked again and he couldn't see anyone else,

Stone silently opened the door just as Rambler cursed and turned away.

"I'm in here," Stone said softly. Rambler squealed and jumped in fright. "Step inside and I'll turn the light on."

Rambler did as he was told, and once the two men were in the room together, Stone closed the door and flipped on the light. "You didn't need to scare me like that," the grubby little man complained.

"I'm just being careful," Stone said. "Now let's have it."

From the soiled pocket of his tattered jacket, Rambler pulled out a package. "It's all in here," he said as he held it out to Stone.

Stone ripped the package open and examined the contents while Rambler watched. The passport looked real to him. So did the driver's license and visa. Whoever was behind this strange thing was good.

Still examining the documents, Stone handed Rambler an envelope of bills. Rambler thumbed quickly through the money, making sure it was all there. Then he backed toward the door. "I'll be going now," he said nervously.

"Not just yet," Stone said as he suddenly turned and grabbed the man, his right arm around Rambler's neck, squeezing tightly. "I need to know who created these documents."

Rambler struggled, but Stone was too strong. When Rambler had given up struggling, Stone eased the pressure on his neck, and Rambler said, "I can't. I was told not to."

"I think you can," Stone said as he again tightened his arm around Rambler's neck and pressed his head into his hip. As Rambler continued to struggle, Stone said, "Do you know why I was sent to prison?"

He released some of the pressure, and Rambler said, "'Course I do. Murder."

"That's right. Now you might consider your dilemma. I have what I want. I don't need you anymore."

"He'll do something to me," Rambler whined.

"Would you rather that I do something to you?" Stone asked coldly.

"No, please don't, mister."

Feeling the panic in Rambler's voice, Stone released the pressure. What was he doing? Injuring this man could lead him straight back to prison. "You are a coward," Stone said darkly. "I don't like cowards much, so get out of here."

Rambler fled.

After he was gone, Stone packed up his few belongings and slipped away from the motel. He wasn't about to stay here for another minute and be a sitting duck. He'd learned in prison that there were far worse men than him in the world, men who couldn't be trusted.

That night, under his newly assumed identity, Karl W. Faulk, Stone slept in a clean bed in a nice hotel several miles from the place where he'd met with Rambler. First thing in the morning, he'd begin making travel plans.

# CHAPTER FIVE

AFTER ARRIVING IN COPENHAGEN AND being escorted to a hotel where they checked in, Aubree and the twins decided to see some of the sights within walking distance. They didn't have to catch the ship until the following morning. Though Aubree was still a bit nervous about being on her own with the twins, she felt safer than she had in days, knowing she was thousands of miles away from her father.

They were walking down Pedestrian Street when Ryan spotted a group of street performers. The twins were amazed by the colorful costumes and antics of the performers. Ryan turned to Aubree, a puzzled look on his face. "How come they have Indians here?" he asked.

"I don't know," Aubree said, keeping her eyes on the young American Indians. "But they're amazingly talented, aren't they?" Others in the surging crowd had stopped as well, and a few minutes later, when the performers had stopped, a wave of applause rippled through the audience.

After a moment, Aubree and the twins moved on along the ancient cobblestone street. Pedestrian Street was aptly named, Aubree soon realized—only pedestrians were allowed on this street that ran for several blocks through the older part of Copenhagen. Shops lined both sides of the narrow, busy street, offering an astounding variety of goods. Aubree stopped in a little shop selling handmade purses. She felt a pang of homesickness, knowing her mother would have loved the beautiful leatherwork.

To keep from getting lost, Aubree had picked up a small map of Copenhagen at the hotel before setting out. One place they wanted to visit before they left Copenhagen on the ship was the Round Tower.

Following the map, she guided the twins away from Pedestrian Street and led them toward the tower. As they walked, the satellite phone in Aubree's bag vibrated. It was Reginald on the line, checking in to make sure that everything was going well. "I'm jealous," he joked after he'd asked about their flight and arrival. "I wish I was there with you."

Aubree smiled, touched that he had called. "I wish you were here too—I know the twins miss you already. Here, I think they want to talk to you." Brandi and Ryan nodded eagerly, and Aubree passed each of them the phone.

When Reginald hung up, they continued onward.

"Why do so many people ride bikes here?" Ryan asked as several bicycles passed them.

"Probably because it's cheaper and easier to get around," she told him. She too was fascinated by the hundreds of bikes they saw parked in front of the stores and businesses here and by the people, both young and old, who rode them.

Brandi watched a young woman go past on a rosy pink bike. "I want a new bike."

"You two got new bikes just a couple of months ago," Aubree reminded her. The twins loved to ride around the Kern estate and on the hilly streets of Malibu.

"But our bikes don't look like these," she said plaintively.

Aubree chuckled. "That's because yours are more expensive, much nicer than these," she said.

They soon arrived at their destination and stared up at the tall tower and large building it was part of. The Round Tower made up one end of an imposing structure that had been built in the seventeenth century. Aubree picked up a small brochure and read it, learning that the tower was made of stone cut in the shape of bricks and had been designed for use as a place of learning, a church for students, a university library, and an observatory. It rose over a hundred feet into the sky above them.

"Let's go," Ryan said anxiously as he tugged on Aubree's hand. With excitement they started up the wide cobblestone ramp, one that wound seven and a half times around the tower's hollow core. They were breathless after hurrying upward for almost seven hundred feet on the cobblestone path. The view from the top was breathtaking. As the children looked down on Copenhagen at the red tile roofs, the many church spires, and the narrow cobblestone streets, Aubree sighed happily, grateful to Reginald and her mother for allowing them to come to this beautiful place and escape their troubles at home. A nagging thought at the back of her mind caused her to think about what would happen when they returned home, but she shrugged it off as she took a few pictures and tried to point out to Ryan and Brandi a few landmarks they had visited earlier.

When they finally started back down the long spiral ramp, a group of young people of about her age came toward them. They were laughing and speaking what Aubree assumed must be Danish. As they passed, two of the girls, both with bright red hair and twinkling blue eyes, pointed at the twins, obviously charmed.

"Such beautiful children! They are twins?" One of the girls asked Aubree in broken English.

"We sure are!" Ryan piped up, smiling widely.

"We are twins also!" the second girl said. "My name is Abigail, and this is Ada."

"It's nice to meet you," Aubree replied. "I'm Aubree, and this is Brandi and Ryan." Abigail turned to the rest of the group and repeated their names, then said something in Danish to her friends as they smiled and waved, then started again toward the top of the tower.

Aubree waved back, her eyes following the group of young people until it disappeared around the core of the tower.

The twins had continued on shortly after she'd stopped, and she felt a bubble of panic rise in her chest when she couldn't see them. She began to run down the ramp but didn't catch up with them until she was almost to the bottom. When she did, she said with a touch of anger, "Hey, you guys. You can't run off alone like that. You could get lost. Remember, we promised Mom and Dad that we'd stay together all the time."

"You're the one that stopped," Ryan said, shrugging. "I thought you wanted to talk to those guys."

Aubree reached out and tousled Ryan's hair. "Next time stick close, okay? Come on, it's later than I realized, and I'm starving. Do you guys want something to eat? It's almost dinner time."

"Yeah," both children cried, and so they set off once more in search of something to eat.

Aubree started to walk, making sure the twins were right with her. The crowds were getting thicker, and at times it was difficult to maneuver through the wall of pedestrians. Catching sight of a promising-looking café, Aubree took a few steps to the right in an attempt to see the sign. "Café Luna," she read, "I think I remember reading about this one. What do you guys think?"

"Sure, I guess so," Brandi said.

"How about you, Ryan?" As Aubree turned to face him, she realized that only Brandi was standing next to her. As she gasped in alarm, Brandi turned to look about her as well.

"Ryan? Ryan! Aubree, I can't see Ryan!" Brandi shouted, her eyes growing wide.

Aubree looked around in alarm as her heart pounded. The crowd was surging now, going in both directions. He had to be close by. "We've got to find him quickly," Aubree said firmly. "I can't believe he isn't right with us. He knows he's supposed to stay close. He was here a minute ago."

But he wasn't there now. Everywhere Aubree looked there were blond heads in the crowd. But none of them was attached to a little person Ryan's size. Clinging tightly to Brandi's hand, she hurried back the way they had come, calling Ryan's name and frantically looking in every direction. She suddenly realized that she had again passed the street they had traveled on from the Round Tower, and she turned back. Five minutes passed, and Aubree realized that she had lost her bearings. Her breath coming in panicked spurts, she forced herself to stop and pull out her map to try to figure out where she was.

After a minute or two she regained her bearings and started back in the direction of the café. Aubree wondered if maybe Ryan had somehow gotten ahead of them, and so she hurried faster, keeping the map in her hand so she wouldn't get lost again. As the two of them walked and even ran, Aubree kept a tight hold on Brandi's hand.

They again reached the street where pedestrians surged by the hundreds. "I don't know what to do!" she screamed into the crowd as she came to a halt in the middle of the wide, busy street.

A few heads in the crowd turned, but no one asked what the matter was. "We've got to find him," Brandi wailed.

"How? I don't know how!" Aubree cried, clenching her fists in front of her chest. "Why couldn't he have stayed with us?"

"I wish Mom and Dad were here," Brandi sobbed, her little eyes wide with fright and wet with tears.

"But they're not," Aubree said sharply. "What can we do?"

"I know—you can call Lieutenant Jensen," Brandi suggested, her face brightening. "He said we could call him."

Not knowing what else to do, Aubree quickly reached into her pocket and retrieved the satellite phone. If nothing else, Lieutenant Jensen's calm, reassuring voice would help keep her from falling apart. As she dialed the number, Brandi stood with her fingers crossed in front of her face.

"What are you doing?" Aubree asked as she listened to the phone ring.

"I'm wishing him to answer," Brandi said.

Aubree was wishing the same thing, but the phone continued ringing and then went to voice mail. She slowly closed her phone without leaving a message and then began to cry in earnest. She had failed her little brother. Aubree threw her arms around Brandi, who was sobbing as well.

\* \* \*

Kevin and his family were on their knees for morning prayer when he felt his cell phone vibrating in his pocket. Resisting the temptation to answer it, he listened more intently to the prayer. Toward the end of the prayer, Rosanne, who was mouth, said, "We ask thee to bless Aubree and Ryan and Brandi. Please keep them safe, Heavenly Father. We can't help them from here if they need it, so we pray Thou wilt watch over them."

A moment later she closed the prayer. As they all got off their knees Kevin pulled out his phone with one hand while looking at his watch with the other. He was going in to work early this morning, even though he'd been up late the night before, and he had been surprised when his phone had vibrated during the prayer. The children and Rosanne sat down to breakfast while he looked at his phone. "Aubree called from her satellite phone during the prayer. I'd better call her right back. I hope they're okay," Kevin said.

A minute later, Aubree answered the phone. Kevin could tell she was crying. "Aubree, what's the matter?" he asked.

"Oh, Kevin. I've lost Ryan," she sobbed. "I don't know what to do."

"Where are you? And is Brandi with you?" he asked urgently.

"We're in Copenhagen, and Brandi is here with me. So was Ryan, but a few minutes ago we noticed that he wasn't with us anymore, and he just had been. And there are people all over. I'm so scared. I don't know what to do. Ryan must be terrified. What should I do?"

"What time is it there?" Kevin asked, trying to keep his voice calm, hoping that it would rub off on Aubree while he gave her some advice.

"It's about five o'clock. We were going to find someplace to get dinner when Ryan disappeared. He was with us one second and gone the next," she said.

"I'm sure he's fine. He's probably as worried about finding you as you are about finding him. Now listen, Aubree, here's what you need to do. Find someone who can help you contact the police. Go into a shop—there are shops near where you're at, aren't there?"

"Yes. There are shops all over the place."

"Go in one. I suspect that the owner will know English. Ask for help in contacting a police officer. While you're doing that, I'll stay on the phone with you, okay?"

"Yes, okay." Aubree paused a moment then said, "We're going into a little doll store now. Just a second and I'll ask someone if they know how to contact the police," she said.

"What's happening?" Rosanne asked urgently.

"The kids are in Copenhagen. Ryan was with them and then he just disappeared a few minutes ago," Kevin explained. "Aubree is scared to death."

Kevin noticed that none of his family was eating. All eyes were on him. Everyone looked as worried as he felt. He could hear Aubree asking someone for help. Then she said into the phone, "The owner speaks English. She's calling the police for me right now." A sob shook her voice again and she said, "Do you think they can find him for us?"

"I do, Aubree," he said as a calm assurance settled over him. Then, after a moment's hesitation, he added, "The reason that I didn't answer the phone when you called the first time was because my family and I were having morning prayer. You remember how we prayed when you were with us?"

"I do," Aubree responded.

"After the phone quit vibrating in my pocket, my wife, who was saying the prayer, asked Heavenly Father to bless you three. Aubree, I know that He will."

"Thank you, Kevin," Aubree said sincerely. "When I was going out of my mind, Brandi said that I should call you. I'm glad she thought of that."

"So am I, Aubree. Has the woman in the shop reached the police yet?"

"Yes. Her name is Pansy. She says they'll send someone right away," Aubree said. "She's very kind. She says for us to stay right here with her."

"That's good. You do that. And then you do whatever the police say when they get there. I'll let you go for now, but when they come, call me back if you need to. And try to believe this," he said. "The Lord is watching over you. You'll get Ryan back."

After ending the call, Kevin finally sat down at the table with his family. Rosanne looked up at him, her expression somber. "As I was praying, those kids suddenly came to my mind. I was prompted to pray for them. I know the Lord is watching out for them."

* * *

On a rare break, Vanessa heard her cell phone ringing faintly from within the purse she had left on a nearby chair. Hurrying to answer it before it went to voice mail, she picked it up and hurriedly said hello.

"Vanessa? It's Lieutenant Jensen. I don't want to worry you, but I received a call from Aubree . . ."

Vanessa felt her heart sink as Kevin relayed what had happened in Copenhagen. A few moments later, she numbly hung up the phone, her head swimming. Ryan was gone. Kevin Jensen had been trying to contact her for the past hour, and as she looked through her phone, it was clear that Aubree had been trying to call as well. So far the police had been unable to locate Ryan. She listened to the voice mails Aubree had left, each one more desperate than the one before.

"Back to work, darling," came a voice from behind her, and Vanessa whirled around to see Miles standing impatiently behind her. When Miles saw the expression on her face, however, an eyebrow shot up. "Not a good call?"

"No," she snapped, feeling like she might collapse. "My son, Ryan . . . he's missing."

Miles frowned. "Have they called the police?"

"Of course . . . and they've been trying to call me . . . but they couldn't reach me until now. I'm sorry, but I have to call my daughter."

Miles nodded slowly. "Yes, call her. But, then, darling, I don't mean to sound callous . . . but there's not much you can do from here. The police will find him. I'm sure he just wandered off."

Her eyes blazing, Vanessa took a step toward him. "You're right. There's nothing I can do because I'm not there with my children when I should be." She gave him a hard look then added, "We're finished here. I'm not going to risk being away from my phone for the rest of the day."

"But your flight doesn't leave until tomorrow!" Miles spluttered, "Leave the phone on; we'll do whatever you need."

"I'm calling my daughter, and then I'm going home. Period." Turning toward the door without waiting for him to respond, Vanessa collected her bag and hurried away, dialing the satellite phone as she walked.

*  *  *

"Please call me as soon as you know anything."

"I will, Mom," Aubree promised Vanessa again. There was still no sign of Ryan, and though Aubree was grateful she had finally gotten in touch with her mother, Vanessa had proceeded to call every ten minutes like clockwork.

"I'll have my phone right next to me waiting to hear from you . . . I just can't believe they haven't found him yet. What if something happened? I'd never forgive myself." Vanessa broke down again, and Aubree swallowed back fresh tears of her own for Brandi's sake.

"I'm sure we'll find him soon, Mom. I'll call you as soon as I know anything."

Aubree hung up the phone, struggling to remember the calm that had settled over her when she had talked with Lieutenant Jensen earlier. It was like nothing she had ever experienced. She had somehow sensed that they would find Ryan—she just didn't know when and where. She clung to that thought as she looked out of the open doorway and watched the surging throng of people. The police had been out looking for Ryan for an hour and a half now. *Heavenly Father, please help us,* she cried out in her mind.

It was then, with a start, that she recognized the two girls she had seen earlier at the tower. She stepped out of the door and the two young women saw her. They grinned and began to wave as they pushed forward. "Aubree!" one of them—Ada, Aubree thought—cried out.

Pansy followed Aubree outside. The twin Danes started to talk slowly in English then gave up and began speaking rapidly in Danish. They appeared excited about something. Pansy listened for a moment, and then her wrinkled face broke into a broad smile. "These girls have been looking all over for you. They say they know where your brother is," she said happily. "They want you to come with them, and they'll take you to him. They say that one of their friends is waiting with your brother. The rest of them went looking for you. But I don't want you to leave. You wait here and I'll notify the police and have the girls bring your brother to us."

Aubree felt dizzy with relief. She was more grateful than she felt she could adequately express. But she did her best, saying to Abigail, "Thank you."

"You are welcome," Abigail said, her English broken but understandable, then she turned with Ada to go back in the direction she had come.

Pansy put an arm around both Aubree and Brandi as they waited. "You are a lucky girl," she said to Aubree. "It can be a very bad thing for one as young as your brother to get lost. There are lots of people here, and not all of them are good. I was beginning to worry something had happened. God must be watching over you."

"I think He is," Aubree said in a quiet voice as she reflected on the Jensens' family prayer as well as her own plea for help.

Fifteen minutes later, just as a pair of police officers arrived back at the shop, the redheaded twins and the entire group of friends they had seen in the tower pushed their way through the crowd. Ryan was holding Ada's hand tightly. When he saw Aubree, he shook free of Ada's hand and flew into his sister's arms. He hugged her so tightly it hurt her neck, but she held him as he sobbed, ignoring the pain, just grateful to have him back. When he finally released her, he looked up through tearful eyes and said, "I'm sorry, Aubree. I didn't mean to get lost."

"I'm sure you didn't," she said through her own tears, "but we were so worried about you. Something could have happened to you. From now on we've got to be more careful than ever to stay together. Will you promise me?"

"I promise," he said shakily, and then he turned to Brandi. "I promise you, too," he repeated. And with that, Brandi opened her little arms to him.

Aubree turned and thanked the police officers who had been searching for Ryan. They nodded with relieved expressions on their faces and then turned to speak to Pansy for a moment. Then Aubree did something the likes of which she had never done before with a complete stranger. She hugged first Abigail and then Ada, thanking them for helping her. As the police officers left, Pansy spoke to the girls in Danish. Their smiles grew broader as she spoke. Then Abigail said something in return. Pansy turned to Aubree and said, "Abigail said to tell you she is glad she and her friends could help. She says they are going to go eat and wonder if you three are hungry. As you know, they can speak a little English. It will be fun for them to try to talk to you. They will show you a good place to eat just up the street, and they'll buy your meal."

"We were thinking about finding a place to eat when Ryan disappeared," Aubree said. She checked her watch and, turning to Abigail, said, "We still have a couple of hours, so we'd love to go with you. But I will buy for all of us."

Ada smiled. "That is kind of you."

"You don't know how thankful I am that you found him," Aubree replied sincerely. "If you'll wait just a moment, though, I need to call my mother and our friend Lieutenant Jensen."

Vanessa was beside herself with relief, and Kevin was equally grateful for the happy outcome. Before Aubree hung up with Kevin, he told her, "The Lord was with you. He loves you very much."

Those words seemed strange to Aubree, and yet she felt like there must be some truth to them. She hoped there was.

Later, in a crowded sidewalk café, Abigail and Ada helped Ryan tell Aubree what had happened. Between them, they spoke enough English to make passable conversation.

"Why did you fall behind?" Aubree asked, looking sternly at her little brother.

"I saw a weird coin on the ground while we were walking on that busy street. I just wanted to pick it up," he said. "When I looked up,

I couldn't see you or Brandi anymore, but a man was standing there. There were a lot of people around, but he was looking at me funny, so I thought the coin must be his. I tried to give it to him. I wasn't trying to steal his money. But he shook his head and said—"

Before he could finish the sentence, Aubree cut him off. "What did he look like?" she asked in alarm, suddenly fearful that her father had somehow found them here. Ryan had never seen Stone and wouldn't know him.

Ryan thought for a moment. "He was short. He was older than you but way younger than Dad. And he had blond hair like me and Brandi."

Aubree breathed a sigh of relief. "I'm sorry I interrupted you— what did the man say to you?"

"He said I should hurry and catch up, that I shouldn't get lost from my sisters," Ryan said. His lips puckered in a frown as he remembered. "That scared me, Aubree. How did he know you're my sister? I dropped the coin and ran, trying to get away from him."

"I'm glad you did," Aubree said, wondering with new fear who the blond stranger had been.

Ada laboriously explained that they had been walking down the street when they saw Ryan run past them. He had seemed frightened, and they had darted after him. However, Ryan was fast, and in the crowd it had taken two blocks to catch up with him.

Ryan broke in and added, "When I felt someone grab me from behind, I screamed and started kicking, but then I saw that it wasn't the blond man but one of the girls from the tower. She smiled at me, and I knew it was okay." His eyes narrowed. "But I looked behind me and saw the blond man again. He kept watching me."

Abigail nodded and told Aubree that she had seen the blond man as well. It made her shudder the way he had been looking at them.

Ada explained that they had hurried Ryan along then, trying to get back to Pedestrian Street where there would be lots of people, thinking it would be safer for them in a crowd. The blond man had followed them at a distance, though he never tried to overtake them. Once they felt like they were safe, they left Ryan inside a store with one of their friends while the rest of the group went looking for Aubree and Brandi. They hadn't seen the blond man since then.

"You guys probably saved my brother's life," Aubree said softly as she looked at the two redheaded twins.

Ada answered. "I am glad we helped."

Aubree kept looking around as they ate their meal. Finally, Ada asked if she was still watching for the blond man.

"I am. I can't help it," she said. "What you told me scares me to death."

After they had eaten, the group of young Danes walked Aubree and the twins back to the hotel. Though everyone kept a close eye out, no one saw the man again.

At the hotel, the new friends said their good-byes and exchanged e-mail addresses. Aubree was surprised to feel tears prick at her eyes as she gave Ada and Abigail a last hug. She wished she had more time to get to know these girls and their friends. She felt a special bond with them after all that had happened in the past few hours. Still, she was grateful they would at least be able to keep in touch by e-mail.

Back in their hotel room, Aubree tried to call her mother and Reginald again. She continued her efforts for the next hour. She suspected that Vanessa was either on a plane and had her phone turned off, or that she had been delayed again. She assumed that Reginald was in court. Finally, she placed a call to Kevin Jensen. When she related to him what had happened and how badly it frightened her, he told her that she and the kids should stay in their hotel room for the rest of the evening. He promised to call the hotel and get them to have their security people keep a close eye on their room that night. When he called back later, Kevin informed Aubree that someone from the hotel would personally escort them to the ship in the morning.

When Vanessa finally called an hour later, she listened in horror to Aubree's story. "This is scary," she said. "You do exactly what Detective Jensen told you."

Reginald also called. He also sounded upset about what had happened to Ryan that day. "Aubree," he said sternly. "You keep the kids right with you all the time. I wish this case hadn't been moved up. I should be there with you guys. I'm sorry that I'm not."

Aubree was a little more relaxed that evening. She played with the twins, and after putting them to bed, she even spent a few minutes thumbing through the book Kevin had given her at the airport—the

Book of Mormon. Finally, restless but anxious for the next day to come, she went to bed.

When they approached the boarding gates of the *Stargazer* the next morning, Aubree and the twins looked up at the massive cruise ship in awe. Thinking she heard her name from somewhere behind her, Aubree turned, scanning the crowd, and was surprised to see the Abigail, Ada, and their group of friends. "We thought we would be your send-off party!" Ada called. "Have a wonderful trip!"

Aubree smiled and waved, and the twins called out good-byes as well. When they turned back toward the gate, Aubree smiled and looked at the hotel security officer who had accompanied them. "Thank you," she said gratefully.

"You're welcome," the short, balding man replied, tipping an imaginary cap and smiling. "You children be careful now."

"I'm beginning to think we can't be careful enough," Aubree agreed as she scanned the crowd one last time before she and the twins made their way up to the ship.

# CHAPTER SIX

TORBEN DAVIDSEN STOOD ON THE concrete pier and watched as the passengers filed out of the huge building where they had left their luggage to be transported on board later by ship personnel. As the new security officer of the ship, he took his job seriously. He wanted to get a good look at all the new passengers to familiarize himself with their faces.

The passengers boarding the ship were of all ages and from all walks of life. Several times he found himself being smiled at by pretty girls, and he always smiled politely in return. He hoped that he looked professional in the brown and tan uniform the shipping line required him to wear whenever he was on duty. He wanted to represent the *Stargazer* well.

It seemed like the procession of people would never end as literally hundreds of new passengers boarded the ship. Torben felt a swell of pride as he heard many passengers comment on what a beautiful vessel it was. The *Stargazer* was a relatively new ship, and it was indeed large and luxurious.

An older couple passed him, and then three young people came hurrying from the building. The young lady who was holding the hands of two towheaded children had long, slightly wavy black hair. The girl moved with natural grace, even as she hurried along with the two children. Her dark brown eyes met his for a moment when he said, "Good morning, Miss. Welcome to the *Stargazer*." She gave him a halting smile and a brief, studying glance before she ducked her head and moved past. He followed her with his eyes, disturbed by the glint of fear he'd seen in hers.

The girl seemed tense and withdrawn, and she kept looking back, beyond him and the other employees of the ship who were greeting passengers like he was. It was almost as if she were afraid there was someone following her. He also noted how tightly the two children clung to her. Unlike other passengers, these three were clearly tense and worried. Something wasn't right here. He made a mental note to keep an eye on them.

Torben turned back to greet the other arriving passengers. But even as he studied each face that passed him, his thoughts drifted back to the trio and he wondered why there were no older adults with the black-haired girl and blond children. Perhaps she was a nanny, he decided, and was being paid to take the two youngsters on the cruise.

When all the passengers were on board, Torben spoke for a moment with Lieutenant Hild DeHaven, the third ranking officer of the ship and a man who'd befriended Torben as soon as he was introduced as the new security officer of the *Stargazer*. He told Hild briefly about the boarding in general then added, "There was one other thing that piqued my curiosity. A teenage girl and two younger children boarded. The girl looked me in the eye when I spoke to her," he said, "but I don't think she even saw me. I'd swear she's scared of something."

Hild reached up to smooth back his black hair, which was flopping into his eyes, and nodded. "I'm pretty sure I know who you're talking about . . . I had the same impression," he said in English. Although Torben was Danish and Hild was Dutch, they both spoke very good English, and it was easy for Torben to talk to him.

"Keep an eye on them," Hild suggested as they entered the ship together. "It's part of your job to make sure the passengers are okay."

"I'll do that," Torben agreed.

"Let me know if you find something out," Hild said as the two parted company once they had reached the fourth deck of the ship.

In a few hours they would be heading out into the Baltic Sea on the first leg of the journey, and Torben busied himself with making his rounds, going from deck to deck, studying the passengers and visiting with people, helping them feel welcome and comfortable as they began their experience. He didn't see anyone who stood out as a possible troublemaker. However, he knew from his past limited experience that when some of them started drinking alcohol, difficult and troublesome personalities often emerged. And although his two years as a Danish police officer had prepared him for dealing with trouble, he hoped the voyage would be free from as much of it as possible.

\* \* \*

Cord placed a call to Nadif. "They are on board," he said.

"Excellent. Their first port of call is Tallinn, Estonia. You will fly there and watch for them when passengers get off the ship. If the three children get off, you will follow them again. Keep close track of them. Your job will be to make sure they get back on the ship."

"Isn't there anything else I should be doing?" Cord asked with a shadow of irritation in his voice. "I'm getting bored here."

"It may be that I will require your more . . . specialized services soon," Nadif replied. "But for now, your job is to watch and wait. It is of the utmost importance that they be on the ship a few days from now."

Still grumbling, Cord shut the phone and watched the cruise ship prepare to depart, hopeful that his assignment would soon be more interesting.

\* \* \*

The view from their seventh deck suite was breathtaking, and Aubree and the twins spent most of their first hour on their private balcony enjoying the harbor and the city beyond it. Later, she and the twins moved inside to further explore their suite. Their room was fairly large, and Aubree was sure they would be comfortable here even though it was nothing compared to the luxury to which they were accustomed. There was a bed for each one of them and sufficient room to move about.

Aubree actually began to unwind and vowed to try to relax now and enjoy the trip and quit thinking about her father and the blond man. She had lectured Brandi and Ryan again as they boarded the ship, reminding them that they needed to stick together. After the previous evening's frightening experience, they didn't argue with her; however, she knew that Brandi and Ryan would be itching to explore once they became more comfortable with the ship. And after all—how far could they get on a cruise ship? Perhaps they wouldn't have to be quite so careful once they got their bearings and the ship was out to sea.

The twins enjoyed the practice drill they were required to participate in to make sure the passengers knew what to do in the event of an emergency that would require everyone to abandon the ship. As Aubree looked around at the people who made up the group they were assigned to, there was a party atmosphere. She wondered if anyone was paying any attention. Some people joked about the *Titanic,* causing a shiver to run up her spine.

Back in their room, Ryan and Brandi jabbered excitedly about the lifeboats and how fun it would be to ride in one of them. Aubree reminded them that if that were to happen, it would only be because the *Stargazer* was sinking. "It could be days or even weeks before we were found," she said darkly.

The twins were unfazed and continued giggling and talking about the orange lifeboats as Aubree again wandered onto the balcony and watched as the huge ship began to slowly move away from the dock. About a half hour later, the ship was far out into the sea, and she and the twins made their way down to the fourth floor where tons of food was available.

As they rounded the corner toward the long buffet lines, Aubree's heart leaped into her throat. There, standing a few feet away with his back turned to them stood a tall, black-haired man.

Aubree stifled a scream and roughly grabbed Ryan and Brandi by their arms as she attempted to pull them back the way they had come.

"Aubree! Let go!" Brandi cried, and several passengers turned to face them, including the dark-haired man.

As Aubree looked up, her panic dissolved into embarrassment when she realized that the man she had assumed was her father was a stranger. Humiliated, she let go of the twins' arms and tried to avoid the glances of the other passengers.

"I'm sorry, Brandi, Ryan . . . I just . . . maybe it would be better if we get some snacks and take them back to the room."

The twins nodded obediently and then stood in line to fill their plates. Suddenly not hungry, Aubree didn't make a plate for herself but quickly ushered the twins back up to their suite when they were ready.

While her siblings ate, Aubree attempted to collect her thoughts.

*I can't fly off the handle every time I see a man who vaguely resembles my father,* she chastised herself. *We're safe now . . . we have to be. It's just . . .*

A knock at the door broke her train of thought, and she felt her heartbeat accelerate once more. Brandi and Ryan raced to the door as Aubree cried, "Don't open it! I need to see who it is first."

The twins backed away from the door. How quickly they seemed to forget. She slipped past the twins, who both muttered, "I'm sorry," under their breaths, and she peered through the peephole.

She was relieved to see someone in a tan and brown uniform standing outside her door.

"Hello?" she said tentatively after opening the door slightly and looking up at the smiling young man standing there. His hair was almost exactly the same color as Abigail's and Ada's—and her mother's, for that matter. His was cut short and neatly combed except for a little tuft that stood up on the back of his head. He was very attractive, and the thought caused her to blush. She was surprised that she noticed, as tense as she'd been.

For a moment, the young man didn't speak, but his bright blue eyes gazed into her own. When he spoke, his voice was deep and pleasant. "My name is Torben Davidsen. I'm a member of the ship's crew," he said with a slight accent. "I don't mean to intrude, but I wanted to make sure you were all right. I saw you walk into the dining hall a few minutes ago, but something seemed to upset you badly."

Aubree's blush deepened. "Oh . . . that. We're fine. I just . . . I thought I saw something," she finished lamely.

Looking unconvinced, Torben began, "Are you sure? I'm security officer on this ship, and if there's anything—"

At that moment, Brandi peeked around Aubree and said, "You can come in if you want." Turning to Aubree, she added, "He's got a uniform on, so he's safe, right?"

Aubree wasn't sure about that, but the guy seemed harmless. In fact, he was very charming and quite impressive in his distinctive uniform. She said, "Okay, sure," and stepped back, signaling for him to follow.

Torben hesitated a moment, then nodded and stepped inside. Seeing Ryan, he reached out and tousled the boy's blond hair. "I'm Torben," he said. "And what is your name?"

"I'm Ryan Kern."

"And I'm Brandi Kern," his sister added. "We're twins."

"I never would have guessed," he said with a wink at Aubree that made her skin tingle.

"Well, we are," Brandi said. "You should be able to tell. Even though I'm a girl and he's a boy, people say we look a lot alike." As Torben spoke with the twins, Aubree studied his face, noticing his strong square chin, high cheekbones, and straight nose.

"That you do," Torben said with a chuckle. "I'm pleased to meet both of you." Then he looked at Aubree again. "I take it you're Aubree," he said, raising a bushy red eyebrow.

"Yes, I'm sorry. I'm Aubree Lansing. These two are my little brother and sister."

"Ah, I see," Torben said. "Well, it's nice to have you guys aboard. Are the three of you traveling alone?"

Aubree suddenly felt uncomfortable. She didn't want to reveal anything that could cause her and the twins problems later. But she wasn't sure how to dodge the question. As it turned out, she didn't have to. Brandi spoke up again. "Yes. We're on a vacation. Our mother is coming, but she couldn't get here yet. Our dad had to work, so he couldn't come. But we're glad we're here, because it helps us stay away from Aubree's dad." Torben's eyes swung to Aubree as Brandi spoke. She frowned and gave a slight shake of her head.

"Torben's not interested in our problems," Aubree said sternly. "His job is to make sure we are comfortable and that we have a good time. Isn't that right, sir?" she said, looking Torben in the eye, daring him to disagree with her.

"Of course," he said sincerely. "But I was being serious earlier—I'm here to help if you need anything at all. My main responsibility on the ship is security." He smiled at the twins.

"I guess we'll be seeing you around the ship, then," Aubree said, moving toward the door. Torben nodded, taking the hint. A moment later, he left.

Aubree had no sooner shut the door than she turned toward the twins, unable to contain her frustration. "Don't ever mention my father to anyone again. No one needs to know our personal problems. We don't talk about my father, we don't talk about that guy in Copenhagen, and we don't talk about any problems we might have. Do you two understand?"

The twins nodded, even as tears filled their pale blue eyes. When neither of them spoke, she realized how harsh she'd sounded, and she felt bad. "I'm sorry, kids," she said, sighing. "I didn't mean to get angry. But we do need to be really careful."

She dropped to her knees and held out her arms to them. They rushed to her, clinging to her neck as the stress from the previous few days caught up with all of them. After the three held each other for a couple of minutes, Aubree said, "Torben seemed like a nice guy, didn't he?"

Brandi pulled back and offered a tiny smile. "He was cute, too."

Ryan pulled a face, and Aubree chuckled. But really, she couldn't have agreed more.

\* \* \*

Torben walked slowly away from the suite, troubled. Although Aubree had stopped the twins from saying anything further, he sensed that there really was some kind of trouble with her father. And whatever it was, it was clearly upsetting her. He recalled the sudden fear and panic in her eyes at the buffet, and how, minutes later, she and the twins had carried their plates back to their suite. Concerned, he had followed. Somehow, he needed to get them to tell him more so he could be of help to them if it was needed.

A few moments later, he arrived back on the main deck, but he couldn't get Aubree and her little siblings out of his mind. Clearly, they were on this ship alone with some kind of threat hovering over them, and he didn't like it. He resolved to do everything he could to gain their confidence and become their friend. Later, he shared his concerns with Hild. Both men felt that it would be wise to keep a close eye on the three young Americans, although, as Hild pointed out, it was unlikely that they were in danger here on the ship. At least they both hoped that was the case.

\* \* \*

"Please, Aubree! Francesca always reads us at least one story before bedtime," Brandi pleaded.

Aubree shook her head but smiled and said, "Then I guess we'll go see what we can find out." It was now far past the twins' usual bedtime, but since the time change had them all a little thrown off, Aubree decided not to worry about it. A few minutes later, they found themselves on the deck just below the top of the ship where they found a library filled with books and movies. There were even computers for the personal use of the passengers.

"While you kids find a book you'd like me to read to you," Aubree said after helping them find the children's section, "I'll check my e-mail."

She sat down at one of the computers and soon had her e-mail account open. She was delighted to see an e-mail from Lieutenant Jensen. He wanted to confirm that they had made it safely onto the ship and wondered if they were having a good time. He reminded her that if she felt the need, she was welcome to call him anytime.

Aubree typed a reply, telling him that everything had gone well after the incident with Ryan getting lost. However, she didn't mention her almost constant worries.

There was another e-mail from an address that she didn't recognize at first, but she grinned when she realized it was from Abigail. She wrote in broken English, just like she'd spoken. But Aubree's excitement faded and deep gloom settled over her when she read Abigail's report of what had happened after she and Ada and her friends had seen them off at the harbor. As Aubree read, she bit her lip so hard it hurt.

Abigail and Ada had seen the blond man at the harbor—and he had been watching the cruise ship. Abigail and her sister had been standing nearby and had heard him mutter something in German as Aubree and the twins boarded the ship. When the ship doors were closed, the man had climbed into a taxi that had been waiting nearby and left.

Although the e-mail seemed to give credence to her continued worries, Aubree was also relieved in a strange way. At least she didn't have to worry about the man being on board the ship.

After sending a short response to Abigail, thanking her again for her help, Aubree turned back to the twins to see if they had located a book. "Come on, guys. It's time to get back to our room."

Carrying their books, the three of them returned to their suite. After they had finished getting ready for bed, Aubree read the twins a story then tucked them in for the night. She was about to turn off the light next to her bed and fall asleep as well when, on an impulse, she reached into her bag and pulled out the Book of Mormon. She longed for the sense of comfort she had felt at the Jensens' home, and somehow this book was connected to that feeling. As she began to read rather than just thumb through it as she had in the hotel, Aubree was surprised to find that even though she didn't understand a lot of what she read, it was quite interesting. The worry and tension she'd felt after reading Abigail's e-mail faded away as she became engrossed in the story of Lehi and his family as they prepared to sail across the ocean into the unknown.

# CHAPTER SEVEN

THE LIGHTS OF THE STUDIO burned brightly. Vanessa posed for several more photos before heading back to her dressing room. Anxious to be with her children, she was now booked on flight that left later that day. Her manager, Miles Jordan, had scheduled the shoots she had reluctantly agreed to be to that morning, including the one that was to begin in an hour. But she was about to do something she'd never done before—cancel a session that was underway. Her manager was angry, but she was firm about it.

"You can't afford to offend our clients," he said sternly, his dark brown eyes flashing a warning. Miles had been with Vanessa for most of her career, and he had a tendency at times to think that he was the final decision maker. And quite often he was.

She set him straight, saying angrily, "They are *my* clients, Miles, and I will offend them if I like."

"You are risking your career," he warned, clenching one fist.

She studied him for a moment, wondering why it was so important that she work right now when he knew she had a plane to catch. Miles was about fifty now, a stocky, short man who worked out every day. The veins in his thick neck stood out when he was angry. They stood out now.

"My career is secure," she said confidently. "You will make sure it is."

His dark face grew darker, but he bit his lip. Rubbing his shaved head and then unconsciously flexing his huge muscles, he finally said, "Your kids can get along without you for a few days. They have done so plenty in the past."

"You are not going to stop me from making my flight. I promised to meet them in Tallinn, and I plan to do so," she said. "I'm going now.

You take care of things for me here while I'm gone. That's what I pay you for."

"Whatever you say," he answered as he marched away. She knew he would calm down. He always did. She headed for the door.

Since she'd gotten up that morning, she'd worried about her children. She was supposed to have left with them a couple of days ago, and yet she was still in LA because of Miles scheduling shoots she hadn't wanted, first on Catalina Island, and now here in LA. He would have to cancel what was left of the schedule. She was determined to catch up with the kids like she had promised. She was not going to risk missing her flight and causing another delay. It was bad enough that Reginald had been forced to miss the trip. There was no way she was going to do the same.

She arrived home an hour later. Her bags were packed, everything was in order, and she was more anxious than ever to be on her way. Even with servants bustling about the large mansion, the huge house felt empty without her children. As a last-minute impulse, she decided to call Reginald on the off chance that he might be able to answer.

Surprised when he picked up the phone, she said, "Hi, honey! How are you?"

"Oh, busy as ever," he replied, sounding distracted.

"I just wanted to say good-bye before I left. My flight leaves soon."

"About that . . ." he began, and she heard papers shuffling in the background, "I was actually just about to call you. It looks like there's a storm brewing over the Atlantic—I'm surprised there isn't a flight advisory. Are you sure you want to leave now?"

"Of course," Vanessa replied, surprised. "The children need me and I promised them."

"I'm just worried about you, Vanessa."

She paused and then said, "I was actually just going to ask if you were sure *you* couldn't come. Isn't there anyone in the firm that can cover for you?"

"I wish that were possible, Vanessa, but there isn't anyone else who doesn't already have a full calendar. And the judge made it clear that he expected me to be here personally. I'll have to try to make it up to the kids later. Are you sure *you* have time?"

"Honestly, honey, I don't, but I've decided to make the time. I really feel like I need to be with the kids—especially after what happened with Ryan."

Reginald sighed. "Once you make up your mind, there's no changing it, is there? Be careful at least, for me."

Vanessa agreed that she would then hung up the phone. Heading to her computer, she checked the weather and saw that there was indeed a severe storm building in the Atlantic. Concerned, she checked her flight. It was still scheduled for departure as planned. She was soon on her way to the airport.

\* \* \*

Torben watched Aubree and the twins as they walked toward him. She was smiling and chatting with Ryan and Brandi, and she looked much more at ease than she had yesterday. Her dark hair swayed as she walked, and she unconsciously reached up to tuck a strand behind her ears. He was relieved to see her looking so happy. As they came closer to where he was standing, a plate of food in his hand, she caught him looking at her. Her smile widened, and she steered the twins toward him.

"Hi, Torben," she said brightly. "They let you eat here too?" She cocked her head to the side and grinned.

"My job is to mingle with the guests," he said. "As security officer, I'm supposed to make sure everyone is happy and safe—and you three seem happy today."

"We are," she said as she turned her attention to the twins. They were eyeing the long lines of delicious food.

"Would you like to join me when you get your plates filled?" he asked on an impulse.

"Sure, that would be great," she agreed.

"I'll be right over there," he said, pointing at a table near the window. "I'll save all three of you a seat."

When they joined him, the twins rushed toward him, their eyes wide. "Torben! Look what we found!" Their plates were heaped with food—mostly pastries, Torben noted with a grin. "They let you take as many doughnuts as you want!" Brandi said in amazement and proceeded to take a bite from a bear claw.

"I'll be amazed if you two eat half of what you took," Aubree said with a smile, rolling her eyes. She sat down directly across the table from Torben and began to eat her more sensible meal. The twins sat beside her, but they only lasted a moment before they were on their feet again. "We forgot to get juice and milk," Ryan said, and away they went.

Torben noticed how Aubree's eyes followed them, and when Brandi and Ryan disappeared around the corner, the worried look she'd had the day before returned. "I'll be right back," she said, and in an instant she too was on her feet.

He watched her disappear around the same corner as the twins. He had only taken a few bites of his less than sensible breakfast before the three of them returned, each carrying two glasses. After they were again seated across from him, they all began to eat.

"So," Torben began, "I can tell you guys are from the United States. What part of the country are you from?"

Aubree swallowed a bite of bagel and then said, "California."

"Oh, the warm state," he said with a grin. "Not like my country."

"Where are you from?" she asked, her eyes meeting his.

"I'm from Denmark," he replied.

Ryan looked up from his plate and said, "Abigail and Ada are from Denmark too. But they don't speak English as well as you do."

"Who are Abigail and Ada?" Torben asked.

"We met them in Copenhagen—they saved me from the bad guy," Ryan said as he picked up another pastry from his plate. "They knew—"

Aubree cut him off. "Ryan, did you forget?"

Ryan's cheeks turned red and his eyes dropped until he was looking at the top of the table.

"Abigail and Ada are some friends we met yesterday before we boarded the ship," Aubree said, patting Ryan on the shoulder. "They watched us board the ship. But, anyway, you're from Denmark? What's it like there?"

Wanting to know more about what Ryan had been talking about but sure he shouldn't pry, Torben said, "It's a beautiful place—as I'm sure you saw from your short time in Copenhagen. Someday you'll have to go back to see more of the country. Outside the city the rolling hills are beautiful and green, and I could spend all day at the beach. My father and I often fish from the shore."

Aubree nodded. "That does sound nice. Malibu is really beautiful as well, but I've never been fishing from the beach there."

For the next few minutes they talked about their respective countries, settling into a relaxed and easy conversation. A couple of times, the twins went for more food, and Aubree laughed when she realized that they had indeed finished off their plates.

They ate in silence for a moment, and then Aubree said, "You speak very good English. Do a lot of Danish people speak English?"

"Yes. Many do. It's a very useful language."

"I wish I could speak another language," she replied.

He took a bite of his pastry and, after swallowing, said, "You'll find people in most of the countries you visit who speak English. English is probably the closest thing there is to an international language. By the way, how many countries do you plan to visit?"

"I think it's about six or seven," she said as she sat her glass of juice on the table.

Torben nodded then asked, "So tell me more about yourselves."

"Like what?" Aubree asked warily.

He smiled, hoping to put her at ease again. "Like what your parents do for a living or what you plan to do with your life. I'm guessing you're out of high school?"

"I'm going to UCLA this fall," Aubree said.

"UCLA?" He raised a bushy red eyebrow.

"Oh, sorry. The University of California at Los Angeles."

"It sounds impressive. Is it a big university?"

"One of the biggest," she said.

For a few moments, they talked about what she planned to study. Then he asked, "What do your folks do?" The look on her face reminded him of the comment Ryan had made about her father, and he wished he hadn't asked. But it was too late for that. "Our mother is a model," she said after a slight hesitation. "In fact, she's a very successful one. She'll be here soon. She's planning to meet us in Estonia."

"That's great," Torben said sincerely. "I'll look forward to meeting her. I don't know any famous people."

"Surely you meet a lot on this ship," Aubree said.

"Actually, I've only been the security officer for the *Stargazer* for a few days now. This is my first cruise with them."

"Really? I'm surprised. You seem to have a pretty good handle on things." She smiled at him. "So what did you do before you came here?"

"I was an officer in Denmark," he said as he slipped a bite of scrambled egg onto his fork.

"Really? What was that like?"

"I enjoyed it very much"

"Did you get to stop a lot of bad guys?" Ryan asked, his interest piqued.

"I did get to stop my fair share of bad guys," Torben replied with a chuckle, "but, actually, Denmark has one of the lowest crime rates in the world."

"That must be a good feeling" Aubree said with a shrug. "Malibu isn't far from LA—which I'll bet has one of the highest crime rates in the U.S."

"We have a friend who's a cop," Brandi piped up. "His name is Kevin Jensen."

Torben smiled at Ryan, and then he said. "I'll bet he's a good cop, too."

"He is," Aubree broke in. "He's a homicide detective for the Los Angeles Police Department. He actually works with my mother sometimes—he's provided security at some of her high-profile events." Then, before Torben could ask about that, she questioned, "So why did you leave the police force to become a security officer? Travel?"

"No, I left because they pay a lot more here," he said slowly. "My father is recovering from a severe heart attack, and he can't work for another year or so. He's a mechanic, and the doctors told him that he had to be completely healed before he started crawling around under cars again. I have little brothers and sisters, and my mom needed some extra help financially," he said.

"So you are doing this to support them?" Aubree asked with a look of unabashed admiration.

"It's what anyone would do," he said modestly, not wanting to seem like he was bragging.

"I don't know about that," Aubree replied, shaking her head. "I think it's pretty amazing."

He felt himself blushing, and she grinned. "I have a great family," he said seriously. "By most standards we'd probably be considered poor, but we've always been happy, and that's what counts.

"I'm just glad I can do a little something to help my family when things are tough for them. Don't get me wrong, I'm also grateful for the opportunity to travel. I look forward to seeing some of the places this ship will be going." His eyes softened and he finished with, "Maybe I'll even get to visit your country sometime."

"I think you should," Aubree said, nodding. "I bet you'd really like California."

"I bet you're right," he said. Then, knowing he should really get back to checking things out around the ship, he stood and said, "I've got to get going, but I hope I get to see the three of you again soon."

"We'd like that," she said, nodding, and the twins voiced their approval as well.

"I really am glad to see you guys are having fun today," he added as he prepared to move away from the table. "You seemed so tense and worried last night."

Surprising herself, Aubree opened up a little. Shrugging and not quite looking him in the eye, she said, "I was worried. I have full responsibility for these two on this trip until my mother gets here, and it's a little overwhelming. That's a lot of responsibility for someone who just barely finished high school."

"I'll say it is," Torben agreed.

"Thankfully, our mom will be here soon," Aubree added, flashing a bright smile. "Then she can worry about these two and I can relax a little."

Brandi had been listening carefully as they spoke. She broke in, saying, "My mom has the same color hair you do. It's really, really pretty."

"Thanks, Brandi. You know, there are a lot of people with red hair in Denmark, and a lot of blonds, like you two," he said, tousling Ryan's hair. He looked back at Aubree. "But girls with hair like yours are a little more rare in my country. You have beautiful hair."

"Thank you," she said, lowering her eyes and smiling shyly.

Just then, an older couple passed them. They said something to Torben in broken English, and as they struggled to find the right words, he answered them in a foreign language. Their faces lit up. They had apparently noticed his uniform and were looking at him expectantly. He pointed to the right, and the couple hurried away from them.

Aubree watched his face intently. "Was that Danish?" she asked. "It doesn't sound like the way Ada and Abigail were speaking."

"Actually, that's German. Those people needed to know how to find medical help. He's not feeling very well," he said with a frown.

"You speak three languages? Holy cow," she muttered, then waved and began to walk away. However, a moment later, she was unable to keep herself from glancing back. When she saw that he was watching her, she waved once more, grinned sheepishly, and quickly turned around.

* * *

Stone's session with his parole officer had gone very well that morning in Los Angeles. Stone had been cooperative, answering each question sincerely and openly, and he had told the man that he was looking for work. The only tense moment in the meeting had come when the officer had asked him about his ex-wife and daughter, However, Stone was quite sure he'd convinced the man that he would stay away from both of them. When the officer had asked him if it was true that he had threatened his daughter's safety because of her part in his conviction, he'd said, "She's my daughter. I love her. I would never do anything to hurt her or her mother." When the man looked at him doubtfully, Stone had simply stared back at him, daring him to respond.

The parole officer had sighed and reminded him to stay away from them.

"Whatever you say," Stone had replied. "I don't want any trouble."

When the officer had told him to report back in two weeks, it had set an unexpected roadblock in Stone's path. He thought he'd have a month. But he hadn't argued. His mind was made up; he'd simply have to do what he had to do overseas and report in when he could. Let the cards fall as they may, he thought grimly. Eleven years had been taken from him, and the time to set things right was now. Eventually, he would put it all behind him. But not before he was finished.

Fortunately, Stone had already succeeded in making travel arrangements. The papers Rambler had given him were excellent. He still felt uneasy not knowing who had fabricated them, but he intended to take full advantage of the generosity, if that's what it was. He would also watch his back at all times.

Four hours after leaving the office of his parole officer, Stone, aka Karl W. Faulk, was sitting on a jet at LAX waiting for the flight to take off. His travel plans had stated a final destination of Copenhagen, Denmark. But when he landed in Atlanta to change flights, he intended to modify his destination. He didn't want anyone to know his exact travel plans. It might take an extra day for arrangements to be made, but he planned to be in St. Petersburg, Russia—one of the stops of the cruise ship, before she left port there.

Settling back in his seat, Stone closed his eyes. He felt confident about his plan.

# CHAPTER EIGHT

THE BAIT HAD BEEN TAKEN. Stone was on his way to Copenhagen. The American didn't know for certain how Stone planned to catch up with the ship after that, but he was confident that Stone would figure those details out on his own. He knew the assumed name Stone was traveling under.

Humming to himself, pleased with the way things were working out, he called Nadif. "You'll need to have one of your men in place in Copenhagen a bit longer. They are to watch for a man by the name of Karl W. Faulk at the airport."

"My man has already left for Tallinn," Nadif protested.

"Then send someone else," the American said as he poured himself a glass of wine. "This is critical."

Nadif mumbled his assent but then said sharply, "I hope you can keep the woman contained. I don't want to focus any more of our energy watching her."

"Unfortunately, that's going to be a problem," the American said, taking a sip from his glass. "She left already. There's nothing I can do about that."

"But she was your problem," Nadif responded angrily. "You said you could keep her there."

"I was wrong. She's your problem now," the American told him. "So deal with it." Before Nadif could make a further protest, he disconnected.

* * *

Vanessa finally relaxed as she settled into her first-class seat. Miles was still angry with her, but she didn't care. Thinking about their last conversation, she shook her head. He'd urged her to change her plans and return to the studio. He'd tried to convince her that if she didn't, the angry clients would find a new model. She didn't care at this point. Maybe it was time to get a new manager. Miles had become a real pain lately. Sighing and cinching her seat belt over her lap, she turned her mind to more pleasant thoughts.

She was on her way now. And she was leaving behind, at least for a few days, the worry of what her ex-husband was up to. The delight she'd heard in her children's voices when she'd called them on the way to the airport to tell them she was finally on her way made her smile. Who knew? Maybe she'd even extend the cruise a little longer, she thought, to make up for the time they'd had to travel without her. She allowed herself another little smile. Miles wouldn't like that, but she didn't really care. Maybe he'd quit and save her the difficulty of firing him.

Closing her eyes, she tried to make herself comfortable for the flight ahead. A stewardess in first class came around offering beverages, and Vanessa nodded that she'd like some orange juice. Vanessa had been all over the world, thanks to her professional career, and if there was one thing she knew how to do well, it was travel. This was old hat to her. But despite that, she couldn't help but wish that when she opened her eyes, she would at last be on the *Stargazer* with Aubree, Ryan, and Brandi.

* * *

Stone fiddled with the buttons on his seat's armrest as he anxiously waited for takeoff. He had been one of the first to board and had selected a seat near the back of the plane, but his anxiety continued to rise with each passing second that somehow someone might realize he was flying under an assumed name—and breaking his parole.

As the airline's safety video began to play, Stone relaxed a bit. No one had come to drag him away. The falsified driver's license and passport had worked. He pretended to pay attention to the monitor displaying information on how to properly inflate a life vest, all the while running through his plans once his plane reached Atlanta.

A few minutes later, the plane rumbled down the runway and took off. Realizing he had to use the restroom, Stone waited until the seat-belt light went off, then made his way to the plane lavatory a few feet away. Apparently, other passengers had been waiting for it themselves, because three people arrived to wait in line before he had reached the door.

Frowning, Stone looked farther up the plane's aisle and saw that only one person stood in line at the lavatory there. Making his way toward the front of the plane, he reached the door as the person inside the lavatory exited and the next person went in.

As his eyes swept across the plane noting the flight attendant coming down the aisle opposite of him, he glanced inside the first-class cabin, which was directly in front of him. An old man sat reclined in one seat reading a sports magazine. Directly in front of him sat a woman with long, red hair.

Stone felt his stomach drop. Though the woman wasn't facing him, there was no mistaking that shade of red. *Vanessa,* he thought as he studied what he could see of her.

At that moment the lavatory door opened, surprising him so much that he stumbled backward, bumping into a large woman sitting behind him in an aisle seat.

"Watch it!" she cried out and reached for her Diet Coke to keep it from spilling.

"I'm so sorry," Stone muttered, red-faced, as he shut himself in the lavatory. He didn't think his ex-wife had seen him, but even so his heart pounded and his anxiety remained acute for some time. *Had* she seen him? Why wasn't she on the cruise with the children? His mind whirled with questions, and conflicting emotions battled within him. What he would have given to see her face after all this time . . . and yet, fresh anger swelled in his chest. She had betrayed him. She was married now to the pompous lawyer whose very name made his skin crawl.

Vowing not to let himself be seen, Stone left the lavatory, hurried up the aisle, and sank back into his seat. She couldn't know he was here.

\* \* \*

Aubree and the twins had discovered earlier that afternoon that, to their delight, the ship offered numerous activities for all ages. The twins signed up for several classes and activity groups, and Aubree was walking them to their first group now. They would be learning how to paint pictures of the ocean, and they couldn't be more excited. Afterward,

Aubree planned to take a walk by herself on deck to watch the setting sun. Although she loved her little siblings, the strain of watching and worrying about them every moment was taking its toll on her.

They had just rounded a corner on the third deck when they saw Torben walking toward them. He grinned broadly when he saw them. "Hey, it's my three favorite passengers."

Aubree smiled and said in return, "And it's our favorite security officer."

"Have you done any securing today?" Brandi asked cheerfully.

Torben laughed. "Actually, the answer is yes."

"And what did you secure?" Aubree asked with a grin, knowing she was flirting—and enjoying it in spite of herself.

"I escorted a drunk who was creating a scene in one of the lounges to his room," he said.

"Hmm," Aubree said, raising an eyebrow. "How did that go over?"

"Actually, I felt bad I had to be so rough on the guy. He *really* didn't want to go, and I sort of had to make him. But I didn't hurt him and he didn't hurt me, so I guess everything turned out okay."

Aubree nodded. "Good. I hope that an occasional drunk is all you have to deal with on this ship."

"So do I," he said. "When I was a police officer, dealing with drunks was usually the least of my concerns." They were standing in the hallway and had to move to let a couple pass by. "Hey, where are you three headed? I was just checking things out on this deck—I'd love some company."

"We're going to a painting class!" Brandi exclaimed, and Ryan nodded eagerly. "It starts now."

Torben's look of disappointment made Aubree's heart accelerate just a bit, and she quickly added, "They're going—I'm not. I was actually just planning to take a walk here on deck while I wait for them. I love the view."

The smile returned to Torben's face. "It is beautiful. And I'd love to accompany you on your walk."

After they had dropped the twins off at the painting class, Torben and Aubree went outside to the walkway that encircled the entire ship at this level. They strolled at a leisurely pace, watching as the sun began to turn the sky a pale shade of orange.

"So have you heard from your family at all?" Aubree asked him as they walked.

He nodded. "I got an e-mail from my dad this morning." He cast Aubree a glance. "He wanted to know if I'd met anyone interesting on the cruise yet."

"What did you tell him?"

His deep blue eyes met hers, and Aubree quickly looked back out at the setting sun. "I told him I certainly had—three people, to be exact," Torben said.

"More interesting than the drunk guy?"

He laughed. "Most definitely more interesting than the drunk guy." He shook his head. "I felt bad for his wife . . . she was so embarrassed. She just followed behind me as I escorted her husband back to their room, shaking her head and looking mad enough to spit."

Aubree laughed and he added in a softer tone, "But, seriously, I'm glad I met the three of you. Although I couldn't tell my family much, because I don't know much about you."

Aubree nodded, both flattered and nervous. Torben was definitely cute—and he seemed like a nice guy—but she wasn't quite ready to open up yet. "You know, I'm getting a little bit sleepy. I'm still getting used to the time change. I might go back to the suite and rest for a minute while the twins finish up their class."

"All right," he said with a smile, but the disappointed look was back in his eyes. "If you don't mind, could I walk you back to your suite?"

"That would be nice," Aubree replied.

When they reached the suite, Torben lifted a hand in farewell and turned to leave. But before he could walk away, Aubree called out, "You can come in for a minute, if you'd like—for a treat. We bought some really good cookies earlier." She blushed furiously, unsure why she'd followed the impulse and sure she sounded ridiculous.

However, to her relief, Torben didn't seem to think she was silly at all. He stepped into the suite and proceeded to eat three chocolate chip cookies as the two of them stood on the balcony watching the waves far below them reflect the lights from the ship. It was a beautiful and peaceful sight. The waves were much larger than they had been earlier, but the increased rocking of the ship only added to the contentment Aubree felt.

"I should let you get your rest now and go check the lounges again," Torben said after a few minutes. "That's where trouble usually is—since it's where everyone drinks."

As she followed him to the door, her eyes fell on the Book of Mormon by the bed. Although she'd tried reading it, she really hadn't been able to get into it very much. She saw Torben glance toward the book as well. Then he stopped and said, "The Book of Mormon. Are you reading that?"

"I've read a few pages," she admitted. "The police officer the twins mentioned gave it to me. He and his family are Mormons." Then she shrugged. "I think it's over my head, though. I'm not really a religious person."

"It's one of my favorite books," Torben said softly. "I read in it every day. It helps guide my life."

"Are you a Mormon?" Aubree asked in surprise. "Do they have Mormons in Denmark?"

"Yes to both questions." He considered a moment then added, "Maybe later, if you'll let me, I'll tell you more about that book," he said. "And if you have questions about what you've read in the Book of Mormon, I'd be glad to try to answer them."

After Torben was gone, Aubree sank to the sofa. She pictured Torben's smiling face and the color of his hair, which was so close her mother's. Then she thought about the sacrifice it must have been leaving both a job he loved and his family so he could support them. She felt a twinge of guilt at the thought. Her family had far more than they needed, and it made her slightly uncomfortable. She remembered what he'd said that morning at breakfast—that his family was poor but happy. And she could tell he really meant it.

She was surprised to find a tear working its way down her cheek as she thought about her own family. Yes, they had money and a luxurious home—servants, even—but they'd never known happiness of the kind Torben was referring to.

Aubree realized she was already looking forward to seeing him again. She knew that at some point, he might be someone she could confide in. And in moments such as this she admitted to herself she could use a trusted friend, someone she could talk to.

She reached for the Book of Mormon. If Torben liked the book so much, maybe she could try reading it again, just for a few minutes, before she went to pick Brandi and Ryan up.

\* \* \*

Out in the hallway, Torben stood at the foot of the stairs, his gaze toward Aubree's suite. Was it coincidence that he'd met her and the twins? He didn't think so. He had experienced enough in his life that he was certain the Lord was behind it. Perhaps they needed his help in some way. And maybe he could help them and their mother, when she got here, to learn more about the Church. Having served a mission, he was always looking for opportunities to share the gospel. But whatever it was that they needed, he vowed that if he could help them, he would.

That night he prayed for them. He asked fervently that he would receive the inspiration he needed to know how he could assist them, and especially how to share the gospel without being too pushy. As he drifted off to sleep, Aubree's dark, smiling eyes were the last thing he saw.

\* \* \*

Vanessa awoke as she felt the wheels of the plane touch down in Atlanta. Pleased that she had slept almost the entire flight, she quickly gathered her belongings then exited the plane a few moments later. She quickly stepped into a restroom near the gate to freshen up a little, knowing that her connecting flight left in a couple of hours. She wanted to locate the proper gate early, and she knew from previous experience that she would have to travel some distance across the airport to reach it.

As she stepped from the restroom, she glanced up and saw a man step out of the line of passengers still streaming from her flight. Her breaths came quick and shallow as she took in the man's build and hair color. *Stone?* Had he followed her somehow? Trying to get a better look but unsure whether it would be wise to move closer or not, she took a few tentative steps forward. However, at that moment the man began walking in the opposite direction without turning to face her.

Even as a tremor of fear ran through her, Vanessa scolded herself for being silly. Surely her fears were causing her to see her ex-husband in every man who remotely resembled him. But even as she chided herself, she craned her neck to see through the crowd as she moved forward, trying to see where the man had gone. Unfortunately, he was now lost in the throng of people.

Still shaken, she slowly turned and went in search of her next gate. As she waited there, a new thought struck her. If Stone had somehow followed her, he'd be boarding her connecting flight. With that thought in mind, she determined to be the last passenger aboard. Keeping an eye on the customer-service desk at all times, Vanessa anxiously awaited the call to board.

A few minutes later, the first-class passengers were called to board the plane. Even though she was traveling first class, she waited. Next they called for families with children and, finally, coach passengers. Although she carefully scrutinized each passenger who boarded the plane from a vantage point near the gate but at an angle where she herself would not be noticed, no one even remotely resembling Stone passed the gate.

A second boarding call was made, inviting any remaining passengers on the flight to Copenhagen to board now. Vanessa scanned the surrounding area once more and remained seated. Five minutes later, the intercom speaker made a final boarding call.

Rising from her seat, Vanessa strode toward the flight attendant who was checking boarding passes. Handing her pass to the woman, she asked breathlessly, "Are there any more passengers who still need to check in?"

The woman checked the computer in front of her then shook her head. "No, Mrs. Kern. You're the last one."

Breathing a sigh of relief, Vanessa hurried forward to find her seat. It had all been in her head.

# CHAPTER NINE

VANESSA FROWNED AT THE PHONE she held as she sat down on the side of the bed and slowly replaced the receiver. She had arrived in Copenhagen without incident about an hour ago, and she had checked into the hotel thinking she'd be here only a short time before boarding another plane to Tallinn. However, to her dismay, Reginald had been right about the storm causing problems with her travel plans. She had been on the phone since she arrived, trying to find a flight to Tallinn, but all flights had been either delayed or outright canceled due to the storm now raging over much of the Baltic region.

She had a decision to make. She could either continue to attempt to find a way to Tallinn, or she could fly to St. Petersburg, Russia—the ship's next port after Tallinn—and meet her children there. It wasn't what she wanted, but the chances of getting to Tallinn in the near future were almost nil. And if she didn't get on a plane to St. Petersburg soon, the storm would likely prevent a flight there as well.

Seeing little alternative, Vanessa picked up the phone once more to call her travel agent, and few minutes later, she had secured a flight to St. Petersburg leaving the next day, weather permitting.

Glancing at her watch and seeing that it was seven in the evening, she decided to call the children now. It would be later than that wherever the *Stargazer* was at, since the farther east they went, the later it was, but was sure they would still be awake, and the sooner they knew, the better. They would be disappointed—as was she—but there wasn't much to be done about it now. All she could do was look forward to seeing them when at last she was able to meet the ship.

* * *

"Boy was I surprised to see that bear again!" Chad Jackman exclaimed, gesturing animatedly as the twins laughed at the conclusion to his story.

Aubree giggled as well, especially because at that moment the ship pitched slightly, causing her to fall sideways into Brandi, who laughed even harder. They were enjoying a later dinner together in the dining hall, along with their assigned table companions, Chad and Leah Jackman. Dinner had been postponed that evening due to rough seas caused by a storm raging farther to the east, and when the captain had finally announced that they would be still be serving the meal, Aubree and the children had dressed in their finest and hurried down to the dining hall. They had felt somewhat seasick earlier as the waves grew in size and the ship began to rock more, but taking Dramamine had helped, and by evening they were famished.

As Chad began telling another story about his wilderness survival adventure in Alaska, Aubree's phone rang in the bag next to her and she quickly pulled it out to see who was calling. When she saw that it was Vanessa, she almost left the table to answer, but not wanting to interrupt Chad's story, she silenced the phone and dropped it back into the bag beside the table, intending to call her mother back in a few minutes.

Aubree took a bite of her chocolate mousse, reveling in the delicious dessert and in relaxing with her siblings. She was finally beginning to believe that everything would be okay. Chad and Leah Jackman had taken an instant interest in Aubree and the twins and had made them feel very welcome. It comforted Aubree to know that there were more adults on the ship she could consider friends.

The head steward, an Indonesian man by the name of Padli, approached their table to see if anyone needed anything. He had kept the twins entertained all evening and was constantly smiling and joking with the passengers as he served them. He was easy to like, and Aubree too had enjoyed visiting with him and learning about his country.

They had also met Padli's assistant, Farid, and the man who served the drinks, Eko. The twins had quickly memorized their servers' names and giggled in anticipation whenever one of the men walked by. And they were never disappointed—at each pass, one of the men would tweak Brandi's nose or make a joke.

"We're sure looking forward to meeting your mother," Leah said to Aubree as Padli left the table. A smile lit up her narrow, attractive features, and she lifted a slender wrist to gesture toward the twins. "We feel like we've known you three for years already; you've been such good company." She looked wistful for a moment then said, "Isn't it fun to eat in such a formal setting each night? It's definitely not something we're used to."

"Yeah, the missus and I are factory workers," Chad explained. He was a well-built man of nearly six feet. His hair was light brown like his wife's, and he was every bit as friendly as she was. "This kind of fancy thing is a once-in-a-lifetime opportunity for us. We won the trip through a drawing from our employers," he told them. "We could never have afforded it otherwise."

Padli appeared at the table once more, brushing the crumbs covering the table in front of Ryan. "You make big messes," he said with a grin. "Maybe if you eat the crumbs you spill, you will get full."

Ryan smiled and said, "They're just little crumbs, but I wish I had another cookie. They were so good!"

"For you I get another cookie," he said. "You are a cute kid. What about the little girl?" he asked, turning to Brandi.

"I don't eat as much as Ryan," she said primly.

"I can see that. You may be twins, but he's bigger than you. Maybe you need another cookie so you can grow like him."

"I don't want to be as big as Ryan," she said, pulling a face. "I'm a girl. I want to look like Aubree." She looked with admiration at her big sister.

Eko appeared as well and began refilling the Jackmans' drinks. He grinned and said to Ryan, "If you are such a big a boy, maybe you need some of this." He waved the bottle he was holding. "But your big sister will probably say no." He smiled again and headed for another table.

"He's right about that," Aubree said to Ryan with a smile. Then she turned to the Jackmans. "It's been so nice talking to you—I'm glad we were assigned to your table. It's getting a little late, though, so I'd better get the twins back to our room so they can go to bed."

"Can't we just stay up a little later, Aubree?" Ryan begged.

"It is getting pretty late," came a voice from behind them. Aubree turned, a smile already on her face, and saw Torben walking toward their table.

"Torben!" she greeted him enthusiastically as the twins called out greetings of their own.

"I'm sorry I got here just as you're about to leave. Hi, Mr. and Mrs. Jackman," he added, nodding to Chad and Leah.

"I promised Francesca that I'd get them to bed by a reasonable time each night so they won't develop bad habits by the time we get back home," Aubree said with a wink toward Torben. "I'm afraid I've already let them stay up way past when they should have gone to bed. I just hope the ship's rocking doesn't keep us all up tonight."

Torben nodded. "The captain says he's hopeful that we'll skirt the worst of the storm, but it's still possible we could run into it if it changes course. Cross your fingers—although this ship is as tight as they come. Hopefully, you'll just be rocked to sleep tonight."

Wishing she could linger a little longer and talk to Torben but knowing she should really be going, Aubree bid Torben and the Jackmans farewell, then led the twins to their room to get them ready for bed. She figured that when they were ready, they'd call Vanessa back and say good night. Glancing back one last time at Torben, who stood by their table with the Jackmans watching her leave, she gave a little wave then turned toward the door to the hallway.

\* \* \*

After chatting with Chad and Leah a moment longer, Torben turned to continue his rounds. However, as he began to walk away, he heard Leah say, "Oh, dear, Aubree left her cell phone."

Turning back, he saw her holding the small black satellite phone in her hand, having picked it up from off the floor near where Aubree had been sitting. "I'd be happy to take it back to her," he offered.

"That'd be great," Chad replied, patting his stomach. "I don't know if I could move if I tried right now."

Torben chuckled, then he took the phone and began walking toward Aubree's suite. He felt slightly silly for how pleased he was that an opportunity had presented itself to see her again, but he shrugged it off. She was just a friend. She'd be leaving to go back to her country soon.

The satellite phone in his hand began to ring. On an impulse, he opened the phone to see who was calling. However, to his dismay he quickly realized that he must have hit a button by mistake and answered the call by doing so.

"Hello?" he heard a distant voice calling through the receiver.

Quickly putting the phone to his ear, Torben said, "Hello?"

"I'm sorry," a male voice said clearly into the phone. "I must have misdialed. I was trying to reach Aubree Lansing."

"I'm sorry, this is Aubree's phone. She left it at dinner, but I'm in the process of returning it to her now."

"Who are you?" the voice asked in an authoritative manner.

"My name is Torben Davidsen. I'm the security officer for the *Stargazer* cruise ship," he said, trying to sound equally authoritative.

The voice on the phone immediately shifted from one of authority to one of concern. "Security," he said. "Actually, I'm glad I reached you, then. My name is Lieutenant Kevin Jensen. I'm an officer with the Los Angeles Police Department. I just wanted to check in with her before I left for work this morning."

Knowing he should probably just end the call and take a message for Aubree but unable to set aside his curiosity, Torben asked, "Are you the police officer who gave Aubree a Book of Mormon?"

"Yes, that was me," Lieutenant Jensen replied, sounding surprised. "Why do you ask?"

"I'm a Latter-day Saint as well. I saw it in Aubree's room the other day."

"That's wonderful. I'm glad to meet you—in a sense, at least." The lieutenant chuckled. Then his voice turned serious and he said, "Listen, though. I'd like to ask you a favor. Please keep a close eye on Aubree and her siblings, would you? They're such good kids, and they've really gotten a bum deal here."

"What do you mean?"

"Well, law enforcement to law enforcement—and without going into too many details—Aubree's father is a pretty bad guy. He just got out of prison—for murder no less—and he's apparently still pretty ticked at Aubree for testifying against him. The poor kid is terrified, and I don't blame her. He tried to hunt her down at her house before she left, and it gave her a pretty bad scare." He sighed then finished. "Anyway, please just keep a close watch on her and the twins. They could really use a friend."

"I see," said Torben, though he really didn't. He had a million other questions to ask, but, sure it wasn't his place to ask them, all he said was, "You can count on me to watch out for them."

"I appreciate that," Lieutenant Jensen said. "And if you don't mind, I'd like your number if you have one. I'm pretty certain Aubree isn't in any sort of danger, but since we're talking, I'd still feel better if you knew what her father looks like, just in case." He then described Stone before adding, "If you have an e-mail address, I'll send his picture to you."

"Sure," Torben said. After giving the lieutenant his phone number, he said, "Would you like me to leave a message for Aubree to call you? I think she's getting the twins ready for bed at the moment."

"No, I won't bother her now. I'll call back tomorrow. You've been a great help," Kevin said.

A few minutes later, Torben knocked quietly on the door of their suite on the seventh deck. Brandi answered, peeking through the locked chain. When she saw it was Torben, her face broke into a wide grin. Her hair was still dripping wet from her bath, and she held a fluffy pink towel under her arm against her pink pajamas.

"Is Aubree here?" Torben asked.

"She's helping Ryan with his bath," Brandi stated. "Then we're reading a book."

"That sounds great." Wishing he could stay but knowing that he should probably get back upstairs before he was missed, Torben slipped the phone through the doorway. "Will you give this to your sister?" he asked. "She left it downstairs at dinner."

Brandi nodded, and Torben hurried back downstairs, trying to process the information he'd just learned about Aubree. He paused on the stairway, both concerned and saddened, as the ship rocked more forcefully for a few moments. Her father had been in prison for murder—and he was out for revenge. Torben shook his head angrily. How could anyone want to hurt such a beautiful young woman? Swallowing his anger and determining to be the friend she needed, he offered a silent prayer for her, asking the Lord to help ease the terrible burden she carried. Now he understood why she looked as if something might suddenly jump out at her. Apparently there was a very real possibility that it would.

* * *

"The children seem to be very content on the cruise. I just have one thing to report. My source on the mainland tells me there's no way the mother will be joining them in Tallinn. All flights have been canceled. The soonest she'll be joining the ship is St. Petersburg."

"Fine," Nadif replied indifferently. "Cord will adjust as necessary."

"They don't suspect a thing."

"Of course they don't—why would they?" he shot back in annoyance.

"They plan to leave the ship for a tour of Tallinn. Should I keep an eye on them?"

"That won't be necessary. Cord will take care of that. Just continue monitoring their activities aboard the ship," Nadif instructed him. "Any information you gather could be useful. And remember, I need you to be on board at all times and ready to act when I give the word. Until you hear from me, there will be no further communication between us unless you have an emergency you can't handle. And keep an eye on our colleagues. They must be ready to act as well. Timing is of the essence."

"I'll take care of things," Nadif's man on the *Stargazer* promised.

* * *

"All right, you guys, you're clean and ready for bed. What do you say we call Mom and then read a story?" She grinned wearily as she stepped out of the bathroom and deposited Ryan's old clothes into the hamper. "I'm about to fall over I'm so tired, so I think I'll go to bed too."

"Good thing Torben brought your phone back," Brandi said, handing her the small black satellite phone.

"What do you mean?"

Brandi shrugged. "You left it at dinner. He brought it back while you were helping Ryan."

"That was nice of him," she said softly, wishing she'd seen him.

Brandi and Ryan stood next to her, excitement apparent on their faces, as she dialed Vanessa's number. However, when their mother picked up the phone, she didn't sound very happy. In fact, Aubree suddenly realized, she should have been on a flight to Tallinn by now.

"Mom? What's wrong?"

"I'm sorry, sweetie. I don't know how to tell you this, but the storm has caused all flights to Tallinn to be delayed or canceled." She paused then said in a slightly more hopeful voice, "But the good news is that I will be able to fly to St. Petersburg and join you on the ship there. I'm sure the weather will clear up in time for me to do that."

"That's okay, Mom," Aubree said, not wanting her mother to feel bad, although on the inside she felt an acute twinge of disappointment. "We'll still get to see you pretty soon."

"I'm sorry, sweetheart. I really am. I wanted to try to find a way to Tallinn, but there was simply no way."

"I understand, Mom. I really do. But, hey, I think Brandi and Ryan want to talk to you. It's late for them, and they wanted to say good night to you. We'll see you soon. And don't worry, we're doing fine."

"I love you, Aubree. And thanks for taking care of everything."

Passing the phone to the twins, Aubree listened to their end of the conversation as they told their mother good night and realized she wouldn't be joining them as soon as intended. Although they were disappointed, they seemed to consider the news a small setback, and they spent most of the conversation talking about their waiters' antics and their painting class on the ship.

When the twins had hung up, Aubree herded them toward their beds. "It's story time," she said. "What book do you have for me tonight?"

"Oh." Brandi's face fell as she looked toward her nightstand. "We only picked out two books last night—and we already read them both yesterday."

"Can we please go to the library and pick out a book for tonight? We'll be really, *really* fast," Ryan said, batting his clear blue eyes.

Although she was tired, she didn't want to deny the twins the pleasure of a bedtime story after the bad news Vanessa had given them. So, resigned, she hurried Brandi and Ryan up to the library.

As they entered the room and hurried toward the children's section, neither of the twins noticed the young man who was sitting at one of the computers, but Aubree did. Torben seemed engrossed in the screen as she tiptoed up behind him, grinning to herself, pleased that their paths had intersected once again this evening. She smiled as she studied him from behind. His red hair was neatly combed as usual, but the stubborn cowlick in the back had managed to spring free.

Sneaking up behind him, intending to surprise him, she tiptoed closer. But before she could say his name, she saw the screen he was looking at, and it knocked the breath right out of her. *Torben was looking at a picture of her father.* And it was printing even as he studied the photo.

For a minute, she couldn't speak. Questions raced through her mind. How did he know about her dad? What did he know about her dad? Who had sent the picture—and why? And perhaps most importantly, what right did Torben have to go behind her back this way? Why hadn't he told her he knew? Anger began to boil inside of her.

"What are you doing?" she cried. "You have no right!"

Torben jumped and looked around. Her eyes met his, and her anger mounted further when she saw that he looked taken aback. "Aubree," he said meekly. "I'm sorry. I know this must look like—"

"Like you're sneaking around behind my back, prying into my private affairs? Exactly. And I thought you were someone I could trust," she said, feeling tears prick at her eyes.

Torben got to his feet, his expression stricken. She had wounded him, but she was too angry to care. "Would you please explain what you are doing with my father's picture?"

For a moment he didn't answer. He just looked at her, his eyes full of pain. "Well, are you going to tell me?" she demanded. The twins, who had noticed what was happening, hurried back to Aubree's side, a book clutched in each of their little hands.

"Aubree, I'm not trying to sneak around behind your back," he said as he pushed his chair back and stood up, his eyes going to the twins. "You can at least let me explain. I was only—"

However, her anger had not yet run its full course. She cut him off tersely. "Then why are you printing a picture of my father without my knowledge?"

He looked down then said softly, "I was trying to learn what he looks like in case something happened."

That slowed her down. "But he's in LA."

Torben nodded. "I know. But your friend Lieutenant Jensen, who sent me the picture, by the way, is still concerned. He cares a lot about you guys. While I was bringing your phone back to you, it rang, and I accidentally answered the call when I opened the phone." He paused, seeming to expect an interruption. When Aubree remained silent, he continued. "I tried to tell him I'd give you a message, but he said he'd call back later. When he found out I was a security officer, he sent me this picture—just in case. He didn't tell me much—just to watch over you three."

Unsure what to think, Aubree took a step backward, pulling the twins—who had remained silent throughout the exchange—with her. "We're going back to our room," she said shakily, ignoring the further hurt she knew she was inflicting. "I need time to think about this."

"Please, Aubree. Talk to me," he said, his eyes pleading.

"I need to think this through myself," she said, averting her eyes. "Come on, kids. Let's go." Blinking back tears, she spun on her heel and led them toward the hallway, leaving Torben where he stood.

# CHAPTER TEN

THE COMMANDER OF THE PRESIDIO of Monterey, California, sat staring at the orders he'd just received under the signature of the commander. He double-checked the information regarding the weapons shipment. The shipment in question had arrived less than a week ago at the Presidio, not something usual for them, as they were a language training center. The weapons were only being held there temporarily while awaiting shipment overseas to U.S. army units in Iraq. He had expected the order to come so they could be moved.

Within two hours, the crates had left the Presidio on two large military trucks headed south. Two hours later, the captain had gotten a call from a major in the general's office, telling him that he was to prepare the rifles for shipment to Fort Benning, Georgia, where they would then be shipped directly to Iraq. The rest he was to keep where they were until further word.

Surprised, the captain informed the major that he'd already sent the entire shipment in trucks as per the order he'd received from the general hours earlier. When told that no such order had been given, the captain replied that he was looking at the signed document even as they spoke.

Ten minutes later, the commanding general himself was holding the order in his hand, shaking his head angrily and declaring that it was a forged document. Word was sent out and law enforcement agencies in the area were issued an urgent bulletin to locate and stop the trucks. But the vehicles seemed to have vanished, along with the soldiers who had been driving them.

As it stood, a great number of automatic weapons had been cleanly stolen from the United States Army. Their destination was of concern to military brass all the way to the Pentagon.

* * *

During the night, the *Stargazer* had docked in Tallinn. After the captain had assured all passengers that the storm had abated on the mainland, Aubree, Ryan, and Brandi ventured out as part of a tour group from the ship to go see the city. The Jackmans accompanied them as well, for which Aubree was grateful. She'd been expecting her mother to join her here, and the stress of keeping her siblings safe and together felt like an ominous task.

Their guide for the outing, Kerttu, was a tall, attractive young woman of about twenty-one. She spoke excellent English and was a very pleasant person. However, as she pointed out various landmarks on their walking tour, Aubree found herself listening only halfheartedly. She found it impossible to stop looking over her shoulder.

Kerttu escorted them through a castle and a large cathedral. When they were inside the buildings, which were packed with people, Aubree felt more at ease. Standing in the cathedral, near the back, she watched as other tourists filed in, oohing and aahing at the beautiful artwork. A mother and her son stood a few feet from her, point at a painting of an apostle, and Aubree smiled. A few feet away from them, a man who must have been the boy's father momentarily met Aubree's eyes. She smiled and turned away, happy to see a family together enjoying the sights Tallinn had to offer.

As Kerttu led the group into a part of Tallinn known as Old Town, Aubree felt the familiar, unwelcome paranoia creep back. People thronged them on all sides, and she kept her eyes trained on Brandi and Ryan at all times. As they walked down the narrow cobblestone streets, Aubree tried to concentrate on what the guide was saying. She looked closely at the ancient red-roofed stucco buildings of yellow and pink that rose two or three stories on either side of them. This was a fascinating place, and Aubree was angry that she couldn't give it her full attention. However, her irritation turned to icy fear a few minutes later when Ryan bolted away from where he'd been standing just a few feet ahead of her and ran back to her side, wrapping his arms around her waist and burying his head against her stomach. "Ryan, what is it?" she asked in alarm.

"He's here," Ryan said in a whisper. "The blond man who talked to me in Denmark is here! I just saw him." Aubree felt faint. Ryan's little body was shaking, and he began to sob.

Brandi also grabbed hold of Aubree's arm, and the three clung together as Aubree frantically looked about, but she didn't see anyone who fit Ryan's description of the blond man.

"We will all gather here again in thirty minutes," Aubree distantly heard Kerttu say. "Don't go too far, but enjoy yourselves." Aubree turned around, unsure what was going on. She assumed that the group was on its own for a little while, and the thought terrified her.

The Jackmans came over to them as Aubree looked about in confusion. Kerttu also stepped beside them and said, "Is something wrong? Can I help you?"

Brandi said in a trembling voice, "There's a guy here. He scared Ryan in Denmark. And now he's here. We think he's after us."

Kerttu's green eyes narrowed. "I'll summon the police at once," she said.

"Hold on," Chad Jackman interrupted. "What did this fellow look like?"

Ryan looked up from Aubree's side. "He has blond hair. He's really strong looking."

Chad nodded, but he looked unconvinced. "There are lots of blond people around, Ryan. Are you sure it was him?"

"I . . . I think so," Ryan stammered.

"It's all right, dear," Leah soothed. "I'm sure everything is okay. Chad's right—maybe you just thought you saw someone."

"I don't think we should take chances," Kerttu said firmly. "We will stay together until the rest of the tour group returns, and then we will get on the bus together and go back to the ship."

Aubree nodded, relieved that they would be staying together and also somewhat relieved that the police wouldn't have to be called here as well. She found herself wondering if maybe Ryan had mistaken someone else for the blond man.

"Come on," Kerttu said to all of them with a smile. "Let's wander around together for a little while. We'll be gathering here again as a group in less than thirty minutes. And you can watch for that man. If you see him again, you can point him out to the rest of us," Kerttu directed Ryan.

"We'll stay with you too," Chad Jackman declared. "There's safety in numbers."

"You don't have to do that," Aubree said, although her hands still shook slightly.

"But we want to," Leah told them. "So it's settled."

The time passed quickly as Kerttu gave them a private tour. Aubree and the twins began to relax. When the group had again gathered, they all made the walk to the bus together. The even sat together on the bus for the short ride to the port. Aubree sighed with relief when the bus was moving. Ryan hadn't seen the blond man again, and soon they would be on the ship again, safe.

Aubree kept a keen eye out as they got off the bus and approached the ship, remembering what Abigail had said about the man watching them board in Copenhagen. However, as she scanned the crowd walking near the ship, one face stood out as looking familiar: it was the man from the cathedral, but his wife and son were nowhere to be seen.

At that moment, Ryan made a quiet whimpering noise. "That's him," he said in terror, pointing directly where Aubree was already looking. Aubree's stomach clenched as she realized that the man she'd seen earlier did indeed have blond hair. When he saw that she continued to stare at him and that he had attracted Ryan's attention as well, he hurried into the crowd, disappearing before Aubree could cry out.

"Come on, we need to get on the ship now," Aubree told the twins urgently. The Jackmans, who stood a few feet away, hurried along with them.

As they entered the door, Aubree looked back one more time. The blond man had vanished completely. Unable to keep a tear from sliding down her cheek, Aubree held onto her siblings tightly. *He had been watching them in the cathedral. He had followed them to the ship.* Who was this man? What did he want from them? Those questions swirled around in her head as she tried to explain things to the Jackmans.

Chad and Leah attempted to comfort them, but all Aubree wanted to do was return to the suite with the twins, lock the door, and stay there until their mother joined them on the ship. Without tarrying, she thanked the Jackmans and hurried the twins back to their room.

Aubree had barely sat down when there was a knock on the door. Her first reaction was to leave the door unanswered, but then she considered that perhaps it might be Torben. To her surprise she found herself wishing fervently that it was him. Her anger had finally dissipated, replaced by increasing fear. She hoped he could forgive her for being so upset with him the day before. She had believed him when he'd said he was only looking out for her. It had just been so jarring to see him looking at a picture of her father. She hurried across the room and down the little hallway and looked through the peephole. Relief washed over her. She swung the door open.

"Torben," she said. As his name left her lips, the emotion from the past few hours overcame her, and to her chagrin, she began to cry.

"Hey, what's the matter?" he asked, worry evident in his clear blue eyes.

"It's terrible," she said.

"Is it your father?" he asked, urgency in his voice as he entered the suite and shut the door behind him.

"I don't know," she sobbed. "I just don't know."

"I saw you when you came back on board the ship. All three of you looked like you'd seen a ghost. What happened to upset you so much?" he asked, placing a hand gently on her arm. She didn't attempt to shake it off and, in fact, leaned closer to him.

"It was the man who frightened Ryan in Denmark," Brandi said in a small voice, coming to stand beside Aubree. Ryan sidled up beside her as well.

"You saw the guy who was in Copenhagen?" Torben asked with a furrowed brow while gently rubbing Aubree's arm.

She nodded, stricken. "He's in Tallinn now. I saw him in a cathedral, and I later recognized it was the same guy when Ryan spotted him by the ship. Oh, Torben, he must have been trailing us all day!"

"Something is going on," Torben said. "I think we should call your friend Lieutenant Jensen and ask him what we should do." He waved in the general direction of Tallinn. "And what about your mother? Don't you think she should know about him?"

"You're right; I should call them both," Aubree agreed shakily. "And I better let Reginald know, too. He'll wish he'd never let us come on this trip." She turned to look at Brandi and Ryan, who had lain their heads against her shoulder, clearly exhausted from all the worry. "I think I'd better let these two rest first. It's been a hard day for them too. I can make the calls after that."

Torben nodded but also suggested, "Why don't they take a nap in the Jackmans' room? I'm sure Chad and Leah wouldn't mind. And I know they have a large suite. I just think it's important that you let your family and officer friend know what's going on."

Aubree nodded slowly. "Will you take them to the Jackmans' and then come back and stay with me for a little while?" she asked quietly.

"Of course I will," he said firmly, then guided the sleepy twins out of the suite to talk to the Jackmans, holding their hands firmly to keep them steady as the ship pitched slightly.

When he returned a few minutes later, he lightly rapped on the door and Aubree opened it. "They were more than willing to take them in," he said. "Are you ready to make your calls now?"

She nodded. "I am . . . and thanks, Torben," she said as she looked deep into those clear, light blue eyes of his. "Thanks for looking out for us. After the way I treated you last night, I don't deserve it."

He shrugged, grinning a little. "Forget about that," he said as he hesitated, then pulled her toward him for a quick embrace. "I can't imagine the stress you are under."

Turning to pick up her phone to hide her blushing cheeks, Aubree dialed Vanessa. After she had explained what happened that afternoon, Vanessa replied, "You must have been so frightened . . . who is this man?" Her voice took on an angry edge. "I want you to promise me you'll call Lieutenant Jensen right after you speak to me. He'll know the best course of action. And I also want you to promise me you won't leave the ship in St. Petersburg. I'll meet you at the *Stargazer* the day after tomorrow, and then we'll finally be together."

Aubree readily agreed. "We're really looking forward to seeing you, Mom," she said softly.

"You too, baby," Vanessa replied. "Give my love to Brandi and Ryan. And before you know it, we'll be together again."

Moments later Aubree called Reginald, who was also worried and angry.

"I just wish I knew what was going on," he repeated several times, sounding upset and frustrated. "In the morning I'll look into it." To her dismay, Aubree realized she'd forgotten the time difference and woken him up.

After assuring him that she and the twins were fine, and after filling him in on the past couple of days, she disconnected. Aubree slumped back against the chair. "I think I'm as tired as the twins," she said with a halfhearted smile. "Telling people unpleasant news isn't the most energizing thing I've ever done."

"Would you like me to call the lieutenant for you?" he asked gently.

She considered for a few seconds then shook her head. "We can't call him quite yet. It's too early there. I'd like to talk to him, but I'll call later. I have a hard time keeping track of the difference in time. But thanks for the offer." She looked at him thoughtfully then said, "You know, if you have any questions, you can ask me now. I wasn't ready to talk to anybody about what's going on before. But you've really been a good friend to us, Torben."

He smiled softly and scooted closer to her. "I don't want to pry at all, but I have been curious and worried about you. Will you tell me a little of what's going on?"

Aubree took a deep breath and, keeping her eyes down, said, "When I was a little girl, my father was tried for murder. I was the key witness who sent him to jail. The murder happened in my house. I was playing in the closet at the time." She swallowed then continued. "To make a long story short, my father was in prison for more than ten years. He was recently released, and now he wants revenge. There's a restraining order against him . . . but . . . I don't know if that makes much difference to him."

A tear slipped from Aubree's lashes, and Torben tentatively placed an arm around her shoulder and drew her to him. "I can't imagine how hard this must be for you," he said quietly.

"What if this man who's been following us has something to do with my father?" she asked fearfully as she looked up into his serious eyes.

At first he didn't reply, but finally he said, "I don't know, Aubree. But I do know that I've kept the three of you in my prayers since the day I met you."

She nodded, touched. "I've never prayed much," she said quietly. "Sometime, will you teach me how?"

"Of course," he said sincerely. "I can teach you now, if you'd like. It's pretty simple. You address your Heavenly Father, and then you talk to Him just like you would talk to someone you respect and love. You can thank Him for blessings you have, ask Him for things that you need, or just tell Him what you're feeling. Then you close the prayer by saying 'in the name of Jesus Christ, amen.'" He smiled then added, "You know, I actually spent two years teaching people full time about my church and helping them learn to pray."

"I thought you were a policeman."

He grinned. "It was before that."

"Did it pay much?" she asked innocently, glad to turn the topic away from her situation for a moment.

Torben chuckled. "It didn't pay at all. I made a commitment to go wherever the Lord wanted me to and served at my own expense."

"But your family is poor," she said in dismay. "How could you afford to do that?"

"I couldn't afford not to," he said, his face growing serious. "And, anyway, we weren't as poor then as we are now. Dad was healthy then, and he worked hard and I had some money of my own saved."

"Of course, I guess if you took your meals at home and didn't rent a place," she concluded, thinking that he must have spent those two years in his hometown.

"Actually, I didn't see my family for those two years. You see, I was in Russia. I was teaching people there."

Aubree was stunned. "But how could you do that? How could the people understand . . ." She didn't complete her thought as understanding dawned. "Don't tell me you speak Russian, too?"

"That was a hard language to learn, but with the Lord's help, I managed," he said modestly. "I still have my Russian Book of Mormon. I read from it a lot so I can keep the language fresh in my mind. During my mission, the Book of Mormon was the teaching tool I used most— you know, that book you had on your nightstand the other night. I also taught people about Joseph Smith—the man who restored the gospel."

Keeping his gaze steadily on her, he said, "I'd love to tell you more about him sometime. But for now I want you to rest." He looked toward the door then added, "I'm going to check on the twins while you relax." Guiding her to the bed, he gently helped her to sit down on the side and pulled an afghan around her shoulders. "I'll be right back, okay? And, Aubree, everything is going to be all right."

Looking up into his face, she could almost believe it was the truth.

\* \* \*

Two hours after her call from Aubree, Vanessa's phone vibrated. She recognized the number—her manager's. "What do you want now, Miles?" she asked sharply.

"I warned you about this," he began without preamble. "You are this close to losing a very lucrative job. It's those people from Venice. They woke me up to tell me that they want you, but they said that unless you get back here *immediately,* they'll find a different model."

"Then I guess they'll just have to find someone else," Vanessa replied sharply, her emotions already pushed to the brink. "You should have already told them that."

"What's the matter with you, Vanessa?" Miles asked angrily. "This is your career we're talking about here."

"And it's my *family* I'm talking about. I'm not coming home for those people or anyone else."

"Have you lost your mind?" he asked.

"No, I think I've finally found it," she said. "Tell them we'll fly to Venice later if they'd like. But if they decide they can't wait for a few weeks, then I guess that's how it will be."

Miles changed his tone, sounding pleading when he spoke next. "Please, Vanessa. Think about this. Come back. They want this thing done now. Your kids are fine."

"Miles, for the last time, I'm not coming back. Deal with it." She closed her phone with an angry snap.

# CHAPTER ELEVEN

KEVIN'S ALARM CLOCK HAD BEEN set for six, but he shut it off five minutes before that. He slipped out of bed, hoping not to disturb Rosanne, but she mumbled, "I'll go get some breakfast for you. I take it you're going into the office early."

"Unfortunately. There's a lot I need to do today," he said, stifling a yawn.

Kevin's cell phone began to ring as Rosanne slipped from beneath the sheets, and he grabbed it from the nightstand and flipped it open. It was Aubree.

"Lieutenant Jensen? I know it's pretty early there, so I'm sorry if I woke you up, but I wanted to talk to you before you headed off to work."

"Don't worry, you didn't wake me—what's going on?" he asked, the last remnants of sleep fleeing, overtaken by his worry at a call this time of morning.

"We're all safe," Aubree responded, "but we had a bad experience in Tallinn today. I wanted to know what you thought."

What Aubree told him over the next few minutes was highly disturbing. He didn't know what was going on, but he intended to do everything possible to find out. It all seemed far too complicated for all of the problems in Aubree's life to have been orchestrated by her father seeking revenge. And yet . . . it was a good place to start digging.

"For now, I want you to stay on the ship at all times," he told her. "Stick close to the security officer you've befriended—Torben, wasn't it? And let me know the second you see anything amiss. I'll call you back when I know more."

"We'll do that," Aubree told him. "That's what I thought you'd tell me, but I still wanted you to know what was going on."

Fifteen minutes later, Kevin Jensen got in his car, hoping he'd be face-to-face with Stone Lansing within the hour.

* * *

That evening, the waiters' antics were as animated as ever, and so were their tablemates, the Jackmans. The waters were much calmer than they had been earlier, and Aubree and the twins hadn't even needed to take motion-sickness medicine before dinner. But still, Aubree couldn't relax. Everyone seemed to understand; however, the mood at the table eventually became more somber. Leah finally said, "I'm sorry about what happened today. But you kids really don't need to worry. You're safe on the ship."

Her husband echoed her words. "If there's anything we can do to help, all you have to do is ask."

"Thank you," Aubree said, "it was so kind of you to let the twins take a nap in your room earlier. I really appreciated it." Still, she was glad when they'd finished their dinner. She and the twins hurried to their suite.

As the twins played quietly together, she thought about what Kevin Jensen and Torben had told her about prayer. Although she felt slightly awkward, she felt confident enough from what Torben had explained to her that she could pray out loud herself. A little uncertainly, she invited Ryan and Brandi to kneel with her. For the first time in her life she offered a vocal prayer. In that prayer she asked that God protect her, the twins, and their mother. Then, a few minutes later, she sought the privacy of the little bathroom where she knelt again. This time, though praying silently, she was more specific than she had been in front of the twins. She made particular mention of the blond man in Tallinn and of her father. She asked God to protect her and her siblings from those two men. Although she still felt worried, a warm glow of peace edged out the darkness that had seemed to cloud her mind all that evening.

An hour later, she and the twins went up to the library to check out a movie and to use the computer. She settled the twins down in a pair of large chairs, with a book for each one, just a few feet from the computers. "Don't you guys leave your chairs," she warned, then turned toward the computers.

However, before she had reached them, she saw a familiar handsome redhead walking in the door. After the twins had woken up from their naps, he'd left to attend to some passengers who were locked out of their room, and she hadn't seen him since.

"I'm sorry that took so long," he said, shaking his head. "We really had to jimmy that lock, and by the time we got the door open, someone else needed help."

"It's okay," she told him, not wanting him to worry. "We just hung out in the suite and then went to dinner. But we didn't stay very long . . . I don't think any of us has much of an appetite."

"Understandably," he said, nodding. "Have you had a chance to call the lieutenant yet?"

"I talked to him for a few minutes before he left for work. He's looking into things from his end, and he wants us to stay on the ship for now—and stick close to you."

A grin tugged at the corner of his mouth. "Sounds good to me." But his serious expression returned quickly, and he said, "I've been thinking, though, Aubree. It would be a good idea to let the ship's captain know what's going on as well."

"You're probably right," she said slowly then frowned. "I just don't want to worry the twins any more than they already are."

"Would the Jackmans be willing to stay with them for a few minutes while we go talk to him?"

"I hate to put them out again so soon, but they did offer at dinner, and it would only be for a little while."

A few minutes later, Aubree called the Jackmans' room. They had not yet gone to bed. "Yes, we'd love to watch the twins. But let us come to your room," Leah offered. "That way the kids can go to bed if they get tired before you get back. And you and Torben can take whatever time you want to."

"Thank you so much. I'm sorry to put you out again after you just watched them, but they shouldn't be much trouble. I found a movie for them. They can watch that, if you don't mind," Aubree said.

"We'll be there in five minutes," Leah informed her. "We're delighted to spend a little more time with those sweet children."

The Jackmans got to room 737 at about the same time as Aubree. They didn't ask for an explanation of what Torben and Aubree were going to do, and Aubree wondered if they suspected it was a sort of date. She decided that was fine with her. She and Torben left the suite, thanking the Jackmans, and headed toward the captain's office.

Before they had even left the seventh deck, Torben's beeper went off. He listened to the message, frowning. "It looks like there's trouble in one of the lounges," he told her, taking her hand and hurrying faster. "A couple of guys had too much to drink and are picking a fight with each other."

Aubree hurried along by his side. For once, she wasn't afraid for herself, just for Torben. She didn't want him to get hurt.

Two men in their midtwenties were wrestling on the floor when Aubree followed Torben into the lounge. "Wait here," he said to her and waved at a large chair near the door. He then went straight toward the men and said, "That's all, guys. Break it up."

Seeming to do as he asked, the men pulled apart and stood up. But only half a second had passed before the first man again swung violently at the other. The other man quickly retaliated, heedless of his split lip and bloody nose.

"I mean it, guys. Break it up or I'll break it up for you," Torben said, his hands both held lightly in front of him, his palms open.

"Stay out of it," a young man in the small group of onlookers near the fighting men said.

"Stay back," Torben warned him with a black look. Then he stepped in close to the fighters. He grabbed the nearest one by the arm and pulled him back.

"Look out!" Aubree screamed as she saw the third man suddenly lunge toward Torben, his fist raised.

The blow never landed. Torben moved deftly as one of his feet came up and threw the man's blow off course. Losing his balance, the man stumbled backward over a chair and went down like a rock. The man Torben was holding tried to get loose, swinging at Torben. But he too met the floor with a resounding crash. The last man standing turned on Torben even before his adversary quit rolling across the carpet. But Torben somehow grabbed the man's swinging arm midflight. Then, in one swift movement, Torben turned his back into the man's chest, leaned forward, and with what appeared to be no effort at all, lifted the guy into the air and over his head. In the blink of an eye the offender had joined the others on the floor with a thud. Torben stepped back and surveyed the scene. Convinced that the three were not moving for the moment, he addressed the small crowd of onlookers. "Would anyone else like to try something?" he asked.

He'd made his point. The crowd of onlookers slowly dispersed, but Torben called out, "Are any of you friends of these guys? Someone needs to take them to their rooms to sober up. If you don't, I'll have to take them to the brig," he said, referring to the small jail cell on the ship used for just such occasions as this.

Three young women and a couple of men stepped forward, and Torben instructed them to take the intoxicated men to their rooms and sober them up. "If this happens again, someone is going to be locked up," he promised.

Aubree stared at Torben, dumbfounded. She'd leaped up from her chair when the first man had launched his ill-fated attack on Torben, and she was still standing. But she slowly lowered herself back into the chair and waited while Torben jotted down the identity of the drunks and the lounge staff began to clean up the mess they'd created. Once the offending men were gone and order had been fully restored, Torben came over to her.

"I'm sorry about that," he said, rubbing his arm. "Alcohol sure can make people mean."

He held out his hand, and she took it and rose to her feet. "That was incredible," she said. "How did you do that?"

"Do what?" he asked. "Help you to your feet?" He grinned and she felt herself relaxing.

"No," she said, pulling a face. "I mean, how did you take those three guys down like that without getting hit even once?"

He chuckled. "Let's just say I've had some training and experience," he said. "But apparently they haven't. I got lucky."

"What kind of training and experience?" she persisted as he led her out of the lounge and back into the hallway.

"I studied martial arts from the age of about ten," he said. "There was a man from China living in my town, and he taught classes. I was lucky enough to be able take them. I even made some money as an instructor when I got good enough. I never knew when I started studying it that it would ever be anything but sport for me, but it definitely came in handy in police work, and now, I guess, as a security officer on this ship."

"Do you have a black belt?" she asked.

He grinned. "Yeah, I do, actually. Let's get to the captain's office. I'm going to need to explain what happened in the lounge as well as discuss your situation. I don't suppose he'll like any of what we have to tell him."

* * *

It had been a busy morning. Kevin had contacted Stone's parole officer as soon as he'd arrived at work, but no one seemed to be able to locate the man. His consternation growing with each passing minute, Kevin had finally taken a break while he considered what to do next. As he took a bite of the candy bar he'd got from a vending machine a few minutes earlier, his cell phone rang. Intending to hit the ignore button, he quickly changed his mind when he saw that the call was from Vanessa Kern.

"Vanessa, how are you?"

"Well, worried, frankly. Aubree called you this morning, didn't she?"

"That she did," he told her, "but I'm afraid I don't have much to tell you yet. I didn't tell Aubree this, but I wanted to contact Stone to ask him if he knew anything. It was a long shot, but it was a place to start. I didn't think anything would come of it, but I have to admit I'm getting a little suspicious now. He seems to have vanished."

He heard Vanessa's sharp intake of breath on the other line. Then she said hesitantly, "I was sure I was seeing things, but . . . it couldn't have been him . . . he didn't get on the connecting flight."

"Hold on, Vanessa. What are you talking about?"

"It's probably nothing, and I didn't think to tell you before now because I was sure my imagination was getting the best of me. But on my flight to Atlanta from LA, I saw someone who looked just like Stone— from behind, anyway—get off the flight. But I never saw his face. And I waited to see if he would board my connection to Copenhagen, but he didn't. I was sure I'd been mistaken."

Kevin mulled over this information. "You might be right, but then again I think you might have just given me a lead. And if so, there'll be a warrant out for Stone Lansing's arrest as soon as I can confirm it."

Hanging up with Vanessa, Kevin grabbed his candy bar and drove directly to the LA airport. After speaking with security personnel and gaining access to the passenger records and security tapes, he set to work.

A mere forty-five minutes later he hit pay dirt. There on the screen he watched as a man with black hair, a polo shirt, and khakis stepped up to security. He kept his head turned until he began to walk up the ramp toward the plane. And then, at the last moment he turned, and Kevin paused the tape. *Bingo.* There, in front of him on the tape, was Stone Lansing.

Within the hour, Kevin had a bulletin out on Stone and was in contact with a number of agencies. By the time noon rolled around, he'd secured a warrant for Stone's arrest for breaking his parole. Stone was now a wanted man, nationwide and beyond. He'd already made dozens of calls, but none of them had yielded him any concrete information. His conversation with the Atlanta, Georgia, airport had been somewhat helpful in determining that Stone had not been on Vanessa's flight to Copenhagen, but where he'd gone after that was anyone's guess. It was clear that Stone had used an assumed name to travel, but determining which of the passengers that was could take days.

Kevin sighed and rubbed at his eyes, unhappy as he thought about the calls he had to make next—to tell Vanessa, Reginald, and Aubree that Stone was indeed missing and that things might very well get worse.

\* \* \*

The trucks that had been carrying the shipment of automatic weapons had been found. However, the vehicles, left in the mountains of Big Sur, were empty. The soldiers that had accompanied them were bound and gagged in the back of the trucks, and the weapons were gone. When questioned, the soldiers could not give any description of the thieves except to say that they were dressed in black with hoods over their heads. They had blocked the truck with a pair of vans they were driving. At least a dozen men had spilled from the vans with automatic weapons trained on the truck drivers and the soldiers who were providing security. They made their demands, and the soldiers had no alternative but to surrender themselves and their weapons. Moments later, more trucks had pulled up, and the thieves had transferred the crates of rifles and sped away. The army was calling it an act of terrorism, and a search for the thieves and for the stolen weapons was launched nationwide.

* * *

Stone's pulse sped up as he considered his situation. The anonymous phone call he'd just made to the LAPD made it clear that the authorities knew he had broken his parole, and he knew he had a choice to make. Things were only going to get worse for him from here on out. If he turned himself in now, the penalty would be much less severe—after all, he'd currently only broken his parole. Closing his eyes and trying to weigh his options, his daughter's face came unbidden to his mind.

His resolve strengthened, he knew he would continue, but not before he'd taken some precautions. Twenty minutes later, he had obtained scissors, peroxide, and glasses with clear lenses. After doing his best to alter his appearance, he looked into the mirror to survey the change. Even as he winced, he knew that his appearance was the least of his worries now.

* * *

Torben and Aubree stepped out of Captain Newkirk's office and began the walk back to the suite in companionable silence. Although the captain had been sympathetic to their story, he had offered much the same advice as Kevin Jensen had: the children should stay on the ship at all times, and he was to be notified if anything seemed amiss. Other than that, there wasn't much he could do. Still, Aubree felt better knowing he was aware of their situation.

When Aubree's cell phone began to ring, she pulled it from her bag and, seeing it was Kevin Jensen, answered.

"Aubree, I'm afraid I have some bad news," he began.

Aubree's chest tightened as Kevin explained the situation, and before he had finished speaking, she found that the pounding in her ears from the beat of her heart kept her from processing much more. "I think I need to hand the phone to Torben," she whispered in a barely audible voice as she numbly handed over the phone.

Torben, his expression deeply concerned, put a hand on her shoulder as he got on the line with Kevin. A few minutes later, he hung up, and Aubree realized she hadn't even been listening to what he was saying to Kevin on the phone.

"Lieutenant Jensen is going to call your mom, Aubree, and Reginald," Torben said softly. "I'll—"

Before he could finish, she leaned into him. Stopping midsentence, he hesitated only a fraction of a second before drawing her to him and stroking her hair softly. Safe in his arms, the tears finally began to fall. *Maybe he just wanted to start a new life away from us,* she told herself desperately. *Maybe his disappearance has nothing to do with me.* But it was no use. Her father was coming after her.

She felt her legs begin to buckle, but Torben pulled her closer, keeping her from falling—in more ways than one.

"Do you think you can walk to your room?" he asked her after a moment had passed.

"Yeah, I think I'm okay," she said, even though she felt very light-headed. "Lieutenant Jensen told you about my father?"

He nodded, his expression grave. "He told me they're doing everything possible to locate him—that there's a warrant out for his arrest. I'm sorry, Aubree," he said quietly.

Aubree's phone rang once more, and with a shaking hand she looked to see who was calling. It was Vanessa.

Although Vanessa attempted to console Aubree, it was clear that she was quite distraught herself. "I could kick myself for not calling the police in the airport when I thought I saw him. This could all be over now if I had—I just keep hoping that maybe, since he didn't get on the flight with me, he's just skipping town—not trying to follow you or me."

"I hope so too, Mom," Aubree replied softly. "And please don't blame yourself. I would have done exactly what you did."

"I wish I was with you right now, sweetie. But I'm glad you're out of his reach."

"I feel the same way. Torben and I were just talking to Captain Newkirk. I guess we'll need to let him know about this as well. He didn't seem too worried about the blond man who was watching us off the ship, but I'm sure he'd want us to tell him about anything that might be . . . a problem."

"I'm glad you did, Aubree. And remember, I'll see you in St. Petersburg."

A few minutes later, Aubree hung up, and Torben accompanied her to the suite, where they bid the Jackmans a brief good night. Aubree didn't feel much like talking to anyone right now, but it was with marked hesitation that she watched Torben walk back down the hallway as she entered the darkened room, her mind once again filled with threats of revenge and bloodied hands.

# CHAPTER TWELVE

LIEUTENANT JENSEN HUNG UP THE phone and shook his head. It had already been quite a day—and it hadn't slowed down even as six o'clock rolled around. He had just been briefed on the theft of the weapons, and although it had occurred far from his jurisdiction, everyone in law enforcement was being informed. The FBI and other federal authorities had made this daring theft a top priority, and he certainly understood why.

Turning his mind back to matters closer to home, he looked over the papers scattered across his desk with a grim expression. No new leads had surfaced concerning Stone yet, but Kevin was hopeful that he would soon be receiving another call from the LA airport. They had offered the possibility of synching the security tapes with the electronic record of passenger check-in data to find out exactly when Stone had given the attendant his boarding pass—and thus what false name he was traveling under. Although the airport security officer had told him it wouldn't take too long and Kevin had stressed the importance of the information, he still hadn't received a call back.

As he drummed his fingers on his oak desk, he tried to make sense of it all for the hundredth time. If it truly was revenge Stone was after, why would he arrange to have someone follow and watch Aubree and the twins? If he knew their location, why wouldn't he just go there himself and leave the mysterious middleman out?

But if Stone Lansing wasn't behind the recent troubling events, who was? And why had he broken his parole by leaving the area? Kevin had no answers. He was a homicide detective who had three squads of detectives working for him—and he'd been allowed to look into this matter on a purely provisional basis. The captain had been very under-standing, but he didn't know how much longer that would last.

*Unless.* He had a thought. It was a stretch, but it was worth a try. The plight of Aubree Lansing and her brother and sister had weighed heavily on his mind over the past few days, and he was willing to explore any angle he could think of.

He walked into the captain's office a few minutes later and, relieved his boss was still in the office at this hour, made his request. To his surprise, the captain was in agreement with him, and permission was granted to open Stone's file to see what it might reveal.

\* \* \*

The *Stargazer* had docked in St. Petersburg, Russia, in the early morning hours. The weather was good since the storm had moved farther out to sea, and Aubree and the twins' mood was bright as well. Although Aubree had promised her mother that they wouldn't leave the ship when she had called to tell them she had made it to St. Petersburg, she was sure that Vanessa wouldn't mind if they waited outside for her car to arrive in the harbor, especially because Torben had offered to go with them.

Brandi and Ryan were bubbling with excitement as they were funneled into and then passed through a small building just a short ways from the ship. Despite the somber expressions of the customs officials, who were wearing dark, severe uniforms, the twins giggled amongst themselves, playing a rhyming game as they walked.

Torben led them toward the gate, where a heavyset woman took each of their passports and issued them a red card, which they were told to surrender when they returned. Torben explained to the woman in English that they were going to meet an American woman on the dock who would be entering the ship with them in a few minutes.

"We're not actually planning to leave the harbor at all," Aubree assured the woman. "We'll only be a few feet away from here." But the woman's cold grey eyes remained impassive. In the end, she insisted on taking the passports, but Torben and Aubree were allowed to keep their visas. Aubree helped the twins tuck their red cards securely in their pockets.

As they left the Russian checkpoint to await Vanessa's appearance a short distance beyond it, Aubree heard her phone ring. Seeing it was Vanessa, she quickly answered and announced, "We're standing right outside the ship!" She listened a moment as Vanessa expressed her concern that they had left the ship then said, "Don't worry, we're in front of a Russian checkpoint right by the gates. Torben, the security officer I told you about, is here with us. You'll need to come past some big piles of shipping containers before you get to us, though," Aubree explained. "They're in straight rows and stacked two or three high. The road comes right past them, and as soon as you see them, you can see the ship. You can't miss us. We'll be watching for you."

"I should be there in about five minutes according to my taxi driver," Vanessa said excitedly.

"Just keep an eye out for the blond man we described to you. We haven't seen him, but I wouldn't be surprised if he's here somewhere," Aubree warned.

"I'm sure I'll be fine," her mother assured her then disconnected.

\* \* \*

"I'm hidden behind some big crates," Cord said on his phone. "I haven't seen her yet, and I'm getting tired of waiting."

"She'll come, so stay where you are," Nadif snapped. "I thought you wanted to see some action. This is your chance."

"I don't think you were ever clear on what you wanted me to do with her," Cord replied.

"Whatever you want to. Just stop her from boarding the ship," Nadif said darkly. "We needed her in California, but it's too late for that now. The American has failed me. Just make her disappear. And when you've finished with the woman, watch for the man I mentioned. His name is Karl Faulk. And, as always, make sure the children board the ship. Then get out of Russia and return to Berlin."

"Here comes a taxi now," Cord said excitedly. "I think it's her." He watched for a moment. "The windows are tinted, though."

"Keep watching," Nadif said. "Do you still see the children?"

"Yes, but there's a guy with them, a man in a tan uniform." Cord fell silent again then said urgently into the phone. "She got out of the taxi; it's her."

"Go!" Nadif barked.

Cord shut the phone and rushed from his hiding place between the shipping containers.

* * *

Aubree momentarily felt as if the wind had been knocked out of her. Then, gasping as she found her voice, she cried, "Torben, it's him!"

Without waiting to be told twice, Torben darted away, running straight for Vanessa. But the blond man was closer. He grabbed Vanessa and hit her hard on the back of the head as the car driver watched in horror, his mouth agape. Vanessa's large purse and the one piece of luggage she was carrying fell to the ground. Her red hair fanned down across the pavement as she slumped in his arms. Then the blond man threw her over his shoulder like a sack of grain and ran for the containers. Torben raced after them.

Aubree, who had been frozen by fear until this moment, suddenly snapped out of it. "I've got to help them," she cried to the twins, whose expressions revealed their terror. "Run back to that little building as fast as you can. Have them take you into the ship and then run to the room and stay there," she ordered them, and then she ran after Torben as fast as her legs would carry her.

She looked back once, just in time to see the twins disappear into the checkpoint. She could only pray that the officials inside would take care of them. When she looked ahead again, Torben was just disappearing behind one of the large shipping containers. She sprinted faster, pushing her legs forward in great strides in an attempt to keep from losing track of him. When she reached the spot where she had last seen Torben, he was nowhere in sight. Fighting panic and gasping for breath, she ran down the long, narrow alley and looked both ways.

What she saw to her left stopped her in her tracks. Her mother was lying in a heap on the ground, and the blond man was facing Torben, pointing a small black pistol at him not more than two feet from his chest. "You are a dead man," the thug was saying in English. "It was not your place to interfere."

"Please, tell me your name," Torben said in calm, low voice. "If you're going to kill me, at least tell me your name." Aubree was sure he was trying to stall the man, and her thoughts spun frenetically as she tried to think how she could possibly help him without getting all three of them killed.

The man laughed. "My name is Cord," he said. "You can tell the devil when you meet him that I killed you for Nadif, a great man from Somalia. And you can tell him that I also killed the woman with the red hair."

Muttering something in a language Aubree didn't understand, he cocked the gun and raised it slightly so that it was pointed directly at Torben's head.

A scream ripped from Aubree's throat involuntarily as she closed her eyes and heard the gun go off. However, when she realized that the scream that echoed her own was not Torben's but the blond man's, her eyes popped open once more. Quickly taking in the scene before her, she saw Torben crouched on the ground a few feet away from Vanessa and the man named Cord struggling with another man who appeared to be trying to get the gun away from him.

The pistol fired once more, striking a nearby shipping container, and Aubree dashed toward Torben, who was already attempting to pull Vanessa to her feet. Casting a hurried glance toward the two men struggling to the side of her, she desperately tried to figure out how she could help Torben. Another shot went off, and the man who had attacked Cord cried out in pain. Out of the corner of her eye, Aubree saw a few drops of blood spatter to the ground, and for a moment she thought she might faint. Certain that Cord would now turn the gun on the three of them, she braced herself for what would likely be death. However, no bullet came, and she realized that the man who had been shot was still struggling with Cord, though the tan jacket he wore now bore a red gash in the sleeve.

As Torben heaved Vanessa over his shoulder, he simultaneously grabbed Aubree's hand, and the three fled. Just as they had made it behind the corner of the next row of containers, they heard another shot, a sickening scream, and then all was silent except for the sound of their hurried footfalls hitting the pavement.

Aubree's breathing came ragged as she held Torben's hand in a vise-like grip and rushed forward beside him, waiting at any moment to be overtaken. Yet as the ship finally came into view, she nearly wept with relief as she saw several burly police officers in uniform running in their direction from the Russian checkpoint. Torben looked behind them and, seeing no sign of being followed, quickly but gently laid Vanessa on the pavement and placed two fingers over her carotid artery.

"She's alive, just unconscious," he told Aubree, his voice filled with relief.

The police officers drew closer, shouting something in Russian and drawing their large, deadly pistols. Aubree had read books and seen movies about the former KGB, and for a moment she was certain that they were about to be taken and locked away in a cold, dark cell.

Torben, however, began speaking rapidly in Russian, and the three men lowered their guns and then rushed toward the large steel containers where the two men had been struggling. Aubree knelt again beside her mother, whose eyelids began to flicker. "Mom, I'm right here," Aubree said softly, and Vanessa moaned then enclosed Aubree's hand tightly in her own.

A minute later, two of the officers returned, their expressions grim. They spoke to Torben in Russian once more, and his response brought about a rapid-fire exchange.

At last he turned to Aubree, who was still cradling her mother's head. In a low voice he said, "That man, Cord, is dead. They saw no sign of the man who attacked him. They want us to come with them now to answer a few questions."

Aubree nodded, stricken to know that the man was dead even though he had just tried to kill them. Swallowing, she asked quietly, "Are we in trouble?"

"I don't think so," he said glancing at an officer. "These men said that the officers at the checkpoint saw Cord snatch your mother and run with her," he explained. "But they'll want us to give an account of what happened as well as describe the other man."

"I don't even think I could give a good description," she said, shaking her head. "Everything happened so fast—I know he had blond hair and was wearing a tan jacket, but that's honestly it." She shuddered violently. "If he hadn't attacked that man, we'd be dead right now."

Torben took her hand. "I believe Heavenly Father was watching out for us," he said somberly.

Aubree nodded, feeling tears well up in her eyes. Vanessa was beginning to stir once more, and over the next couple of minutes, she became fully conscious.

"What happened?" she asked in a choked voice.

Aubree explained as best she could, and Vanessa shook her head in disbelief, then closed her eyes once more as a wave of nausea and dizziness overtook her. Meanwhile, Torben spoke with the Russian officers, answering their questions and translating for Aubree when necessary.

A few moments later, Torben said, "They want us to go back to the little building where we showed our passports. They want to talk to us inside while they investigate the crime scene further."

Aubree and Torben supported Vanessa as they began walking toward the checkpoint. Suddenly Torben asked, a stricken look on his face, "Where are the twins?"

"I sent them back. They ran into the checkpoint building so they would be safe," Aubree said, but even as she spoke, her stomach began to roll uncomfortably. Surely they had made it back to their room, she thought. Or maybe they would be waiting there in the checkpoint. Vanessa raised her head, a concerned look on her face. "I'm sure they'll be waiting for us there," Aubree assured her.

But they were not there. Not bothering with English, even though the officials in the checkpoint spoke some English, Torben rapidly asked them about Ryan and Brandi. The heavyset woman who had checked their passports told him that they were on the ship and were safe. As she spoke, her expression remained devoid of any emotion. Torben translated what she had told him, and Aubree felt a weight of guilt lift from her shoulders, knowing the twins had made it back to the *Stargazer*.

Aubree, Vanessa, and Torben were ushered into an empty, dingy room. An officer brought Vanessa's luggage and purse and dropped them at her feet. Then, after an uncomfortable wait of ten or fifteen minutes, further questioning began. It was in Russian and directed at Torben, who, when necessary, interpreted for Aubree and her mother, but fortunately, he was allowed to do most of the talking.

It was over an hour before the Russian officers told Torben, Vanessa, and Aubree to board the ship. Grateful that they would be able to leave now, they hurried as fast as Vanessa was comfortable. Torben told them that the questioning had taken so long because a death had been involved and because the man who had shot Cord was still unaccounted for.

"I'm sure it sounds heartless of me, but I don't feel bad about that man's death," Vanessa said with a frown. "I've never experienced anything so horrible in my life." Aubree had no argument to that. Nor did Torben disagree.

"I wonder who the other man was and why he jumped in like that," Aubree said. "Do you think he was just a passerby who saw what was going on? Or do you think he knew Cord somehow?"

Torben shook his head. "That's what the police were trying to figure out as well. He kept struggling with Cord even after he'd been shot. The police are planning to start their search for him in the nearby hospitals." He looked thoughtful and added, "Whoever he was, I'm grateful to him."

"Me too," Aubree said quietly.

Stepping closer to Aubree and her mother as they reached the top of the stairs, he said in a low voice, "I need to tell you two something. The Russians don't know it, but I have Cord's cell phone. It fell to the ground as he struggled with that other man, and I grabbed it. I think it might be useful in helping us find out who Cord was working for, who the man he called Nadif is, why he's been following you, Aubree, and why he attempted to stop you from getting on the ship, Vanessa."

"I can't believe you did that," Aubree said, shaking her head. "But I think it might have actually been a smart move." Then, tilting her head to the side, she gave him a tiny smile. "You know, with everything that's happened in the past hour, I just realized I've never even introduced you two. Mom, Torben. Torben, Mom."

Vanessa smiled and extended her hand. "I don't think we need formalities anymore after this morning, but I'm pleased to meet you, Torben. I really appreciate the friend you've been to my children."

Torben nodded seriously. "It's been my pleasure. I'm so glad you've finally been able to join the ship, although it's been under less-than-favorable circumstances." He began walking along with the two women again then said, "I also forgot to tell you—although I don't think it will be a problem—that the Russian woman instructed me that none of us is to leave the ship again while in Russia. I'm sorry about that. Under different circumstances, I think you would have enjoyed St. Petersburg."

"Maybe so, but I'm perfectly content to stay on the ship," Vanessa said and picked up her pace as Aubree and Torben followed. They all had the same goal in mind right now, and that was to make certain that the twins were safe in suite 737. They had to climb one more flight of stairs before getting on an elevator that took them to the seventh deck. From there it was a long walk toward the front of the ship down a narrow hallway before they finally reached the suite.

Aubree put her electronic key in the door and shoved it open. For a moment, only silence met her ears, but then two squealing eight year olds barreled toward the doorway, and relief flooded through her.

"Mom! Aubree! Torben!" The twins shouted, both laughing and crying. "You're safe!"

Vanessa reached down and pulled her children to her as she shed tears of her own. Torben squeezed Aubree's hand as they watched the tender scene before them, and, in spite of recent events, Aubree felt her heart fill with gratitude.

* * *

Stone gripped his passport in his left hand, gritted his teeth, and began the walk up the boarding gate, where he was issued a plastic ID card. That card, he was told, would now serve as his pass throughout his stay on the *Stargazer*. It would open his room, number 537, and would be used each time he left or entered the ship in any of the countries he would be visiting. Nodding pleasantly at this information despite the fact that his mind was reeling, he told the porters he could carry his own luggage to his room as he only had one bag, then left in search of his room. Once there, he collapsed on the bed, letting the bag fall limply to the floor. He sighed with relief. Although unable to believe it even now, he had made it.

# CHAPTER THIRTEEN

TORBEN SURVEYED THE PASSENGERS AS they made their way across deck. Many entered the ship's several restaurants, and his own stomach began to rumble as he realized that he hadn't eaten much all day.

He felt a buzzing in his pocket, and for a moment he was mystified. It wasn't his beeper, and his own cell phone was currently in his room. Then, with a jolt, he remembered he was carrying the dead man's cell phone. He quickly pulled it out of his pocket and looked at the phone, trying to decide what to do. He glanced around. There was no one close enough to overhear him at the moment, so, taking a chance, he decided to answer.

Attempting to disguise his voice, to make it sound as much like Cord's as he could, he said in German, *"Bitte?"*

"Why are you speaking German?" the man at the other end asked in German. Although he spoke the language passably, it was clearly not fluent to him.

Torben crossed his fingers, then took a breath and asked, "Nadif?"

"Of course this is Nadif," the man answered him, sounding leery. "Now why are you speaking in German?"

Torben thought quickly. "There are Russians around. A lot of them speak English. I prefer that they do not know what I'm saying to you."

"Okay, then speak German," Nadif replied irritably then got to the point of his call. "Did you get rid of the children's mother?"

Torben swallowed but responded confidently. "Of course," he replied, all the while wondering how long he could keep up this charade.

"And did you hide the body well enough so the Russians will not find it until you are long gone from the country?"

"They will never find it," Torben said. "I can promise you that."

"Are the three young people on the ship?"

"Yes, they are."

"And the man you were to kill, Mr. Faulk, have you found and eliminated him?"

Torben had no idea what Nadif was talking about, but he answered in the way he thought would please him the most. "He is dead," Torben said. "Everything went as planned."

"Excellent. Where are you now?"

Unsure what to say, Torben replied, "Russia."

"But I told you to leave," Nadif said harshly. "If the children are on the ship, your job there is done."

"I'm sorry," Torben said. "There . . . was a delay. I will be leaving within the hour."

"Fine. Don't call me unless there's a problem. Once the ship has left port, go back to Germany and stay there until I contact you following the completion of the operation," Nadif said. Then, to Torben's surprise, he switched to English and said, "Do you understand what I want?"

"Yes," Torben said, keeping his answer short, and grateful he now knew Cord had spoken English.

It was silent at the other end for a moment, and Torben wondered what was coming next. But after a moment, Nadif said, "There is one more thing, Cord. Do not attempt to contact anyone on the ship again. And do not accept any calls from them. I want no further communication between you and them unless it is absolutely necessary."

"Of course," Torben said, a battery of emotions running through him at this revelation.

The call ended as the line went dead. Torben looked at the phone in his hand, his heart racing. From what he had just learned, there were people on board who were somehow involved in this mess. He had no idea how many. He had to tell Aubree and Vanessa, and, more urgently, he had to alert the captain.

A few moments later, he found Captain Newkirk and explained what had happened. However, although the captain agreed that something should be done, he seemed distracted as he listened, and finally Torben asked if something was wrong.

The captain looked up at him with steely gray eyes and said, "I'm concerned about what you told me, Torben, but I have to admit that we might have bigger problems on our hands right now."

"What do you mean?" Torben asked with concern.

"That storm we bypassed on our way to Tallinn? It's picked up in intensity and range. There was an advisory out before we left port, but the crew didn't check it until we'd gotten out to sea—they thought we'd already dodged that bullet." He shook his head. "Maybe we'll get lucky again and get only an edge of it, but I'm not willing to be that optimistic yet. I'd like to start questioning the crew right now based on what you've told me, but between making preparations in the event that we hit this thing head on and accommodating so many passengers with the ship's activity in full swing, we've got our hands full." He sighed heavily. "However, if we do hit this storm, it shouldn't be until late evening, so I can promise you that after the dinner hour, I'll personally oversee the questioning."

Slightly disappointed, Torben nevertheless agreed, knowing that there wasn't much else to be done at this point but warn Aubree and Vanessa. As he exited the captain's office and looked out at the ocean, he saw smooth seas and wondered if perhaps the captain had been misinformed. However, looking out to the west, the distant line of purple and gray thunderheads caused him to reconsider.

Hurrying to Aubree's room, he tapped softly on the door. A minute later she answered the door, smiling broadly. "Hey, Torben! Come on in."

Knowing he was about to shatter her bright mood and hating it, he entered the room, waving to Vanessa and the twins, who were reading a book on the couch.

"I'm afraid I have some bad news," Torben began, looking Aubree in the eye and seeing her smile falter. Then he explained what had happened over the past fifteen minutes and what he had learned.

By the time he was finished speaking, Aubree's face had gone white, and Vanessa wore a deep frown. "I don't know what to make of some of what Nadif told me," Torben added when no one said anything. "Like who Mr. Faulk is. But it's obvious the blond man was being paid to follow Aubree and the twins and to kill Vanessa. It's also pretty clear he's been working with someone—or several people—aboard the ship."

"And you're sure the captain won't question the staff yet?" Vanessa asked imploringly as she pulled Brandi and Ryan closer to her on the couch.

"He told me that the soonest we would be able to question anybody was after dinner this evening. He's worried we're going to run into the storm again—only this time full force. The crew is trying to get everything prepared."

"But I don't even feel the boat rocking like before," Brandi piped up.

Torben nodded. "If we do hit the storm, it'll be much later tonight, but we still need to prepare now."

Aubree, who still hadn't spoken, moved toward the couch and faced Vanessa. "Do you think Dad arranged for someone on the ship to . . . to find me?" she asked in a shaky voice.

A pained expression crossed Vanessa's face, and she pulled her daughter toward her. "I don't know, sweetie. I really don't know." Aubree buried her face in her mother's shoulder, and Torben wondered if he should leave to let the family be alone together.

However, as Torben took a step toward the door, Aubree looked up at him, pushing a few strands of ebony hair behind her ears and attempting to compose herself. "Torben, I know you must have things you need to get done right now, but is there any way you could call Kevin Jensen to let him know what's going on? Since you're the one who talked to Nadif, I think it might be best if you explained things to him."

Vanessa nodded. "I'd appreciate that too. I'm going to see if I can get ahold of Reginald."

Torben agreed, and Aubree stood shakily to walk him to the door. She stepped out into the hallway with him for just a moment, and he found himself wishing he could pull her close to him and hold her until he knew she was safe. But instead he simply squeezed her hand and left, dialing Kevin Jensen's number as he walked down the hallway.

* * *

Kevin closed his phone. He'd spent the last ten minutes talking to Torben Davidsen, and he was still trying to digest what he had just learned. It was early, but he knew he wouldn't be able to sleep anymore with this information.

Who was Nadif? And Mr. Faulk? Was Stone really the mastermind behind this ever-more complex web of intrigue?

Not knowing what else to do with himself until he could reasonably go in to work, and sure he wouldn't be able to fall back asleep, Kevin picked up the file he'd brought home to look at the night before. So far, the research into Stone's file hadn't provided any answers or even any solid clues, but there was still more to go through.

After leafing through the papers for some time with no revelations, Kevin sighed then closed the folder and picked up his cell phone to call his work phone to check his messages. He listened intently to two messages that had come in after he'd gone home for the evening. One was from a possible witness to another case he was working on, and the next was from the Atlanta, Georgia, airport.

Kevin listened intently to the message from the airport security officer. They had made a connection between the electronic passenger records and the security tapes—and what's more, they had found a connection to the same passenger on a flight to St. Petersburg, Russia, that same day.

"What's the name?" Kevin burst out, heedless of the fact that his family still slept soundly in the adjoining rooms. However, the message ended simply with a "You can call us back anytime after seven AM, your time," and a click.

Gritting his teeth in frustration, Kevin looked at the clock on the wall. Six AM. One hour. Growling in irritation, he strode back to his room to take a shower and make the drive to work. Something was about to break, and somehow it felt like time was running out. He intended to make the call at six fifty-nine.

\* \* \*

As Aubree, Vanessa, and the twins hurried down to the formal dining room for dinner that evening, Aubree found herself giving more credence to the captain's warning that they would intersect with the storm once more. The sky had turned a murky brownish gray, and the waves visible from the sides of the boat rose and fell in great swells. They could see rain falling on the walkway beyond the windows. She also saw lightning in the distance, adding to the tension she already felt. However, dinner had not been canceled as far as anyone had heard,

and so, despite the increased pitching of the ship, they made their way
down to the dining hall.

Aubree and Vanessa had considered not going to dinner on account of what Torben had learned from his call with Nadif. They had
been unable to reach Reginald yet, but they had left several messages
and expected he would call back soon. However, after waiting in the
room for some time together, they had reasoned that they would perhaps be safer in a crowd of people than they would be on their own,
even if the door was locked. And as they sat down at their usual table,
seeing the smiling faces of the Jackmans, Padli, and Eko, Aubree realized she was glad they had come.

"Some rolls for my favorite passengers?" Padli asked as he arrived
next to their table carrying a basket brimming with freshly baked breads.

"I think I could eat five of those!" Ryan exclaimed. Then he looked
at Vanessa and his face reddened slightly. "I mean . . . yes, please. I'd
like one."

Everyone laughed and Padli offered Ryan and the rest of the table
a roll. "I am glad to see you come hungry," he said. "Some of the other
passengers say they are not feeling well enough to eat much."

"Dramamine has us feeling okay," Aubree said. "We learned from
last time."

Padli nodded, but the smile fell from his face. "I believe this time
may be worse. But we will hope not." Then he moved to the next table.

Vanessa and the Jackmans chatted amiably, getting to know one
another, and after a few minutes Brandi stood up. "Mom, I need to go
to the bathroom," she said. "There's one just outside the door," Leah
said, pointing.

"I'm coming too!" Ryan said.

Vanessa smiled fondly as the twins scampered away. "Twins," she
said. "Whatever one wants to do the other has to do as well"

Leah resumed asking Vanessa more about her modeling career.
However, not more than a couple of minutes had passed before she
was interrupted by cries of dismay throughout the dining hall as the
chandelier lights above them flickered then went out.

"Mom!" Aubree called out, quickly finding Vanessa's hand. All
around her she could hear the voices of people trying to get their bearings amidst the increasingly unsteady, rolling surface of the ship deck,

and a crash split the air as someone's dish went over the side of their table. She heard Chad Jackman call out something to Leah, but their voices trailed away quickly.

"Brandi and Ryan!" Vanessa called out then waited a moment as she and Aubree both attempted to hear a response amidst the growing chaos around them. "Brandi! Ryan!" she called out again, her voice tight with worry.

The captain's voice came on the intercom at that moment, and the frantic noises around them subdued slightly as everyone tried to listen. "This is Captain Newkirk speaking," came the voice. "I regret to inform you that the power has been knocked out aboard the ship due to the storm. Please remain calm and quickly but cautiously make your way back to your rooms at this time. Dinner and the remaining evening activities are canceled, and passengers are advised to remain in their rooms until given further notice. The storm will likely continue to mount in intensity, and, until further notice, all passengers and crew will be restricted from the main deck except in the event of an emergency. The crew will be making rounds while still possible to ensure that you have your needs met to ride out the storm and power outage; please wait for them in your rooms."

As the intercom clicked off, the noise level in the room rose once more, and more crashes and clanks were heard as people hurried to locate one another and began to feel their way out of the dining hall. Aubree watched their dim, shadowy shapes slip past her in the dark, and she struggled to keep a grip on her mother's arm.

Vanessa and Aubree continued shouting Brandi's and Ryan's names, and although only a minute or two must have passed, no tiny voices responded from the dark, shifting mass of people. All of a sudden, the ship pitched violently in the darkness, knocking Aubree off her feet.

"Mom!" she cried as she slammed into a nearby chair, hitting her head on one of its legs with a dull thud. Pain shot through her temple, and she cried out as she blindly attempted to right herself before someone stepped on her.

"Aubree, was that you? Are you all right?" Vanessa asked in a panicked voice from nearby. "Aubree, I still can't find Brandi or Ryan!"

Aubree winced as she put her hand to her head and felt something wet. Suddenly, a beam of light pierced the darkness surrounding them, and Aubree saw a ship's officer—Hild DeHaven—coming toward them. The crowd seemed to settle a bit at the presence of a small light source, and Aubree and Vanessa called out to get Hild's attention.

"Aubree! Are you all right?" he asked as he made his way to them and shined the flashlight on her face.

Vanessa gasped. "You're bleeding!" She turned to Hild. "Can you help us? Please, my two children Brandi and Ryan are missing, and Aubree is hurt."

"I'm fine, really," Aubree insisted. "I'll be okay once I've washed it off. I think I just cut myself a little. We need to find the twins now. They were headed to the bathroom when the lights went out."

Hild nodded. "I can keep looking for the twins while you and your mother go back to your room and get your cut taken care of. It's not safe for you to stay out here right now—you heard the captain's orders. I'll find Torben and let him know what's going on, and we'll start a search for Brandi and Ryan. They can't have gotten far, and as soon as we find them we'll bring them down to your room."

As if to emphasize the import of what he was saying, the ship rolled sideways, nearly sending all of them to the floor. Vanessa nodded, though the panicked look hadn't left her eyes, and Aubree knew that neither of them would be able to rest until the twins were found. Still, having little other choice, and knowing that Hild and Torben would be able to search more effectively with their flashlights, they hurried below deck.

* * *

Torben was doing the best he could to ensure that the passengers got to their rooms safely in the darkness, but he was unable to keep his thoughts from returning to Aubree. Fat raindrops were falling outside the windows, and the wind that had been only a soft breeze that afternoon had turned into a forceful gale. He worried for Aubree's safety in the chaos created by the combination of the power outage and the storm, and he prayed that he would soon see her face.

"Torben!" A familiar voice from the crowd caught his attention, and he turned to see Hild making his way toward him. "I need your help," he said urgently. "The Kern twins are missing. I've been looking for them myself for the past ten minutes, but I haven't found them."

"Hold on. When did they disappear? Where are Aubree and Vanessa?"

"The twins were at the restroom just outside the dining room when the power went out. Aubree and Vanessa couldn't find them, and then Aubree fell and hit her head when the ship pitched forward. Vanessa took her back to the room while I kept searching, but I've got nothing so far."

"Is Aubree all right?" Torben asked quickly.

"I think she'll be all right," Hild said hesitantly.

Torben nodded and said urgently "Let's go. I'm sure wherever those two are, they're pretty frightened right now. This ship is like an out-of-control roller coaster."

The two men searched for ten more minutes, growing increasingly worried and baffled. "I don't know where else they could be," Hild said after they met again a few minutes later. "What do you propose we do? The storm is only getting worse."

Torben frowned, praying for guidance as he tried to find an answer. "I think I need to check in with Aubree and Vanessa. Keep looking, and try to find another crew member to help. Most of the passengers should be safely in their rooms by now, so you should be able to find someone. I'll be back as soon as I can."

Hurrying along the hallway and then up the stairs to the seventh deck, Torben's ears rang with the sound of the storm battering the ship. As he carefully made his way up the stairs in the constantly pitching ship, he almost didn't hear his cell phone ringing.

When he saw that the phone call was coming from Kevin Jensen, Torben debated only a moment then picked up the call as he worked his way toward Aubree's suite. "Lieutenant Jensen? Listen, we've run right back into this storm, so I don't have time to talk. The twins have gone missing and—"

"The twins are missing?" Kevin's voice was charged with urgency. "Torben, I need you to pay attention. I don't have time to explain how I know this, but it may be critical information for you right now. The assumed name that Aubree's father is traveling under is Karl W. Faulk. We found out that he took a flight directly to St. Petersburg, Russia. He may—"

"Faulk?" Torben said, unable to believe what he was hearing.

"I don't know how Stone is connected to this Nadif you were talking to earlier, and it doesn't add up with the theory I've been operating under, but either way, I need you to check the ship's logs for new passengers who came aboard in St. Petersburg. I don't want to think this might be the case, but—"

By this point, Torben stood directly in front of Aubree's suite, breathing heavily in the darkness. "I understand," he said shortly, then disconnected and pounded on the door.

The door opened a minute later, and both Aubree and Vanessa stood there, steadying themselves against the walls, their faces anxious under the illumination of his flashlight. Torben's gaze fell on the red-tinged washcloth Aubree held to the side of her head, and the knot in his throat tightened.

"We haven't found them," he told them, attempting to maintain an air of calmness. "I just wanted to let you know what was going on. And . . ." He held up the phone helplessly in his hand. "That was Kevin Jensen on the line just now."

"Why? What's going on?" Aubree's dark eyes looked at him imploringly as she stumbled backward slightly into the room as a particularly large wave hit.

Torben reached out a hand to steady her, and she continued to grasp his shoulder even after the ship had steadied momentarily. "He believes he knows the assumed name that Stone is traveling under. It's Karl W. Faulk."

Vanessa's brow furrowed. "Faulk . . . as in the Faulk that man asked you about on the blond man's phone?"

"I don't know," Torben replied. "But Lieutenant Jensen discovered that Stone Lansing flew to St. Petersburg, Russia, under this assumed name after he left your flight in Atlanta." He watched Aubree's eyes widen as he said the words. Glancing toward the dark hallway, he took a step back. "That's where I need to go now. Hild is still searching, and I'll be right there with him. But I feel it's critical we know if there are any other factors at play here."

"I'm coming with you," Aubree said firmly, grabbing his arm with a shaking hand.

Vanessa looked at her daughter and then said, "I am too. We can't sit here any longer."

"The captain has ordered everyone to stay in their rooms. I don't know if I can let you do that," Torben faltered.

"You can put us in the brig afterward," Vanessa said firmly. "But we're coming. We've just been sitting there in the dark worrying and alternately trying to call Reginald, who still can't be reached. Let's go."

Figuring it was pointless to argue with the two determined women, Torben led the way to the office, helping them as best he could as wave after wave hit. For a few seconds the lights fluttered, and he thought that perhaps the power might come back on, but then blackness descended upon them once more, and the ship rolled more violently than ever.

"In here," he called to them as they reached the office door. Then, praying that the laptop battery still held a charge, he opened it and waited for the screen to flicker to life. A second passed, then two. When the black screen finally lit up, everyone sighed a breath of relief.

The passenger data system began loading, and Torben tapped his fingers nervously on the desk. When the search box pulled up, he entered the necessary data and clicked the search button.

The cursor froze for a moment, and then the search screen popped into view. Leaning forward to read the information, Torben blinked, hoping against hope that he was imagining the words on the screen.

Karl W. Faulk. Boarding Location: St. Petersburg, Russia. Room 537.

# CHAPTER FOURTEEN

AUBREE LET OUT A LOW moan as she saw the words blinking back at her on the screen. Her father was here. Against all odds, and despite their best efforts to elude him, he had found them.

She heard Vanessa's murmurs of disbelief behind her over the roar of the storm, and she turned to Torben, desperately hoping he'd know what to do. But before any of them could say a word, Captain Newkirk's voice rang out over the intercom. "Passengers, please be advised that two young children are missing aboard the ship—Brandi and Ryan Kern. If you have seen these two children since the power outage, please contact a member of the crew immediately. Otherwise, please continue to stay in your rooms."

*They haven't been found yet,* Aubree realized with sickening dread. *What if my father . . .* The thought was too gloomy to finish, and before she could let herself sink into paralyzing fear, Aubree lifted her eyes to Torben's, and she said decisively, "Let's go. We've got to find them before anything happens."

"First I'm going to alert Captain Newkirk and then head to room 537. If we're lucky, we'll find your father there—alone," Torben said.

Aubree looked stricken. "But what if he has a gun?" she asked in a voice that could barely be heard over the tumult surrounding them.

"I've been trained for exactly this kind of situation," Torben reassured her, but she wondered if he was trying to sound much more confident than he felt.

Vanessa glanced at Aubree before saying, "Please be careful. Aubree and I will keep searching for the twins while you go—we'll stay together."

Torben looked as if he wanted to object, but he only lowered his thick red eyebrows and nodded. Then, grabbing a flashlight from the desk, he handed it to Aubree and led the way to the door. As the three parted ways, Aubree offered a silent prayer that Torben would be kept safe and that the twins would soon be found.

"Where should we look first?" Vanessa asked loudly.

"I don't know," Aubree said as she carefully made her way forward. "Maybe the twins headed down instead of up. They could be on a lower deck. I don't know why they wouldn't have tried to get back to our room, but if they haven't been found yet near the dining hall and on the decks above, it's worth a try."

Vanessa agreed, noting as well that if they were found by one of the ship's officers, they would likely be escorted back to their room despite the twins' situation. Hild had told them in no uncertain terms that the crew would handle the search and that it was too dangerous for the passengers to try to help. However, Hild hadn't known that a killer was on board, Aubree thought with a violent shudder.

As she and her mother made their way down the stairs to a lower deck, all traces of light disappeared except for the dim beam of the flashlight that Aubree held in front of her. They called the twins' names loudly, knowing that the chaos of wind, rain, and ocean would drown out their voices except in the immediate area around them.

As they made their way down yet another flight of stairs, the ship tossed so erratically for a few seconds that Aubree lost her balance and careened headfirst toward the pitch-black darkness at the bottom of the stairs.

Letting out a scream, she grasped desperately for the banister as the flashlight flew out of her other hand. Blind in the darkness, and sure at any moment she would feel her head connect with the sharp edge of a stair step, Aubree hurtled downward.

She gasped in both surprise and sharp relief when she hit the bottom of the stairway with her shoulder, sending only a brief jolt of pain through her side. She'd been closer to the bottom of the stairway than she'd thought, but she had no idea how she'd managed not to injure herself as she fell. She heard the flashlight roll and connect against something with a clunk somewhere to her right. She caught a glimpse of its light as it rolled away and then disappeared.

"Aubree! Are you all right?" Vanessa called frantically from several feet above on the stairway.

"I'm okay, Mom!" she called back, rubbing her shoulder. "But I can't see my flashlight. I'm going to try to find it. Wait there. I'll hurry."

Groping along in the darkness, Aubree saw only blackness for what seemed like an eternity. But as her fingers felt the edge of a wall and she rounded a corner, she saw the faint gleam of her light in a far corner.

Hurrying forward the best she could, Aubree got down on her hands and knees to reach the flashlight. Once it was back in her hand, she retraced her steps. After rejoining Vanessa, she helped her finish coming down the stairs. However, as she turned around, a movement to her left caught her attention and nearly caused her to drop the flashlight again.

*It was just my shadow,* she told herself, fighting the panic that rose in her chest. Moving forward once more, she focused her attention on the twins, willing them to her.

But then, above the noise, she heard a single word. "Aubree."

The voice had come in the direction of the fleeting shadow, and Aubree stopped dead in her tracks as she flung the flashlight beam toward it.

The dim light revealed the unmistakable figure of Stone Lansing standing a few feet away. His dark eyes glittered in the dim light of her flashlight behind unfamiliar glasses, and his hair looked odd, much lighter than she remembered it. But as he reached a hand toward her, she remembered the fear associated with him all too well.

Gagging on a scream, she began to run, crashing into the wall as the ship pitched sideways. "Run, Mom! He's here!" she cried frantically, even as she heard Stone's own cries in the background.

"No!" he called out frantically. "Aubree!" And she was sure that at any moment a bullet would pierce her skull. But as she reached the stairway and stumbled back up a deck, then another and another with Vanessa at her side, Aubree began to believe they'd escaped.

When at last they saw the beam of a flashlight from another crew member, Aubree and Vanessa explained, between gasps of breath, what had happened. Two men were immediately dispatched to the location, and Aubree and Vanessa, despite their protests, were escorted to their rooms. The twins had still not been found, and because of the ever-increasing turbulence, even the crew members were being forced to return to their quarters until the storm broke.

"I'm sorry," the man escorting them said as he guided the two women toward their room. "I want to keep looking, I really do. It's the captain's orders . . . It's not safe. I'm sure your children are hunkered down safely somewhere. They just haven't been able to hear us yet." He sounded sincerely sorry, and Aubree knew it wasn't his fault.

Yet somewhere on the ship, Brandi and Ryan were alone and terrified. And somewhere else on this ship her father prowled dangerously. Tears pricked Aubree's eyes, and she squeezed her mother's hand tighter as they walked, fear and desperation boiling inside her. The one measure of solace she found was that the twins hadn't seemed to be with Stone when she had seen them. Surely they would have cried out to her. *Unless* . . . Aubree muffled a cry, and Vanessa murmured weak assurances as the officer helped them into their room.

Collapsing onto the sofa, Aubree allowed Vanessa to cradle her head in her lap as she had when she was a child. And as the storm raged outside, she closed her eyes against the darkness and prayed with all her might.

* * *

Torben pounded his fist against the office wall in frustration. *What are we supposed to do now?* he wondered angrily. Room 537 had been empty when he and another crew member had searched it half an hour ago, and when he'd learned about Aubree and Vanessa's encounter with Stone from Hild, he'd understood why. Stone was roaming the ship. If he was willing to leave his room in this weather, he wasn't simply going for a relaxing stroll.

Torben knew that the captain had ordered all the crew members and officers to their rooms to ride out the worst of the storm, but somehow he couldn't bring himself to obey. Taking a calming breath, he knelt, knowing he was alone in the office. *Please help me, Heavenly Father,* he prayed. *Help me to know where the twins are, and help keep them safe.*

As the ship shuddered beneath him, he waited to feel any inkling of a prompting. And when a quiet, slight nudge at the back of his mind brought a location on the ship to mind, despite the fact that he knew Hild had already searched there, he didn't hesitate before making his way to the door.

# CHAPTER FIFTEEN

Sitting in the darkened room with her mother, Aubree was more acutely aware of the havoc the storm was wreaking. The ship was rolling so steeply that at times that the floor was at a thirty-five-degree angle above them. Then it would settle back down, roll the other way, and soon be that much below them. The rolling wasn't limited to the huge ship. There was also an uncomfortable rolling in Aubree's stomach. It could only be seasickness, and it was amplified by the worry and fear she was feeling. As the minutes passed, she felt sicker still, and finally, unable to hold back any longer, she leaned over the edge of the sofa and vomited.

"I'm sorry, Mom," she said when the last of it had passed.

"Oh, sweetie, it doesn't matter. I feel sick too," Vanessa replied, stroking her hair once more.

Both women were startled when a sudden knock came at the door. For a moment neither of them moved, but when the ship seemed to level out, Aubree made her way to the door. When she got closer she could hear someone calling to her from the outside. "Aubree! It's Torben. Open the door!"

Relief flooding through her at the sound of his voice, Aubree quickly pulled the door toward her. She was barely able to make out Torben's face in the doorway. And as he moved toward her, she realized that he wasn't alone.

"Aubree! Aubree!" Ryan and Brandi cried out, weeping as they leaped forward and Aubree fell to her knees to catch them.

"My sweethearts!" Vanessa cried out, and despite the ship's pitching, she was at their sides in an instant. "Oh, thank you, thank you,

Torben! Oh, Brandi, Ryan, we were worried sick about you! We didn't know where you were, and we were worried that something had happened to you."

"We were really scared," Ryan said, his lip quivering as Vanessa guided him toward the bed and Aubree, Brandi, and Torben followed. "When the lights went out, I grabbed Brandi's hand and we tried to get back to you."

"But everyone was going crazy," Brandi said, sniffling. "Someone stepped on my foot, and it hurt a lot, so I told Ryan that we should wait by the door. But we kept getting pushed. We thought we saw the stairs that went up to our room, but it was hard to see, and we took the wrong way. The next thing we knew we were going down with other people."

Ryan picked up the story. "We saw some of the ship workers—you know, the ones who feed us dinner and help with our rooms—down where we went. They had flashlights, but no one looked at us and we were scared to talk to them."

Brandi began to tremble more violently, and Vanessa put an arm securely around her. "What is it, Brandi? What happened after that?" she asked gently.

"We saw one guy, the one who was nice to us at the table, but he wasn't nice then. He was waving a flashlight, and he shouted at us," Brandi said tearfully. "He scared us."

Ryan sucked in his breath sharply as the ship tilted dramatically, then said, "He asked us what we thought we were doing down there. He said, 'You kids get out of here. Don't you know you should be back in your room?' We tried to tell him we didn't know where to go, and he said that we'd better figure it out and find our mother."

"So what did you do then?" Vanessa asked gently, but Aubree could hear an edge to her voice.

Brandi spoke again. "We started running, even though it was hard with how much the ship was moving back and forth and how dark it was. We felt along the wall and found a door and opened it, thinking maybe we could get back upstairs that way." She looked at Torben. "It was the room where you found us. We could hear people yelling behind us, so we just jumped in there and shut the door."

"You did the right thing," Torben told them. "I'm glad you went somewhere safe and waited to be found."

"How did you find them, Torben?" Vanessa broke in. "I thought the staff area of the ship had been searched already."

"I was trying to figure out what to do, and as I was praying, the support staff quarters popped into my head. They'd already been searched, but then I realized that nobody the twins knew personally had searched there. I wondered if maybe they were afraid to respond to a voice they didn't know."

Brandi nodded vigorously. "Before you came, someone opened the door and called to us, but by then we were too afraid. We were worried that the bad men—"

"The bad men?" Aubree asked. Then, realizing she might have missed something in Brandi's story, she said, "I'm sorry, keep telling us what happened. How long was it before anybody opened the door?" she asked.

"It was a long time," Brandi said. "And it was really scary being there alone in the dark, with all the stuff in the room rolling around. But nothing hit us hard or anything, and we just huddled in the corner together."

Ryan nodded. "We stayed where we were and listened. We could hear someone outside the room right after we hid."

Brandi looked at Ryan. "We couldn't understand them," she said.

"You mean they weren't speaking English?" Aubree asked.

"Yes," Brandi said. "But they sounded mean. They scared us really bad."

"They sounded like they were telling secrets, bad secrets," Ryan said, his face very somber in the murky darkness.

His sister nodded her agreement and then added, "They were right next to the room we were in, but sometimes we still couldn't hear them over the storm sounds."

"So you don't know what they were talking about?" Torben asked.

"Not then, but then another guy came and we could understand them after that. They started talking like we do," Ryan said.

"They spoke English?" Torben prompted.

"Yeah, and then we got more scared than before," Ryan said, a quaver finding its way back into his voice.

"We just hugged each other and wished you guys would come and find us," Brandi said, and again she began to cry.

"What did they say, sweetheart?" Vanessa prodded.

Brandi thought for a few seconds then said, "One of the guys called one of the others Eko. And that sounded like the guy who told us to go back upstairs."

Aubree let out a little gasp. "Eko is the name of the man who serves drinks at our table in the dining room. He always seemed friendly, but he would have known who Ryan and Brandi were."

"Yes, that's him, the one who told us to get out of there and find our mom," Ryan agreed quickly.

"What else happened?" Torben asked.

"Eko sounded more and more upset. He said that if something happened to the children, some guy named Nadif would be really mad."

"Are you sure they said Nadif?" Torben asked urgently.

"Pretty sure," Ryan answered. "They said that the brats and their sister were going make them and Nadif rich."

Their tears again began to flow, and Torben waited while they wiped their eyes before asking, "What else did they say?"

"One of them said something about taking the ship. I don't know what they meant," Ryan said.

"And one of them said *ransom*," Brandi added.

"Are you sure of that?" Torben asked urgently.

"Yeah, 'cause one of the other guys said it again after that. We've heard that word before in movies. We know what it means," Brandi revealed.

"Did you hear anything else?" Torben asked. Aubree could tell from the look on his face that he was thinking the same thing she was. They were in the company of modern-day pirates. She shuddered and tried to listen as the twins went on.

"There were a lot of banging noises going on, so we couldn't hear them very well, but somebody said they were going to kill someone," Ryan said, and again he had to fight tears, as did Brandi.

Aubree swallowed hard, amazed that somehow their situation seemed to have worsened. "You guys are doing really good," she tried to encourage. "What else did you hear?"

"After a while we couldn't hear the voices anymore," Brandi said tearfully. "But we didn't dare move. We thought they wanted to kill us," she said, and the memory of the intense fear they'd experienced started them crying again. Their mother hugged them both tightly and assured them they were safe now.

"We prayed over and over, like you showed us that Torben taught you, until he found us," Ryan told them.

"God heard your prayers," Torben said. "And ours." He glanced at Aubree, who nodded in agreement.

"What do we do now?" Vanessa asked after a moment, her voice frail.

Torben sighed heavily. "For the moment, nothing. Until this storm calms down a bit, we're going to have to wait. As weird as it sounds, in light of what Brandi and Ryan heard, we're probably safer right now than we would be otherwise. But as soon as we're able, we'll need to alert Captain Newkirk to tell him what you heard about ransom and taking the ship." His gaze turned stony. "I can tell you this—nobody's going to be taking the ship while I have anything to say about it."

"What about my father?" Aubree asked in a small voice. "You know I saw him, don't you?"

"Hild told me," Torben told her, reaching for her hand in the darkness and squeezing it tightly. "I'm sorry I wasn't there with you to help. That must have been terribly frightening."

"It was," Aubree agreed.

"Aubree's dad is here?" Brandi asked in a frightened voice.

"Yes, Brandi," Vanessa said. "He's on the ship, but as soon as the storm calms down, Torben and the other officers will find him quickly. Torben's good at finding people," she said with a touch of a smile in her voice.

"That's right," Torben reassured her. And then, to Aubree's relief, he added, "But let's talk about something a bit happier right now. There's no use worrying ourselves ragged while there's nothing we can do about it. How about I tell you a story?"

"Oh yeah!" Ryan said, clearly relieved as well. And as he spoke the words, the lights flickered on in the cabin.

Everyone held their breath, but the lights stayed on, despite the continued rolling of the ship, and a few seconds later they sent up a cheer.

"I think it's a good omen," Torben said seriously, looking at Aubree, and she felt her stomach flutter despite everything that was happening.

"Now let me tell you a story about another family who was out at sea when a terrible storm came up—one like we are in right now. A man named Nephi . . ."

# CHAPTER SIXTEEN

AT TEN O'CLOCK THE NEXT morning, the intercom came on again. Aubree grimaced and opened her eyes as she tried to listen. But when the captain announced that the passengers would be free to leave their rooms in a few minutes, she became wide awake. Looking around at the chaos in the suite, she remembered last night's events and felt a rush of gratitude that at least one storm had passed. Vanessa sat reclined against the head of the bed, where she'd fallen asleep with Brandi in her arms. Torben sat next to Ryan on the other side of the second bed, where they had dozed off while he told the twins stories to calm them as the storm continued to rage throughout the night. Aubree had finally fallen asleep in the wee hours of the morning on the third bed, but she knew she must have only gotten two or three hours of sleep. She had lain awake long after the others had quieted, turning recent events over and over in her mind.

Torben met her eyes and smiled tiredly, then ran a hand through his disheveled hair. "I bet that was wilder than anything you ever rode at Disneyland," he said, reaching over to ruffle Ryan's hair.

Ryan nodded his head. "I thought the ship was going to sink and that the orange life boats wouldn't help us."

"Me too," Brandi added. "But I was glad we were safe in here with you and Mom and Aubree." A fearful look returned to her eyes and she pointed toward the door. "Is Aubree's dad still out there?"

"We'll find him this morning," Torben told her reassuringly. "Do you remember what we talked about last night before we went to sleep, about Lehi and Nephi and the storm?"

Brandi nodded, and Aubree remembered as well. Despite all the fear and turmoil she had felt, it had slowly melted into the background as Torben began telling the story. The twins had snuggled closer to him as he had talked of brothers building a ship and a family sailing away into the great unknown. When a storm had arisen and nearly swallowed the ship because of the brothers' bad behavior, they had repented and God had calmed the storm.

"There's a lesson there for all of us," he'd said, and Aubree saw that Vanessa was listening intently as well. "We all have storms in our lives, and when that happens, the only way to calm the storm is to rely on the Savior."

Innocently, Brandi asked, "Torben, did you ask God to calm this storm?"

"Yes, as a matter of fact, I did," he replied. "And I'm guessing that a lot of other people on the ship were praying for the same thing."

"It worked," she said. "I was praying too. Aubree taught us how."

Ryan nodded in agreement, and Torben smiled. Vanessa looked at her children in surprise and then said, "Well, it sounds like you might need to teach your mother as well, if it can calm that storm."

Aubree smiled. "Of course we'll teach you."

"Can we say a prayer right now?" Brandi asked. "I think we should tell Heavenly Father thank you."

Torben glanced at Vanessa and Aubree and then said, "Sure. Would you like to say it?"

Brandi nodded eagerly, then folded her arms and bowed her head as she'd seen Aubree do. The others followed her example, and she began to pray. "Heavenly Father, I thank you for helping the storm to go away," she began. "And I thank you that Ryan and Aubree and Torben and Mom and me are safe." She hesitated, thinking for a moment. Then she continued. "Thank you for sending Torben to help us. And . . . and . . ." She hesitated again. "And bless us that the scary things in our lives will be okay. Please keep us safe." Then she closed with, "In the name of Jesus, amen."

After she'd ended the prayer, Vanessa scooted closer to her daughter and enveloped her in a hug. There were tears in her eyes. "Thank you," she said. "That was a beautiful prayer."

At that moment, the intercom came on once more, asking all crew members to report to their respective posts and advising the passengers that they could now leave their rooms and that food would be available in two or three hours.

After the announcement, Torben stood up to leave. Then, as if thinking better of it, he said to Aubree, "Speaking of food, you wouldn't still have some of those cookies left that we were eating earlier, would you?"

"How can you think of food?" Aubree asked, pulling a face. Her stomach was far from accepting anything yet. "Aren't you still a little seasick? The first thing I plan to do in sorting out our room is to look for the Dramamine and take some more," she said, gesturing to the mess that was their room.

"I guess I'm still a little queasy, but I'm hungry enough that I can ignore it."

"Then you can have the rest of the cookies if you'd like, right kids?" she said. "Check in the nightstand there. I think it's the one thing in the room that didn't spill its contents all over the floor."

"*I* don't want a cookie," Ryan said, holding his stomach.

"Me either," Brandi agreed, and so Torben crossed the room and, moving a fallen chair out of the way, opened the nightstand. He pulled out a bag of cookies and extracted a handful of them. "Success. Now I'd better report to the captain." His eyes turned serious. "I know the captain said you could leave your rooms, but I'd like you to stay here a while longer—until we've found Stone."

Vanessa nodded. "We're planning on doing just that. I'd also like to give Kevin a call as soon as possible to let him know what's going on. I'm sure he'll want to talk to you, Torben, when you're able to spare a moment."

"Please be careful, Torben," Aubree told him, feeling her insides twist fearfully in an all-too-familiar way.

"We'll pray for you," Ryan told him earnestly, and Torben smiled gratefully. Then, with a last lingering look in Aubree's direction, he left the room.

\* \* \*

Captain Gabe Newkirk, the Dutch commander of the ship, listened intently to what Torben had to tell him. When he learned what the twins had heard, his face paled as he took in the implications.

"We must act quickly," he said firmly. "If I had an inkling it was this bad yesterday, I'd have made questioning a priority above anything else." He looked at Torben gravely. "I apologize for that. Help me contact the rest of the ship's officers. We need to have as many of them as can leave their current posts to assemble here, and when we are together, we'll have a . . . well, I guess a sort of war council." He thought for a moment then added, "Tell Vanessa Kern and her children that they are not to open their door for anyone except me or you—not any of my staff and no other guests."

"I've already advised them to do that," Torben told him. "I'll start making calls."

The captain cleared his throat. "Torben, I want you to tell the officers everything we know about Stone Lansing, but I don't want anyone but you and me to know about what Brandi and Ryan heard about ransoms and taking the ship. Not yet, at least."

Within a few minutes, most of the ship's officers were assembled. They murmured among themselves at why they had been called in when there was so much to do in recovering from the storm, but Captain Newkirk quickly called everyone to attention then asked Torben to give him the history of Aubree Lansing and the Kern children. When Torben mentioned Stone Lansing and the fact that he was on board, Captain Newkirk held up his hand as ripples of shocked chatter spread among the men and women. Torben stopped talking and the captain said, "It is of utmost importance, as I'm sure you are beginning to realize, that you listen carefully. Torben, do you have a picture of him?"

"It's in my room, but it will be quicker if I can access the Internet from your computer," Torben said.

"Go ahead," the captain said, waving an arm at the computer.

A minute or two later, Stone's picture appeared on the screen. The captain studied it for a moment, and then he turned to his officers and signaled for them to gather around. "Have any of you seen this man?"

When he was only met with murmurs, the captain asked Torben to relate Aubree's run-in with Stone and to describe his altered appearance. Then he added, "This man should be considered dangerous and quite possibly armed. He is traveling under the alias Karl W. Faulk. He is supposed to be in suite 537, two decks directly below the family. I'm now assigning Lieutenant Hild DeHaven and two other officers to stand watch outside his room, and the rest of you, save only a few, will be deployed in a ship wide manhunt until he is found."

With that, he dismissed the officers but said, "Torben, please stay here. We have another matter to discuss." As the last of the officers left the room, he said, "I believe we can trust all of these men, but until we know for certain, it's just you and me." He sighed and said, "Now, we need to determine what we're going to do about the possible pirating threat. I'm praying that somehow the little girl and boy misheard, and that we're mistaken in thinking that 'taking the ship' means there will be an attack, but I'm not willing to take chances at this point. And we don't have enough information to know whether it's related to Stone Lansing or not, but all signs point to that being the case."

They discussed the matter for another minute or two, and then the captain did something most unexpected. "This American homicide detective you spoke of—can you get him on the phone?" he asked Torben.

"I can try," he said.

A minute or two later Kevin Jensen was put on speakerphone and joined them in their strategy session. "I just spoke with Vanessa Kern," he told Torben. "I'm so relieved to hear you're all okay. But you haven't found Stone yet?"

"Not yet, but we expect to find him shortly," Torben replied with determination.

Captain Newkirk filled Kevin in on the details of their situation that he hadn't gotten from Vanessa, then asked, "Tell me our options for stopping this thing—if it is an impending attack, that is—before it starts. We're too far out at sea now to make it back to St. Petersburg. I don't want to alert any of the passengers yet, to avoid panic. Where do you think we should start?"

There was a moment's silence, then Lieutenant Jensen said, "I would suggest that we call the American FBI first and apprise them of the situation. Do exactly what they recommend. "They will know what other agencies in other countries besides mine should be notified. Leave that to them while you arrest the man called Eko. Question him and then hold him. You do have a place to lock someone up, don't you?"

"We have a brig," the captain said. "Fortunately, we don't have to use it very often, but we have it."

"Use it now. When you question him there are at least two things you need to learn from him if you can get him to talk. First, try to find out who else on the ship is part of the pirate gang. It's not likely that he'll tell you, but try. Next, you've got to somehow find out where they're going to strike and how—from within the ship, from a boat coming up from the outside, or a combination of the two. I would assume a combination is most likely."

"Exactly what I was thinking," Captain Newkirk said. He turned to Torben. "Can you get ahold of the one called Nadif on the dead man's phone? If nothing else works, maybe we can bluff him into calling off the attack."

Torben nodded in agreement. "Thinking that he was talking to Cord, Nadif did tell me not to call unless it was an emergency. I suppose this could be considered an emergency."

Lieutenant Jensen was silent for a moment, and Torben and the captain waited anxiously for his response. "That might work, but I'd do that only as a last resort, because I think that he might try something anyway. If there is indeed a pirating attack imminent, I'd wager Nadif is of the Somali pirating class. And they're tougher than you'd like to believe," Kevin finally told them.

"He is Somali," Torben said. "Cord, the dead German, told me that."

"This doesn't sound good. You've been a great help, Lieutenant," Captain Newkirk said. "We'll place the call to the FBI now. Is there anything else we should be doing?"

"You're doing just what you should be. But if you'd like, my detectives and I will start making contacts overseas and try to dig up something on these guys. While you're speaking with the FBI, I'll contact the U.S. State Department. I'm assuming that there are a fair number of Americans on board," Kevin said.

"Just over half of our passengers are Americans," the captain agreed.

"I'll get back with you, Captain. Is there anything else I can help with right now?"

"I can't think of anything. We'll be in touch."

The call ended, and Captain Newkirk turned to Torben. "I don't want you going to take Eko alone. Is there anyone else among the officers you know you can trust?"

Torben nodded. "I trust Hild, sir. He's as good as they come."

"Relieve him of his duty guarding room 537 and have another crew member take his place. Then you two arrest Eko. I intend to get some answers, and soon."

\* \* \*

Kevin hung up the phone, frustrated by his recent conversation with a high-ranking man in the State Department in Washington, D.C. They were monitoring the situation on the *Stargazer,* but so far they felt that the evidence that an attack would occur was somewhat shaky. But since so many American lives could be in jeopardy, they, as well as the FBI, were in contact with Captain Newkirk and awaiting the outcome of Eko's questioning.

He felt more pressure than ever to put a stop to whoever was behind all of this, and he worried that they'd only seen the tip of the iceberg. The conclusion he'd come to that worried him the most was how elaborate it all seemed. Could it really be Stone? Could he have organized this plan, involving members of the *Stargazer* cruise ship and even people in other countries? It seemed unlikely, as Stone had been in prison up until just a few days before, but then again Kevin had no idea who Stone had met in prison. And he certainly would have motive for demanding a ransom—Vanessa had ended up with most of his money. Maybe this was what he had come up with as a way to get it back.

He glanced at the phone on his desk, willing it to ring with news that Stone had been captured aboard the ship and that Eko had spilled all the information he knew. But it sat silent.

Finally, he stood and walked to his captain's office to inform him of the latest news—which wasn't much. The meeting then led to a meeting with the police chief himself. That, in turn, was followed by still another meeting, this one with the special agent in charge of the Los Angeles office of the FBI and two of his agents.

It all led to little action by the FBI. An hour later, frustrated, angry, and sick with worry, he returned to his office. He decided to try to call Reginald Kern once more, but that too led to frustration. Reginald seemed impossible to connect with, and he wondered if Aubree and Vanessa had managed yet. When he'd spoken with them earlier, they'd been out of contact with him for some time. The bored-sounding receptionist at Kern's office told him that Reginald was in court and would be for hours yet.

Kevin stressed the importance of a callback, irritated that Reginald hadn't even checked in with his family. He might have some idea who, if anyone besides Stone, might stoop to the terrible thing that was occurring. He directed the law office to have Reginald call when he got out of court, no matter what time it was.

Kevin felt absolutely helpless as he called his detectives together to brainstorm.

# CHAPTER SEVENTEEN

EKO WAS OF NO HELP to Captain Newkirk and Torben. He insisted that he knew nothing about any planned attack on the *Stargazer*. He also claimed total ignorance about the twins and anyone by the name of Cord or Nadif.

"That's interesting because I suspect that when I confiscate your phone, I'll find both his number and Nadif's on your phone," Torben said, taking a step closer to Eko.

"You won't be taking my phone," Eko said, his face growing dark, for the first time making him look dangerous. "And even if you did, you wouldn't find what you're looking for."

Torben smiled and then pulled the late Cord's phone from his pocket. "I don't suppose you'd have any idea what this is?"

"It's a cell phone," Eko said with a sneer.

"That's right," Torben agreed. "But it's not just any cell phone. I think I'll try a little experiment." He worked with the phone for a minute and then, after locating the number he was after, punched the call button and waited. A moment later a phone began buzzing in Eko's pocket. "Would you like to answer that?" Torben asked mildly.

Rage and hatred filled the Indonesian man's eyes. His lips curled up in a snarl. "I could kill you with my bare hands," he breathed. "I could kill both of you. Where did you get that phone?"

"It used to belong to a man by the name of Cord, a man you claim not to know," Torben said. "He doesn't need this phone anymore. He's in a morgue in St. Petersburg."

A flicker of fear passed across Eko's face. But it was only a flicker. Then he suddenly made a swift move with his hands, striking a hard blow at Torben. But before the fight had even begun, it was over, and Eko ended up on the floor with a broken nose for his efforts.

Captain Newkirk whistled. "I knew you were good—that's one of the reasons we hired you. But I didn't know you were that good."

"He's just really bad," Torben said modestly as he reached down and jerked Eko to his feet and then shoved him back into his chair. "Don't try anything like that again. Captain, this man needs a tissue."

After the bleeding was under control and Torben had relieved Eko of his cell phone and a wicked looking knife he had hidden beneath his clothing, the captain stepped over to Eko. After gazing down at him in silence for a moment, he said, "We have some questions, and if you know what's good for you, you will answer them."

"And if I don't?" Eko asked stubbornly, hatred still burning in his black eyes.

"Let me tell you a little story," the captain said. "Your friend Cord tried to stop a woman from boarding this ship yesterday. This young fellow stopped him." He pointed at Torben, who knew that the captain wasn't telling him the story exactly as it happened, but he wasn't about to stop him. "To make a long story short, your friend is dead now. Think about that." He turned back to Torben and asked, "Mr. Davidsen, would you like to ask him some more questions?"

Torben flexed his wrist slowly, then stepped closer to Eko as well. "Who else on board is involved in this little plot of yours?"

Eko stubbornly said, "I don't know what you're talking about."

"Like you didn't know who Cord was," Torben said mildly. "When is the attack on this boat to take place?"

He saw something register in Eko's eyes and noticed a slight tick at the corner of his mouth, but nothing more. Torben continued to ask questions for several more minutes, but he didn't get one straight answer. Finally, pulling out his ace in the hole, he said, "Since you seem so unwilling to cooperate the easy way, we're going to try something else now. I am going to make another call. This time it is to Nadif. He thinks I'm Cord." Torben waved Cord's phone in front of Eko's eyes. "And *Cord* is going to tell him that you blew your cover aboard the ship."

He opened Cord's phone and selected a number. Eko sat completely still, hatred burning deeper than ever on his face. Torben showed him the number, and Eko paled slightly. "He won't think you're Cord," he said, but there wasn't much conviction in his voice.

"He will, actually. He's already spoken to me once. He thinks I'm heading back to Germany now to await further instructions, but unfortunately, I'll need to interrupt him right now to let him know I've been informed that there are problems aboard the ship," Torben said. "Should I make the call, or do you have something you want to share with the captain and me?"

Eko looked unsure, and Torben pressed him. "Remember this, Eko. I will tell him that you have betrayed him, or rather, that's what 'Cord' will tell him." This statement brought fear to the man's dark eyes, which he shifted rapidly back and forth as if trying to discover a way to escape. "I was told not to call him or you unless it was a real emergency, and he told me you and the others on the ship had the same instructions. If I call him, Nadif will have you killed as soon as you step off this ship, and you know it. Should I make the call?"

"You won't make the call," Eko finally said in a strained voice. But when Torben pointed a finger over the send button, Eko cried out, "I don't know much! Hardly anything, but I'll tell you what I can." Then he sat back in his chair, seething, his face pouring with sweat.

"Let's start with the names of the men on the ship who are in this plot with you."

"I can't. It will get me killed," he said in a low voice.

"And this won't?" Torben asked. He still held Cord's phone in his hand.

Eko seemed genuinely unsure of himself, and Torben prodded. "All I have to do is press this button, Eko." But as Torben held the phone in front of Eko, the Indonesian did a very foolish thing. He tried to kick the phone from Torben's hand. Torben reacted in the way he'd been trained, and in half a second Eko left the chair under Torben's power, flew into the air, and then hit the floor with a sickening thud and crack. The thud knocked the breath out of him. The crack was his right forearm breaking. His broken nose started to bleed again. Eko screamed loudly and rolled onto his back, holding his arm against his side.

Torben grimaced, shaking his head and wishing that Eko would simply cooperate with them instead of lashing out. He felt bad he'd hurt him again, but he knew that Eko was a dangerous man with critical information, and he refused to give up until they'd gotten the information they needed.

As Torben tended to Eko's bleeding nose, the captain called for the ship's doctor. "We have a man with a broken arm in my office," he said. "And he also has a nasty bloody nose."

While they were waiting for the doctor, Torben again began to fiddle with Eko's phone, which had miraculously sustained no damage in the ill-advised attack. To the captain, Torben said, "I really think I should call Nadif."

"Go ahead," the captain said with a nod. "You have my permission."

"No, don't do that," Eko pleaded, wincing in pain. "You can't tell him I blew my cover," he said, his head hanging, his nose still dripping blood onto his lap. He appeared to be a broken man now. It gave Torben no satisfaction, but he knew it was the only way to ensure that the ship was safe.

"When is the attack from the sea to come?" Torben asked, his eyes boring into those of the pirate. "Because we both know that an attack has been planned in order to exact a ransom for the three children."

"Somewhere between here and Helsinki," Eko said in a barely audible voice.

Torben continued, hoping the man would keep talking. "Give us the names," he said firmly.

The captain quickly wrote down three names of his staff as Eko spoke. Then he called in several of his officers, intending to take more of them into their confidence about the attack now that these names had been revealed.

The doctor arrived soon thereafter and was tending to Eko's injuries as Torben placed another call to California. Lieutenant Jensen answered almost instantly.

Knowing that Eko was listening, Torben told Kevin what they'd learned. He didn't tell him how he persuaded Eko to give that information, but he felt confident that he hadn't done anything he hadn't needed to do.

"You did well, young man," Kevin said. "We've also been busy here. I'm sure you haven't had a chance to connect back with the FBI in the past few minutes, but I have good news. Both the FBI and the

State Department are being more helpful now. We have two warships headed your way, and there will be air support as well. The pirates will be taken down quite quickly unless they surrender peacefully."

Torben let out a breath. "That's a relief."

"Are you sure you have all the pirates who are on board?" Kevin asked seriously.

"We're not positive on that one," Torben acknowledged. "But as soon as I get off the line with you, I'm going to be asking Eko a few more questions. I think we can count on him to cooperate at this point. If not, there are three others that I can attempt to persuade."

"Good, good. Have you found Stone yet?"

"No," Torben said, "Unfortunately not. The captain and I have had our pagers on while we've questioned Eko, but Stone is still missing. Vanessa, Aubree, and the twins are safe in their room, however."

"All right. I expect you'll find him soon—he doesn't have many places to run. When you do find him, I have some questions for him. I believe there is a chance he can help us clear up some of the mystery surrounding this matter."

"We'll do that, Lieutenant. Thank you."

Before going after the men Eko had named, Torben secured Eko in leg irons and handcuffed his good arm to a heavy metal desk. He wouldn't be using the other arm, which was now set and wrapped in a sling.

Ten men, nine of whom the captain had brought into their confidence about the attack while Torben talked to Kevin, accompanied Torben to the staff's quarters. Two others stayed to keep an eye on Eko. Each of the other conspirators was then arrested, handcuffed, and escorted to the captain's office. Before the morning was over, one more arrest had been made. No amount of questioning got the men to reveal more conspirators. Although Torben knew that didn't necessarily mean there weren't any, they had hit a dead end for now, until they found Stone.

After speaking with the authorities in Helsinki, it was arranged that all five pirates be turned over to the authorities there when the ship docked next. Until then, the men would be kept secure in the ship's brig and prevented from communicating with anyone until the matter of piracy was resolved.

Torben was exhausted, but his work was far from finished. However, while Captain Newkirk spoke to the FBI once more to discuss
what that they had learned from speaking to the other pirates aboard,
Torben received permission to go to suite 737 and make sure everyone
was safe and well there and to assure them that everything was now
under control. He only hoped he was telling them the truth.

* * *

Aubree was lying down with a cold cloth on her head when a knock
came on the door. She turned her head toward it. "Mom, would you
see who's there? Remember, if it's not Torben or Captain Newkirk,
don't open it."

Her mother looked through the peephole. Torben, with his red
hair shining, was standing there. "It's Torben," Vanessa said.

Aubree threw the cloth at the sink and swung off the bed. She combed
out her long hair with her fingers and said, "Well, invite him in."

Torben entered their suite. His uniform was neat and his short
hair combed. His eyes, however, seemed glazed. He looked like he was
exhausted. He moved slowly toward her, passing Vanessa with a polite
nod of his head. Just seeing Torben gave Aubree energy she didn't know
she had, and unable to restrain herself, she threw her arms around him.
"Oh, Torben," she said. "We've all been worrying about you."

Brandi and Ryan, who had been playing quietly on the sofa, now
ran to him as well. "It's true! We're glad to see you. Did you find Aubree's dad? Are we safe yet? Did you find the bad men?"

"'No' to the first question, unfortunately—but we're still looking.
And 'I hope so' to your second question. I think we're safe. As for the
third question," he said with a tired smile, "yes, we did find the bad
men. I've been busy." Torben pulled back slightly from Aubree's embrace and stepped back, avoiding her hurt gaze. "If you decide to eat in
the dining room tomorrow evening, and if you further decide to take
up drinking, which I strongly urge you not to, you will have to have
someone other than Eko serve you," he said evenly. "He has a broken
arm, a broken nose, a loose tongue, and is now in the brig, along with
his partners in crime—all four of them."

"Was it what we thought? Was there an attack planned on the
ship?" Aubree asked.

"That's part of it," he said. "But there's more. We've learned from Eko and the others that they are part of a pirate gang led by Nadif, who is from Somalia. From what we've pieced together, Nadif and his men plan to take over the ship and hold it for ransom with a separate ransom to be demanded for the three of you—Aubree and the twins." As their eyes widened, he added, "Please don't mention any of this to anyone. The United States government, along with aid from some countries here in the Baltic, is sending help to finish cleaning up the pirate gang on the sea if they show up." He yawned and rubbed his eyes tiredly. "I hate to ask, but do you have any cookies?" he said, glancing around.

Aubree smiled, but Vanessa's expression remained serious. "I have a question for you, Torben," Vanessa said.

"All right, what's the question?"

"If there is a separate ransom for my children, there must be someone besides just the pirates involved. Am I right about that?" Vanessa asked.

"I suspect you are. Lieutenant Jensen and his detectives, along with the FBI from your country, are working on that. They hope to come up with some answers soon," he said. "But I'm afraid that's all I can tell you."

Vanessa looked thoughtful, and she frowned deeply, turning and walking alone to the balcony. Aubree watched her, wondering what she was thinking. To Torben she said, "She's wondering who wants her money. She's convinced that's what this is all about. And so am I. I hope the authorities can figure out who it is."

"I'm confident they're doing their best," Torben assured her.

While munching on a couple of cookies, he visited with Vanessa and Aubree out on the balcony. Two very exhausted twins climbed into bed and took an afternoon nap, sleeping soundly after an extremely trying day. Vanessa and Aubree asked a few more questions, and Torben answered them the best he could. Vanessa said nothing more about her concerns over the children being specifically targeted. Aubree eventually asked, "So when will this attack take place? I mean, can we sleep soundly tonight?"

Vanessa spoke first. "I don't think I'll sleep. I want to know who is after my children and my money."

"We believe the attack will take place between here and Helsinki—and that we've got a little time, so you shouldn't need to worry quite yet. As for who is after your children and your money, Vanessa, we're hoping to know a lot more when we find Stone—which should be soon." Glancing over at the two sleeping children, he said, "You two need to try to rest as well. I don't think anyone got much sleep last night. But I have more work to do," Torben said.

Aubree felt her heart start to thump harder in her chest as she thought of Torben facing her father. "Please let us know when you find my father. I keep worrying something will happen to you."

Torben's eyes softened as he looked at her. "Unless he does something stupid like jump from the balcony, we'll be arresting him anytime now. And believe me, Aubree, I will see to it that he doesn't lay a finger on you. I'm just sorry I let him get on the ship."

"It's not your fault," Vanessa said quietly. She was standing at the railing now, looking down at the ocean, which was mercifully calm for a change. "He's a determined man, and a smart one."

Aubree stood beside her, and Torben joined them. "I don't know what would have happened to us if we hadn't met you," she said softly as she stepped close to him and laid her head against his chest, feeling his body tense at her action. She ignored it. "I owe my life to you, Torben."

"We both owe our lives to you," Vanessa said.

Aubree stepped back and was saddened as she saw the relief on his face as she did so.

"I will let you know what happens," he promised. "But I can tell you this: your father is no longer a danger to you." As he turned to go, Aubree's eyes caught his gaze for a moment—but she was unsure what she saw there.

\* \* \*

Stone was exhausted. He had been on the move for hours now, but the realization that there was nowhere to go finally sunk in as he took a quick look around the corner and saw that two armed security officers were standing in front of his room. After somehow riding out the storm, he had spent the past hours moving from deck to deck, but it was clear that he was being sought after, and he knew the end was near.

He'd attempted to get near Aubree and her mother's room several times, but a guard had been placed there as well, and he was certain that would not change until he was in the ship's brig.

Stone thought of Aubree's terrified expression when she had seen him in the darkness during the storm and of how she had run before he'd been able to do anything but call her name. And he was gripped by a sense of utter failure.

With a last, deep breath, Stone walked around the corner and saw the shocked expression of the two men as he stepped toward them. There was only one thing to be done now.

# CHAPTER EIGHTEEN

TORBEN STEPPED OUT OF HIS office, still unable to believe the notification he'd just received—Stone Lansing had just surrendered himself.

The two officers guarding Stone's room had been taken by surprise when he had simply rounded the corner, a resigned look on his face, and stood in front of them, waiting to be hauled away. Torben glanced around anxiously. They would be arriving any minute, as they had been instructed to bring him to the captain's office.

Mere seconds later, he looked up and stared at the man who had caused so much turmoil for Aubree and her family. Stone didn't look much like the picture Kevin Jensen had sent him. As Aubree had partially described, he now had bleached-blond hair and was wearing glasses. However, there was no mistaking Stone's dark, brooding eyes. Torben swallowed the emotions churning within him, knowing he had a job to do.

"I'll take over from here, thanks," Torben said, shifting his gaze to the two officers. When his eyes met Stone's, he was unable to put his finger on what he saw in the man's expression. "Come with me, Mr. Lansing."

Torben reached out and took Stone by the arm, but as he did so, Stone let out a muffled gasp and tensed.

Alarmed, Torben turned back to the officers as Stone pulled back. "I thought you said there was no struggle. Was he injured?"

The officers exchanged puzzled looks. "He didn't struggle. He walked right up to us. He's fine," the tall officer insisted.

"Are you hurt?" Torben asked him, eyeing the man's arm suspiciously. Stone was still grimacing. "I'm fine," he growled. "Let's go."

Torben shook his head but didn't try to take Stone by the arm again. They were already where they needed to be anyway, and Stone was handcuffed. He excused the other officers after stepping through the door of Captain Newkirk's office.

"Mr. Lansing," Captain Newkirk said, eyeing them as they entered. "I expect you know that you are in a great deal of trouble. You have left your country illegally, you are here with a forged passport and visa, and you have violated your restraining order."

Stone remained silent, and after waiting for a few moments, Captain Newkirk continued as Torben stood by, studying Stone's blank expression.

"If you don't want to talk, it's fine with us. We'll be escorting you to the ship's brig where we'll hold you until we reach the next port. We've already almost filled it to capacity with five men—whom I expect you know well—but I'm sure they'll make room for one more."

Stone's expression darkened slightly. "I don't know what you're talking about." Then he pursed his lips and was silent once more.

"I'm talking about piracy," the captain exploded after a moment, shaking his fist angrily. "And I'm talking about my ship and some of its passengers—your own daughter and her two siblings—being used in a plot for ransom."

A strange expression crossed Stone's face, and he opened his mouth. But the captain wasn't finished. His voice was rising, and his cheeks, above the beard he wore, were getting very red. "I'm talking about five of my own men plotting to take over this ship. I'm talking about your ex-wife being attacked onshore by a man who was in contact with conspirators on this ship. I'm talking about you illegally boarding this vessel and pursuing your daughter, even in the midst of a storm—"

"Enough!" Stone suddenly roared, his eyes blazing. "You have no idea what you're talking about. But I expect you'll be locking me in the brig no matter what I say right now, so I'll answer whatever you want. But I want something in return."

"You're in no position to barter, Mr. Lansing."

Stone shot Torben a deadly look. "Just let me talk to Reginald Kern."

Torben looked at the captain, confused, then asked, "You want us to call Reginald Kern?"

Stone rolled his eyes and growled, "No, I want you to bring him here so I can talk to him face to face."

"Reginald Kern is not aboard this ship, Mr. Lansing," Captain Newkirk said.

Stone looked from the captain to Torben as if trying to divine whether the two men were telling the truth. After a few moments he shook his head slowly, his eyes filled with anger. He released a short, bitter bark of laughter. "Take me to the brig then," he said finally, lifting up his hands. "If you can't fulfill my request, I have nothing to say to you."

But Captain Newkirk still had more to say. Setting his jaw, he pointed at Torben and said gruffly, "Mr. Lansing, this young man saved your ex-wife's life. I know you don't care about that, but he did it at great risk to his own life. And he and I are both intent on stopping you from taking revenge on your daughter. So you're not going anywhere until we settle a few matters."

Stone, who had been looking at the floor, snapped his head up at the mention of Aubree's name. "Like I said earlier, you don't know what you're talking about." He lowered his eyes once more and said in a barely audible voice, "I have no intention of hurting Aubree or her siblings—or Vanessa."

Torben took a step closer to him. "So you're here just to pay a social visit, then?" he asked angrily.

"I'm here to protect them," Stone growled. "And let's get one thing straight, kid. You didn't save Vanessa's life—I did. And I'm pretty sure I saved yours as well."

The captain began to laugh, but as he did so, Stone reached up with one handcuffed hand and pulled back his shirt near the shoulder where Torben had grabbed him earlier.

Torben's stomach twisted as he saw the dried blood surrounding a grisly wound on Stone's shoulder. After staring for a few seconds, he asked, "What are you talking about, Mr. Lansing?"

Stone slowly pulled his shirt back over the wound but remained silent. For a moment it seemed to Torben that he had decided to remain silent again. But then he began to speak.

\* \* \*

"If you're going to listen to this, you're going to hear it all," Stone said, leaning forward, watching the redheaded security officer closely. He'd seen this man before, with his daughter. He knew this might be a mistake, but it was his last shot. "I can promise you right now"—he looked at the officer's name tag—"Torben, that I don't know anything about pirates or taking over ships or anything like that, but that doesn't mean that it won't all fit together in the end."

Torben still looked shocked from what Stone had revealed a few moments before. But now he narrowed his eyes and said, "I'd like someone else to listen to this conversation before you begin. He's much more familiar with your case than I am."

Stone nodded. "It doesn't matter," he said, knowing that he would soon be on his way back to prison no matter what he said to this kid and the captain.

"His name is Lieutenant Jensen; he's a police officer in Los Angeles, California. Hold on." Keeping his eyes on Stone as the captain directed him to a nearby chair then handcuffed him to it, Torben went to the phone and placed the call on speakerphone. When a deep voice answered the line, Torben quickly explained what was happening and that he was on a speakerphone.

When he was finished, Lieutenant Jensen replied, "I'd be glad to talk to the three of you; however, we have some constitutional issues to take care of first. If anything Mr. Lansing says is incriminating, for me to be able to use that information in court here in the United States, I'd need to know he's waived those rights."

At those words, Stone's throat tightened, but he'd known it could come to this all along. "I'm listening, Lieutenant. Go ahead."

Lieutenant Jensen cleared his throat. "Stone, there are some things I need to make clear before we talk. First, do you object to me recording this interview?"

"Not at all," Stone agreed grimly. "In fact, I'd actually be grateful if you did."

"Do you, Torben, or anyone who is there with you, object to a recording?"

"Besides Mr. Lansing, the only other person present besides myself is Captain Newkirk," Torben told him. "And I don't object."

"Nor do I," the captain agreed.

"Then that's settled. Give me just a second here." There was a pause, and then Kevin said, "Okay, I'm ready. For the recording, I need everyone to state their names, titles, and location." That was completed quickly. Then for the next couple of minutes, Kevin took care of the matter of the waiver of an attorney on Stone's part and the waiver of his right to remain silent. Then he asked Torben to write that information down and have Stone sign it.

When they were finished, Torben said to Kevin, "Let's get started, then. Stone, you said you wanted to tell it all. Where would you like to begin?"

Stone looked up at him. "Let's start with the murder I was convicted of committing—one which I did not commit." When he saw the doubtful expression on Torben's and the captain's faces, he again wondered if this was worth the effort or not. But remembering what they'd told him a few moments earlier, he persisted. "Whether you believe me or not, a lot was missed in the investigation," he continued with a touch of anger in his voice as he looked from Torben to the captain.

After a moment, he continued. "I was in prison for a long time following my conviction. I had plenty of time to think things over. When I was released, I finally had the chance to look into the what ifs that had been plaguing me all those years."

"There are rumors circulating that you're out for revenge on your daughter and your ex-wife," Kevin piped in.

"Of course there are rumors," Stone spat. "I was convicted of killing a man, partially due to my daughter's testimony. People run with things like that."

"Not just *people* have been talking, Stone. The information came from your own attorney, George Sedwig. Sedwig said you told him you were out for revenge before you were taken away to prison," Kevin replied.

Stone started to rise to his feet, heedless of the metal digging into his skin, but settled back in his chair at a warning look from Captain Newkirk. "George has been dead for years now, but I can assure you that he never would have said anything like that. One of the last times we discussed Aubree was when I told him to go easy on her in the trial. He and I argued about that right there in court while Aubree was on the stand. He knew as well as I did that she was just a little girl. He was a good attorney and he listened to me. His partner on the other hand?" Stone made a disgusted noise. "Reginald Kern is a piece of work. He never listened to me, never even pretended to believe me when I told him I was innocent. I put up with him to keep George on my case, but that was a mistake I lived to regret."

"You mean because Reginald married your ex-wife?" Torben asked, looking surprised. "I didn't know he was connected to your trial."

"From what I've found out in the past week, I've begun to believe he had a lot to do with my trial," Stone muttered. "And yes, for a long time while I was in prison, I was angry with him for the sole fact that he had married Vanessa—and so quickly after the trial. It blew my mind that she'd even be remotely interested in that guy." He hung his head. "But I guess he seemed like Prince Charming compared to someone with a murder conviction."

"What did you mean he had a lot to do with your trial?" Kevin prompted. "Are you saying you believe that Reginald had something to do with your conviction?" he asked skeptically.

Stone sighed, knowing how all this was coming across, how far-fetched it must sound. "I haven't pieced it all together yet, but everything I've found points to something fishy going on. See, the one thing I had a lot of in prison was time to think. I went over every detail of that trial in my mind, everything that was presented, what was left out, what I was told." He fiddled with the chain of the handcuff. "In light of recent events, I now believe that Reginald somehow steered my defense in a less-than-favorable direction—possibly more than that. I don't know how he did it. I don't believe that George was part of it—but I can tell you right now that Reginald did it."

"Reginald Kern is a well-respected member of the community. But for the sake of argument, do you have anything to back what you're saying?" Kevin asked on the speakerphone.

"I don't know what it means, but I know what I saw," Stone said vehemently. "Like I said, I was upset with Reginald before I went to prison, furious with him when he married my ex-wife afterward, and suspicious of him the more I thought about everything. But it wasn't until I went to his office just a few days ago that I knew for sure that something had gone horribly wrong."

"You went to Reginald's office?" Kevin asked.

"I originally went to confront him about Vanessa and to rattle his chain a little, see if I could get any information out of him. But as I sat there waiting for him to come out of another meeting . . ." Stone shifted in the chair, trying to keep the handcuffs from biting into his wrists. "Lieutenant Jensen, how familiar are you with my case?"

"Actually, very familiar," Kevin responded easily. "Thanks to your parole violation."

"Then you're aware of my statement—that I saw a man in a white T-shirt running along the sidewalk near our house shortly before the murder took place?"

Stone heard Kevin shuffling a few papers in the background. "Yes, I do recall that."

"It never even came up at the trial. Maybe you saw that, too. Reginald convinced George that I was the only eyewitness, that there was absolutely no evidence that anyone else was in the vicinity. He said to my face that I'd just *wanted* to see someone else there."

"What's your point, Mr. Lansing?" Torben asked.

"My point is that the day I waited for Reginald Kern in his office, I recognized the man he was talking to when he exited his office. I couldn't figure out where I had seen him before. The two men were arguing and didn't even see me. But later it hit me like a lead pipe. That man Reginald Kern was talking to? He was the guy I saw that day outside of my house."

For a moment, the room was still as the men digested information. A few seconds later, Kevin started to reply, but Stone cut him off, hoping against hope that he would be believed. "Just let me finish, okay? That's why I'm here on this ship. I didn't come to get revenge on Aubree and Vanessa. I'm here to protect them from that . . . that sociopath, Reginald." He fixed Torben with a steady gaze. "When I followed him outside his office and talked to him, Reginald told me he'd be on this cruise, that he was looking forward to spending time with his beautiful wife and daughter." Stone's voice choked momentarily, but he forced the emotion away. "When I realized later how I'd recognized the man he'd been talking to, and when I realized the possible implications . . ." Stone swallowed but forced himself to continue. "Later that night, when a man showed up and offered to sell me forged papers to travel out of the country, it was too much of a coincidence. I knew something was up."

He shook his head. "I was pretty sure it was a trap someone was setting for me. But tell me, what would you have done?" He looked between the two men in the room as they listened in silence. "Who was going to believe me? Not my daughter or ex-wife, who won't speak to me and who have a restraining order against me. Not a lawyer who's dead. Not the cops, who, considering what a sloppy job they did on the investigation, might have been in cahoots with Reginald. And then I learn that the cops and others think I'm out for blood against my daughter and ex-wife." Feeling despair settle around him once more, he briefly closed his eyes. "I had to come here. Something appeared to be very wrong to me. And from what you've said about pirates and your men turning against you on the boat, it sounds like maybe I was right after all."

Suddenly feeling immensely tired after so little sleep and such great stress, Stone slumped against the back of his chair. "I've done all that I was able to. I'm afraid it was not enough." He raised his eyes once more and looked at Torben and Captain Newkirk, who, he was surprised to see, were looking at him very seriously. He nodded toward the phone. "I can't imagine you believe me, Lieutenant, but I am going to ask you to look into what I've told you. Please, for my daughter's sake more than for my own." He let his gaze fall. "And for Vanessa's."

What Kevin said then surprised Stone. "You've made some very serious accusations, Mr. Lansing. I intend to find out whether anything you've told me can be substantiated. In the meantime, you will remain in the custody of Captain Newkirk. Later, you'll be transferred to civil authorities. I do have another question for you at the moment, though."

"I understand," Stone said. "And if I know the answer to your question, I'll tell you."

"Who made the false papers for you—the visa, passport, and so on?" Kevin asked.

"I honestly don't know that. They were delivered to me by some wino off the street, a guy who called himself Rambler."

Stone heard the scratching of a pen on paper over the speaker-phone and felt the first bit of relief he'd experienced in a long time. Maybe he hadn't failed completely after all. Maybe someone was going to look into all of this.

Torben cleared his throat and spoke. "Kevin, I'd like to ask a couple of questions as well before you hang up." He looked at Stone carefully. "What were you doing during the storm when Aubree saw you? You scared her to death."

Stone nodded. "I heard the captain's announcement that the twins were missing. I was afraid that something had happened. I had to look for them. I didn't even know Aubree was down there until I nearly ran right into her. I tried to call out to her, but she ran in a panic."

Torben nodded slowly. "I've been waiting to ask you this. You said earlier that you'd saved Vanessa's life . . . and mine." He gestured toward Stone's arm. "How did you get that wound on your arm?" He looked at Stone expectantly.

Stone returned a hard look at him. "I know what you're wondering, and yes, it was me." He shook his head. "I was sure that Aubree was going to recognize me, but I guess with my altered appearance . . . Anyway, there was no way I was going to stand by and let that man hurt her or Vanessa. You happened to be on the right side of things, so I saved your skin, too." He clenched his fist at the memory of it. "I don't know if he was one of the pirates you're talking about, but from the looks of things, he was waiting for Vanessa."

"I think you're right," Torben said quietly. "I also think we should have the doctor look at your arm."

Stone shrugged, but when a few moments later Kevin Jensen said that for the time being he didn't have any more questions, Stone allowed himself to be seen by the ship's doctor.

The bullet had only broken the skin and damaged his muscle maybe an eighth of an inch deep. Yet, even though it was superficial, the wound had become infected. Stone was given a heavy dose of antibiotics after the doctor had dressed the wound. Since the infirmary was currently unoccupied and was the most secure place on the ship except for the brig, it was decided that Stone would be kept there for the time being. The ship's brig was pretty well filled up, he was told, and although Stone wondered if he was imagining it, he thought he saw a glimmer of compassion in the eyes of the young redheaded Dane.

When another security officer came to take Torben's place in the infirmary a few minutes later, Stone looked up from where he sat, fighting sleep. "I figure you owe me," he said in a low voice as the young man stood.

Torben looked at him but didn't respond, so Stone went on. "I'd like to talk to my daughter. She likely won't agree. But maybe . . . when she knows what you know, she'll consider it. Just ask her."

Torben glanced at the other officer and turned to leave. But as he did so, Stone thought he saw the slightest nod. With that encouraging image in his head, he was at last able to drift off to sleep.

# CHAPTER NINETEEN

KEVIN JENSEN'S MIND WAS STILL reeling at the unexpected phone call from the *Stargazer* and at the bizarre information he had heard. After replaying the recording of his phone conversation with Stone for his captain, he had received permission to open a full investigation into the murder Stone had been convicted of. He had already sent a couple of detectives to see what they could learn about the victim of that homicide, one Olin Gentry, who had died of a gunshot wound almost ten years ago in the master bedroom of Stone and Vanessa Lansing's home. Another pair of detectives was actively looking into the activities of Bridget Summer, the woman who was Aubree's nanny at the time of Olin's death. They were also assigned to find out what they could about their cook and caretaker, Francesca Bruno, who still worked for Reginald and Vanessa.

A rough sketch of Stone's background sat in front of Kevin now, and he glanced at it again. Stone had married Vanessa when he was twenty-six. She made millions in her modeling career, but his business in advertising also brought in a great deal of income. Following his conviction and prior to Vanessa's marriage to Reginald Kern, Stone's advertising agency had been was sold. Some of the proceeds of the sale had gone into a bank account that Stone now had access to. But the bulk of it went to Vanessa's own estate.

Kevin read something he already knew, that Reginald Kern was part of Stone's defense team, and that following his conviction and the sudden death of Reginald's partner, George Sedwig, Stone had dismissed Reginald and sought a new law firm to handle his appeals.

He scratched his head as he thought back to what the captain had told him on the phone after Torben had taken Stone to the ship's infirmary.

It seemed that Stone had indeed risked his own life to save both his daughter and ex-wife. This fact, above all else, stood in sharp contrast to the picture Kevin had of who and what Stone Lansing was. If he had wanted them dead, why hadn't he allowed Cord to shoot them? Could he be telling the truth? Kevin sighed. What about the murder charge, then? If he was telling the truth now, had he been telling the truth all along? Kevin shuffled the papers in front of him until he came upon Stone's statement of what had happened the day of the murder.

*I came home in the middle of the day to look for some business papers I had misplaced. I saw Olin Gentry's car parked out front, next to the nanny's, Bridget Summer. I had told Bridget that she was not to let him in the house. He was an ex-con. I knew it, and everybody else knew it. I had told her that he was not welcome in my house and that I had better never see him there again. I also had told Gentry that.*

*I had seen Olin's car at a bar a few days before he was killed. I went into the bar and confronted him. I told him if I ever saw him at my home again that he'd regret it. Then I left.*

*After seeing his car out front I went inside looking for him. He ran into my bedroom—to hide from me, according to Bridget. But I found him and told him to get out. Bridget followed me into the room, and the three of us argued. Bridget told him he should do like I said and leave. All three of us left the bedroom together, and I left the house, thinking that he would be leaving right behind me. But then I remembered why I had come in the first place, and I went back inside to get some papers I needed for a client.*

*I saw a man running down the sidewalk at the side of my house as I walked back toward the front door. He was wearing jeans and a T-shirt, and at first I thought it was one of the gardeners, but it seemed strange that he was dressed so casually. I didn't recognize him, but that was not unusual as the domestic help was always hired by Vanessa.*

*In the kitchen, I saw Bridget and told her that if Olin came back, she'd be fired. She didn't say anything, but then I asked her where Aubree was. She said, "The little snot is hiding. You need to teach that girl some manners." I told her that she was not to speak about my daughter that way, but she only said, "I'll find her in a minute," and I dismissed the matter from my mind.*

*I thought I'd left the papers I was after in the dining room. I looked there, and when I didn't find them I wondered if they were on my nightstand in the bedroom. That was why I went back in there. I thought Olin had left the house. And, of course, I had seen him leave the bedroom. But there he was in the bedroom again, on the floor. There was blood all over. I reached down to see if his heart was beating. He was dead. A pistol I always kept in the bedroom was lying on the floor beside the body. I picked it up after I got blood on my hands from checking the body and then quickly laid it back down, thinking that I shouldn't have touched it. I stood up, wondering what to do.*

*A moment later, I went back out of the room and found the nanny. I told her that Olin was dead and asked who it was I had seen leaving the house. She said she didn't know what I was talking about. She said there hadn't been anyone else there. I told her that I saw someone and that he must have killed Olin. She told me that if he was dead, I had done it. She screamed it at me and told me she was calling the police.*

*I looked down at my hands and realized how it would look. Olin had been shot with my gun. It had my fingerprints on it. I had Olin's blood on my hands. The nanny knew I was in the house and that I was angry. I panicked. And then I ran.*

Kevin was grateful he had the full support of the captain and a team of detectives in investigating this matter after so many years had gone by. He knew the task before him was daunting. The job of finding "Rambler" alone would be almost impossible, not to mention the work he intended to do in checking internal affairs records about the officers listed on Stone's case at the time of the murder. And, of course, Reginald Kern had still not returned any calls and his involvement, if any, needed to be investigated. Kevin intended to conduct the investigation as subtly as possible. If word got out, he'd have another can of worms on his plate. That was the last thing he needed right now—because on top of looking into this cold case and dancing around Reginald Kern, there was the slight matter of a pirate attack that was very likely to occur against the ship carrying most of the individuals involved in this case.

* * *

"If Stone's in league with the pirates, why did Nadif ask me—Cord—if Mr. Faulk had been killed?" Torben asked Captain Newkirk as the two men discussed what had happened in the office.

"None of this makes any sense," the captain grumbled.

"You can say that again," Torben said tiredly. He turned to leave, knowing that Aubree would be waiting up for him until he returned with news for her. He was unsure how to give her that news. He knew he couldn't take what Stone had told him at face value and that he had to be careful not to allow himself to be manipulated by the man, but somehow things simply didn't add up in Torben's mind. The man may have saved his life. And Aubree's and Vanessa's as well. That had to be considered.

He had told the captain about Stone's request to speak to his daughter, and although the captain had balked at the idea at first, he'd finally said that as long as Aubree knew that her decision to speak to her father was completely voluntary, he'd allow it.

As Torben opened the door, the captain picked up the phone to speak with the FBI once more. "Don't give that girl any more stress than she's already under," he said warningly, and Torben nodded, determined as well that that was the last thing he wanted for the girl he had come to care so much about.

When he knocked on the door to Aubree's room, she answered right away. "I hope I didn't wake you," Torben said, peering into the dark room and seeing only a dim light on the nightstand.

"Mom and I are awake," she replied, nodding back into the room at Vanessa, who stood to come to the door as well. "We've been talking since you left, trying not to go crazy," Aubree said. "What happened? Is everything okay?"

Torben nodded slowly. "Everything is okay, I think. Your father was taken into custody without a struggle—he actually gave up voluntarily, and we interviewed him in the office for some time. We even brought Lieutenant Jensen in on speakerphone, and he asked your father a number of questions," Torben said, watching the relief on Aubree's and her mother's faces. Then, taking a breath, he added. "Your father said some things I think you need to hear, Aubree. He . . . well, things might not be as they seem."

"What do you mean?" Vanessa asked, her brow pinched in concern. Aubree looked at her mother uneasily then back at Torben, waiting for him to continue.

"He says he didn't commit the murder and that he's here trying to protect you and your daughter."

"Protect us?" Aubree replied in a high-pitched voice. "My dad is a conman and a liar. You really sat and listened to him say that? He killed that man and he wants to kill me."

"If you'll just listen to me, Aubree, I know it sounds crazy—I thought so too at first, but when I realized that he had been the one in the harbor—"

"Mom, shut the door. I don't want to hear this," Aubree said, moving back into the shadows.

Torben swallowed hard. He'd been afraid this would happen, and although he understood why Aubree was reacting this way, he knew he had to tell her what he'd come to say.

"Aubree, there are some things I think you need to hear. Your father would like to speak to you. If you don't want to listen to him, I certainly understand, and I won't make you. But if you do, it will be in the presence of me and of the captain, and he'll be in handcuffs," Torben said quietly, not wanting to wake the twins. "I needed to give you the option, though. If you'll even just talk to me, I can explain what I mean—"

"Whose side are you on?" she said in a choking voice. "I won't talk to him."

"I'm sorry, Torben. I think you need to go now," Vanessa said quietly. A moment later, Torben found himself staring once more at the outside of the door. His shoulders sagging with the stress that had accompanied him since long before the day started, he made his way back to the captain's office.

* * *

Aubree was inconsolable. "Mom, I can't!" she said again as Vanessa gently stroked her hair while she sobbed. "I know too much already."

Vanessa pulled her close for several minutes as her daughter continued to cry. When she spoke at last, she said, "Aubree, I have an idea." She leaned back and looked her in the eye. "You and I both trust Torben, I think, right?" When Aubree reluctantly nodded, she continued. "And if he thinks there's something we need to hear, I'd like to know what that is." She took a deep breath and finished. "I'm going to talk to him first, and if I think he's onto something, *I'll* talk to your father. And then you and I will talk, if there's anything to talk about."

"Mom, there can't be anything left to say," she whispered angrily.

"Sweetheart, I will not let anything happen to cause you more hurt. I'd die before I let that happen. But I really feel like I should do this." She sighed. "It's late, sweetheart. But in the morning, I want to talk to Torben. Do I have your support?"

When she saw the determined look on her mother's face in spite of the fear she saw there as well, Aubree slowly nodded, wiping away her tears. "You have my support. But I'll never talk to him, no matter what he has to say."

# CHAPTER TWENTY

THE CAPTAIN'S PHONE RANG JUST as Torben returned from checking on Stone Lansing in the infirmary early the next morning. He hadn't awoken yet, but the guard on duty said he'd slept restlessly. The captain answered his phone, listened for a moment, and then said, "I'll send Torben to escort you here."

"Was that Aubree?" Torben asked hopefully.

"No, but her mother would like to talk to us. Will you get her?" he asked.

Torben made his way to suite 737, sadly remembering the previous night. He had slept only a few hours and was exhausted both mentally and physically. He was also torn emotionally. His shoulders were slumped, his eyes downcast as he walked, and his arms hung limply by his side.

With an effort, he knocked on her door, his head bent as he waited. Vanessa answered it and simply said, "I'm ready. Let's go."

He looked past Vanessa and saw Aubree across the room where she sat on the bed next to the still-sleeping twins. She looked up at him and their eyes connected and held for a long while. He saw a torrent of emotions there, but then she turned away. Torben sighed and led Vanessa from the room.

* * *

Aubree carefully moved from where she sat on the bed, taking pains not to wake her sleeping siblings, then stepped out onto the balcony overlooking the calm gray sea. She gripped the railing like she was trying to strangle it. She didn't see the beauty of the sunrise or feel the gentle rocking of the ship. As much as she hated to admit it, she was still angry with Torben. At the back of her mind, she realized that regardless of what happened in the next few days, they'd soon be leaving this cruise, and she'd probably never see him again. That thought made her even more miserable.

She didn't know what to do with herself. With Vanessa gone and the twins asleep, she felt all alone. She didn't want to be alone, especially with her jumbled thoughts, and so, on a whim, she quietly went back inside and picked up the book sitting on the nightstand. Then she turned on the corner light, sat on the sofa, and opened the Book of Mormon.

At first she couldn't concentrate, but as she thumbed through it for a few minutes, she gradually became interested. Here and there a verse would catch her eye and she would read it and then look for another page. After a while, she was surprised to realize that tears were slipping down her cheeks.

Feeling the sudden urge to pray, she put the Book of Mormon down and glanced at the twins. Convinced they were still asleep, she bowed her head and concentrated. She thanked the Lord for bringing her mother safely to her. She also gave thanks that her father had been captured.

Aubree paused in her prayer. She hadn't thanked God for Torben or anything Torben had done for them, including risking his life for her mother. Was she really that angry with him? She considered that for a moment, and then she knew what she needed to pray for. So she asked Heavenly Father to help her see past her pain and anger. She also asked Him to help her see clearly.

After closing her prayer, she got to her feet and leaned against the railing for several thoughtful minutes. She didn't feel any answer. She was still angry that Torben would ask her to speak to her father. And she didn't feel like forgiving him just yet. She sighed, puzzled over her own thoughts and feelings. She wanted to forgive Torben. She didn't want to lose him as part of her life. But he wanted her to *forgive* her father.

She caught herself. Where had that thought come from? He hadn't said any such thing. All he'd asked was that she consider *listening* to her father.

Her confusing thoughts were interrupted when she heard the door open. She lifted her head and slid the Book of Mormon back onto the nightstand then looked up to see her mother standing at the foot of the first bed, gazing at her sleeping children. There were tears in her eyes, and it looked like she'd been crying.

"Mom, are you okay?" she asked.

"Not really. We need to talk," she replied, hugging herself tightly as if against a chill. "Let's go out on the balcony so we won't disturb Ryan and Brandi."

With the glass door closed behind them, Aubree asked, "What happened?"

Vanessa took ahold of the railing and looked out at the ocean. "I've been talking to Torben and Captain Newkirk. I haven't talked to your father yet."

Aubree nodded. "Okay."

Vanessa looked at her, her eyes red-rimmed. "But I want you to know right off the bat that I plan on doing so in a couple of hours—when he wakes up."

"I don't think you should," Aubree whispered, avoiding her mother's eyes as she gazed into the distance. "But what is it that you have to tell me?"

Vanessa swallowed hard. "There's a lot to tell. But the one thing I can't stop thinking about is . . . It was him, Aubree. Your father was the man who attacked Cord in St. Petersburg. He saved our lives."

"What?" Aubree asked her, eyes narrowed. "That can't be true." She spun away from Vanessa, her heart pounding. It had to be a lie . . . her mind reeled as she thought back on the blur of memories from that horrible time. It couldn't have been him. Why would he?

Vanessa rubbed tears from her eyes. "I don't understand why he did it. Oh, Aubree, I'm so confused."

"You don't believe him, do you?"

Vanessa stared out to sea. "He boarded in St. Petersburg, right after the attack. He's dyed his hair blond and is wearing glasses now. I'm not sure if you could tell that when you saw him in the dark during the storm." She paused. "He has a bullet wound on his arm, Aubree. Torben didn't realize it was there until he took your father into custody."

"He could have been wounded before . . ." she murmured.

"Aubree, something doesn't add up. Think about it. The name your father was traveling under was Karl Faulk—as in the Mr. Faulk that Nadif asked Torben—who was pretending to be Cord—if he had killed. Torben believes the pirates may be after your father, too."

Aubree couldn't seem to reconcile what she was hearing with what she was feeling. She hated her father. She felt comfortable hating her father. But what if she was wrong? Never before had she entertained the least doubt as to her father's character. But she was no longer certain. A thousand contradictions and questions spun in her head, and she leaned against the balcony for support as she remembered the flash of blond hair she had seen as the mysterious man attacked Cord.

Gathering her courage, she finally allowed herself to say the words she thought she'd never say. "Tell me more," she said quietly.

* * *

Captain Newkirk paged Torben and told him that Aubree and her mother would like to speak with him. Putting the pager back on his belt clip, he slowly began to walk toward their suite, unsure of what awaited him. Although he ached to see and talk to Aubree, he also dreaded it. He was certain she was still angry and was frankly surprised she wanted to see him so soon.

Vanessa answered the door when he knocked, and she invited him in with a smile. The twins bounded over to him as well, and he patted their heads with genuine affection. He couldn't see Aubree, but the drape to the balcony was closed. He suspected that she was out there.

"Aubree's on the balcony, Torben. Why don't you go out and join her? The twins and I were just about to go get some breakfast."

"Sure," he said, and he slipped past Vanessa and the twins as they walked out the doorway. He pushed the drape aside, pulled open the door, and then closed it behind him. Aubree was standing against the rail, staring at the waves lapping against the side of the ship.

She did not turn around, and for a moment he just stood there, not sure what to do. Finally he said, "Your mother said you wanted to talk to me."

She still didn't speak but slowly turned to face him. Her eyes were red from crying, and her dark hair was blowing across her face from the soft breeze off the ocean. For a moment he simply stood where he was, trying to read her dark brown eyes. And then, tentatively, he reached up and smoothed the hair off of her face, tucking it gently behind her ears. His hands lingered there for a moment before dropping to his side.

Finally, it was Aubree who broke the silence. "I'm sorry, Torben. I've been awful."

He shrugged, wanting nothing more than to pull her to him. "You've been through a lot in the last few hours."

She lowered her eyes. "I'm sorry about that. You didn't deserve to be my scapegoat."

Torben reached up and gently lifted her chin so that she would meet his gaze again. "I'm the one who's sorry. I never should have tried to encourage you to talk with your father."

Aubree turned away from him and grasped the railing, staring off into the distance again. Torben watched as the breeze again stirred her long dark hair. For a long time neither of them spoke. It was Aubree who finally broke the silence. Without turning back to him, she said, "I haven't read a lot in the Book of Mormon, but I was thumbing through it and I read a verse that says we're supposed to forgive or we won't be forgiven ourselves. I read it two or three times. But I don't understand it," she said in frustration. "What if our sins are little compared to someone else's?"

He stepped beside her. Without looking her, he said, "It's up to God to judge that. All we're asked to do is forgive and let Him be the judge."

She shook her head in frustration. "It's too hard."

"I know, Aubree. When I was a police officer I saw some really bad things happen. And I really struggled with forgiving folks, especially when they had hurt children. I didn't understand how I could forgive them. But over time, and with the Savior's help, I have." He paused. "It helped me to remember that He forgave everyone, even those who crucified Him. And I know I won't ever have as much to forgive as Him."

Aubree thought this over in silence then asked. "But what good does it do for us to forgive?"

"It makes us feel better," he said. "Carrying hatred around with us is a hard thing, and it wears us down. If we forgive, our burdens become easier to bear."

"Really?"

"Yeah, really. A lot of the cops I know are cynical and bitter. And I know that forgiving has helped me not to become like that."

Aubree moved her head slightly and looked up at him. Her eyes were glistening. They gazed at each other for a moment, and he sensed her deep pain. She turned away again. He reached over and placed one of his hands on hers where she still gripped the railing. They stood like that way for a minute or two. Finally, she spoke in a barely audible voice.

"Torben, will you take me to visit with my father?"

"I will if that's what you really want," Torben answered hesitantly.

Aubree turned to face him again and looked into his eyes. "I'm not sure what I want, but I know that I need to talk to him. But, Torben, I'm scared."

"Aubree, how do you know that your father wants to kill you?" he asked after a moment.

"Because that's what he told his attorney," she answered defensively.

"How do you know that?" he persisted

"Reginald told me," she answered.

Torben sighed. "Kevin Jensen is still looking into everything, and he will be for a while. But so far he can't find any record of George Sedwig ever speaking of Stone wanting revenge. Anyone who has heard of those rumors, it seems, heard them from Reginald." He held up his hand at Aubree's expression. "I'm not saying Reginald lied. But like I said, it's something to think about."

She was thinking, her eyes staring past him. "Mom told me what my father told you and the captain about Reginald." She shook her head. "Mom doesn't know what to believe, and neither do I. Reginald has been good to us." She was quiet for a long time, and once again she turned and leaned against the rail of the balcony, peering at the water below.

She turned to face him then, and her nearness nearly took his breath away. "I don't know what to think right now," she said. "But I'm glad you came to talk to me." She leaned even closer as her arms slowly encircled his waist. He hesitated, and then put his arms gently around her shoulders. "And," she continued, looking deeply into his blue eyes, "I want to find out the truth. But I will feel better if you come with me to talk to my father."

Torben nodded as his eyes moved slowly down to her lips. He heard Aubree's breath catch as he leaned closer, but then he stiffened and pulled away. This couldn't happen, he thought with a jolt of pain in his chest. Aubree watched him as he turned to the railing and gazed at the scene below.

"Torben, are you okay?" she finally asked hesitantly.

He snapped out of his reverie and said, "I'm just tired. Let's go see your father."

Vanessa was waiting with the twins when they came back into the suite, having gotten their breakfast to go and picked up some pastries for Aubree and Torben as well. Mother and daughter exchanged glances.

"I've decided I do want to speak with my father," Aubree told her. "But if you'd like to speak with him first, that's fine with me."

Her mother nodded. "You go first. I'll stay with the twins right now, but regardless of how it goes, I would like to speak to him later."

"That can be worked out," Torben said.

"Are you going to be safe, Aubree?" Brandi asked, looking from her mother to her sister.

"Torben is coming with me, pumpkin. I won't be long." Then, giving Torben a nervous glance, she took his hand in hers and they headed to the ship's infirmary.

* * *

Aubree stood outside the infirmary, her heart pounding painfully in her chest as Torben unlocked the door and stepped inside. He dismissed the guard and then spoke. "Mr. Lansing, if you're well enough, you have a visitor."

Her father replied quietly enough that Aubree was unable to hear his response, and then she found herself being ushered into the room beside Torben.

She looked at her father only briefly and then turned her head away as she tried to still her shaking hands. He looked much different than when she had last seen him. His dark hair was now blond. He was no longer wearing the glasses her mother had mentioned. He looked pale, and a white bandage peeked out of the corner of his shirt at the top. She swallowed, remembering what her mother had told her about her father supposedly rescuing them in St. Petersburg. She had hated him for a long time, and she had feared him. When she spoke, her voice squeaked and she sounded to herself like a frightened little girl. "Hello," she said as she turned back toward him.

However, the eyes that gazed upon her from the man she had feared so much were not the eyes of hatred and anger she had expected. And, to her total amazement, those very dark eyes she remembered so well and that were so much the color of her own filled with tears.

"I'm so sorry, Aubree," were the first words that he spoke in a low, choked voice. She had not expected that. She couldn't speak. He continued, his deep voice trembling, "Before I say anything else, I need to tell you what I've wanted to say all this time. No matter what happened at the trial, you are my daughter, and whoever made you believe that I would ever hurt you was wrong. Aubree, I love you. I wasn't the greatest father in the world, I know that, but I always loved you. Not a single day in these past long years has gone by that I haven't thought about you. I would never hurt you. You've got to believe that."

He began to cry. The man she hated and feared and believed to be a cold-blooded killer sobbed in front of her like a child. She couldn't draw her eyes from his face. If ever she had seen genuine anguish, she was seeing it now. He was either suffering terribly or he was putting on a great act.

She knew that she had to speak again. After looking to Torben for strength and support, she said in desperation, "Mom told me about what you said to Captain Newkirk and Torben." Seeing his look of surprise at the mention of her mother, she pressed on. "But how do I know you're not lying about everything? How do I know it's not all part of your plan for revenge?" She kept her eyes on his face, challenging him.

The look of pain in her father's eyes only deepened. "I guess you don't, when it comes right down to it. I know you don't trust me, Aubree. And I know what I'm saying flies in the face of everything you think you know." His voice choked again. "I know you've . . . hated me all these years."

The pain on his face was so intense that it made Aubree want to cry. She gathered her emotions then asked, "Mom told me that it was you who stepped in and wrestled the gun away from that man in St. Petersburg. Is that true?"

Aubree watched as her father struggled with his feelings. The anguish did not go away, but he seemed to compose himself with a gigantic effort. "Yes. I don't know who that man was, but when I saw what happened, I didn't really have a choice. He was going to hurt your mother, and likely you—and him," he said, gesturing to Torben. "And that's the last thing I would ever want." He lowered his eyes. "I know what this all looks like to you, especially in light of what Reginald has said my motives are." He swallowed hard at the mention of her stepfather's name but continued. "But as I'm sure Vanessa told you if she's talked with Torben and the captain, my motives in coming here were to protect you. Something was wrong, and I couldn't let you down again. Even if it meant going back to prison."

She didn't want to believe him, and yet he looked so sincere.

For the first time, Stone's voice was steady, and he went on when she didn't reply. "I don't know who killed Olin Gentry all those years ago, but I'm praying that in light of what's happened recently, things can be set right once and for all. If I go back to jail, I hope that it will at least be well-deserved this time, that it will be because I kept you safe. Those eleven lost years, very hard years, I'll never get back. But I knew that when it came down to it, I'd go back again if it means you and your mother will be safe. Your father didn't kill anybody," he told her in a quiet voice.

"I hope you didn't," Aubree said very softly as tiny seeds of doubt over what she'd believed all these years sprouted. "I hope you are telling me the truth, but right now, I'm just so confused," she added as her voice broke. Turning to face Torben, who stood silently with a somber expression on his face, she whimpered, "I need to go now."

\* \* \*

"Do you believe him?" Vanessa asked shakily after Aubree had shared a little of what Stone had told her. She hadn't shared all of what she'd heard. It was simply too painful. But she knew she and Vanessa would speak more when her mother had talked to Stone as well.

Aubree sighed. "I don't know if we've been wrong about everything, but maybe we've been wrong about some things." She shook her head. "I'm just so torn up inside." She thought for a moment. "But I'm not as afraid of him anymore. I think I would even be willing to talk to him without Torben sitting there."

"I'm still a little afraid of him," Vanessa admitted. "Will you come with me while I talk to him?"

Aubree thought about it for a second, and then she said, "Yes. But I'd like Torben to be there, too. Let's see if the Jackmans will stay with the twins. I know some of the pirates have been arrested, but Torben says they can't be sure there aren't more. We can't take any chances. I'm just so glad we've gotten to know the Jackmans."

"Let's wait, then," Vanessa said suddenly, seeming more fearful now than she had earlier, especially at the mention of the pirates. "The more I think about this, the more afraid I am of facing him again."

In a way, Aubree felt sorry that her father was sitting alone in the ship's infirmary. But she needed time to think before she saw him again. She had been hit with so much so fast it was almost too much for her.

* * *

Stone thanked Torben when the young man came to tell him that it would be evening before Vanessa would be able to talk to him, if she did at all. "Sorry about the accommodations," he added awkwardly before he left, gesturing to the sterile white room and the guard. "You've been brought food, though, I assume?"

"Don't worry about it," Stone told him. "And, yeah, I've been brought food." Something close to a smile crossed his face. "I'm relieved enough that I got to talk to Aubree that I don't care that I have to sit here."

Torben nodded then turned to leave once more. "I'll be back in a few hours."

"Wait," Stone called, catching his eye and then glancing at the guard. "Could I have a word with you?"

Torben nodded then dismissed the guard momentarily. "What is it?"

"The pirate matter," Stone said in a low voice. "Have you found out anything?"

Torben looked down. "I'm afraid I can't give you any information on that right now. It's what the authorities are advising." He looked torn for a moment then added quietly, "But everything is okay for right now."

Stone looked relieved. Torben reinstated the guard then left to see to his duties on the ship and to check in with Captain Newkirk. However, it seemed to be a matter of time now as far as the pirates were concerned, and he anxiously waited to hear from either the FBI or Kevin Jensen, saying they had new information.

Still, the minutes ticked by, and the only page Torben received was a couple of hours later when the captain let him know that Vanessa was ready to see Stone.

\* \* \*

Stone was relieved when he heard the door lock turn and saw Torben standing in the doorway, motioning to someone outside. He felt his mouth go dry, having told himself for the past two hours that Vanessa would most likely refuse to talk to him. And now she was standing mere feet away. He wanted so badly to clear the air with her as he'd begun to do with Aubree earlier. He wasn't sure exactly why. He still felt some hope that he'd be able to regain a relationship with his lost daughter. But he knew with a certainty that he'd lost his wife forever. She was Reginald's wife now, no matter how much that tore at him. And yet he still wanted her to hear the truth from him, not just second-hand through the captain or Aubree.

When Torben ushered her into the infirmary, Stone braced himself but was in no way prepared. He had remembered her as a beautiful woman, but real life was nothing compared to old memories. Her long red hair fell in soft waves around her shoulders, and although her eyes were filled with worry, they still took his breath away.

"Stone?" Vanessa asked in a strained voice as she took a tentative step closer and sat down in the chair farthest from him. "How . . . are you?" To Stone's surprise, Aubree entered the room a moment later and sat beside her mother.

"I'm doing all right, considering," he said with a smile of his own. "You look beautiful."

Vanessa shifted nervously on her chair at his compliment. Sensing her discomfort, he decided to talk about Aubree.

"And look at our daughter, she's beautiful as well," he said, nodding toward her.

Aubree smiled shyly. Stone noticed Torben's eyes lingering on her face, but he turned his attention back to his ex-wife. "Vanessa, I know you've talked to Torben and Captain Newkirk, but I wanted to tell you a few things myself. I . . . I tried to get in contact with you. I understand why you didn't want to hear from me. It's just . . ." He swallowed back the emotion threatening to overtake him and took a deep breath. He could do this one more time. Then he'd have said all he needed to say, and the cards could fall as they would.

When he was finished, there were tears in Stone's eyes. Vanessa and Aubree were crying softly as well and holding each other.

However, after they had sat in silence for a time, Vanessa attempted to speak past her emotions. She managed to say, "If you're telling the truth, Stone, we have a lot to sort out." Vanessa shook her head and looked at Aubree and then at Torben. She started wringing her hands, but her eyes remained on Stone. "I never thought I'd find myself saying this, but . . ." She swallowed. "I don't know what to think about most of what you've said, but for some reason I know it was you in St. Petersburg. Thank you."

# CHAPTER TWENTY-ONE

"Thank you, ma'am, you've been very helpful." Kevin hung up the phone, pleased at the information he'd just learned. It had taken him nearly all day of back and forth to gain access to Reginald Kern's meeting schedule, but he had finally done it although, amazingly, without once talking to Reginald himself. He'd communicated solely with the reedy-voiced receptionist, whom he had been on the phone with for some time. The receptionist had been unaware of Reginald's activities for the day, since he had canceled all but one early meeting, and she had been reluctant to share any information with the police. Kevin had been forced to get an official subpoena, which had cost valuable time. But now, he finally had Reginald's meeting schedule of the day Stone had confronted him at the office. And, matched with the timeline Stone had given him a few hours earlier when he had called for a few follow-up questions, one name was now circled on the sheet of paper in front of him: Leroy Sanders.

He had just begun a preliminary search on the name when a short, middle-aged Italian woman he recognized as the cook from the Kern mansion walked in. He lifted a hand in greeting as she made her way to his desk, but she looked nervous.

"I was going to call," she said, glancing around. "But I decided to come in and see you instead. You are the lieutenant working with Aubree and Vanessa Kern?"

When he confirmed that he was, the woman looked relieved. "I have spoken to Vanessa. Those poor children . . . and that poor woman. I have been worried sick about them." She looked up at him. "She told me about the capture of Mr. Lansing and that you were reopening the investigation," she added tentatively.

"That's right," Kevin told her, curious as to why she had come. "And please, remind me of your name?" he asked as he offered her a seat.

"Francesca Bruno," she said, sitting and surveying the room. "I know it's late, but I think I may have some information for you. Ever since Mr. Lansing showed up at the house, I've been thinking about what happened all those years ago. Now, with what Vanessa has told me, I knew I should speak to you."

"I appreciate your coming in, Ms. Bruno. What do you have to tell me?" Kevin asked.

"As you know, I work for the Kerns," she said. "But I'm the only one of the current staff who worked for Vanessa when she was still married to Mr. Lansing. I was in my second year there when that man was murdered in the Lansings' bedroom."

Kevin had no idea where this was going, but he decided to let her talk for the moment—maybe he'd learn something. If it appeared that she had anything to add to what was already known about the case, then he would dig deeper, question her more closely, and see if she really could help.

He had promised Rosanne that he would be home by six, but by the time he was finished with Francesca Bruno, it was already five. What he had just learned from the cook was potentially important, especially in light of Stone's story. There was a lot of follow-up that needed to be done to confirm the things he'd just learned, including having several critical points of both Stone's and Francesca's stories checked out. And he now needed more man-hours devoted to locating Bridget, the nanny. So far they hadn't found her, and he was more determined than ever that he needed to interview her. He was also more intent than ever on getting ahold of the elusive Reginald Kern.

He walked Francesca Bruno to the door and then called Rosanne to apologize for the fact that he would not be home when he had intended. He returned to his computer and picked up where he'd left off in searching for Leroy Sanders before Francesca had arrived. As he had hoped, he was rewarded for his long hours on the phone fairly quickly. Leroy Sanders had a record—he was in the system, and an address was on file.

Kevin picked the phone up and dialed again to reach some of his detectives as he walked to his car. He wasn't the only one who would be keeping late hours tonight.

\* \* \*

TORBEN KEPT BOTH CORD'S PHONE and Eko's with him at all times just in case a call came in for either man from Nadif. It was early Sunday morning when he heard the phone ring on the stand next to his bed. Even though he'd only been asleep for a few hours, he was awake instantly and grabbed the phone, Cord's phone. It was now just before three in the morning.

He cleared his throat and his mind before opening the phone, determining who was calling, and then greeting Nadif in German. "I assume you are in Germany by now?" Nadif responded.

"Yes," Torben said.

"Good. The operation is underway. I will call you in Berlin with instructions after we have the children off the ship and the ship itself in our control."

Nadif's words made Torben shudder. He wanted this call over so he could make sure that everything was in readiness to repel the attack and so that he could warn the captain. They had been in constant communication with the FBI, and he believed the attack would be thwarted successfully, but that was still far from certain. "I will be waiting," he said. To his relief, Nadif simply ended the call.

Torben sprang from his bed and called Captain Newkirk. However, after quickly relating what he had just heard, all the captain said was, "You are to come up here right away," in a pinched voice.

A warning bell went off in Torben's head. That wasn't a typical response, and the captain's voice had sounded extremely stressed. Torben had last talked to him before going to bed in the early morning hours, and at that point Captain Newkirk had sounded confident that the pirates would be taken out without any problem and that his ship would be safe. "I'll be right up," he told his commander.

Perhaps he was just startled by the statement from Nadif that the operation was underway. And yet it didn't seem like he'd even had time to fully digest what Torben told him before making his response. Torben would have expected him to ask a question or two before telling him to come up. He hadn't done that.

A chill ran all the way up Torben's spine as he dressed. He had the sinking feeling that something wasn't right. He stopped and tried to think. But at that moment, the other cell phone he'd been carrying began to ring. He picked Eko's phone up and looked at it. It was Nadif calling the former bartender this time. Torben took a steadying breath and then, hoping he was doing the right thing, he said hello in English, attempting to imitate Eko's voice and accent as closely as he could.

"The Jackmans have done their job. The captain and first officer are both in custody," Nadif said. "Gather your men quickly and do your job. A boat will be ready to take the three children in about thirty minutes. The ship's radio system has been disabled, but the intercom is still functional, of which you should be aware. None of the ship's officers will be able to operate the radio for at least an hour. You know what to do during that time."

Torben's mind was racing. *The Jackmans!* But he couldn't stop to dwell on that devastating revelation just yet. Thinking quickly and praying for inspiration, Torben said, "Let's run through the rest of the plan quickly. I don't want to forget anything."

Nadif made an irritated noise but went on. "You'd better make sure you don't miss anything. The most important part is simple: make sure the children are safely removed from their room and taken below. Once they are removed from the ship and my men have boarded the ship, you get on the intercom and order everyone to stay where they are. Anyone who resists is to be killed—passengers or staff. Is it all clear to you?"

Unsure if he could pry any more information out of Nadif without drawing suspicion, Torben made a split second decision to ask nothing more. If he said the wrong thing just now and Nadif discovered he wasn't talking to Eko, the captain could well die. So he answered with one word. "Yes."

"Then get to it," Nadif said, and the phone call was terminated.

Torben had no way of knowing how many pirates were on the ship, how many they had missed when they arrested Eko and his men. What he did know was that there were at least two, and those two had been passengers, the Jackmans, people he had met and trusted. Nothing could be more chilling. He hurried to the cabin of the third-highest-ranking member of the crew, Lieutenant Hild DeHaven. He quickly explained what had happened, and the two men agreed to quickly gather four more senior officers, all of whom were aware of the pirate threat. Five minutes later, they were all assembled in Torben's room, every face there filled with fear and apprehension.

Torben, even though junior in rank, took the lead as they swiftly planned how to approach Captain Newkirk's office and hopefully surprise and capture the Jackmans while keeping a lookout for any other passengers or staff who might be part of the pirate organization. Torben himself led out a couple minutes later, having gotten the rest of the men to agree to let him approach first since he alone was trained in hand-to-hand combat. Hild insisted he accompany Torben when the attempt was made to free the captain and first officer, who they assumed was also a captive when he couldn't be found in his quarters.

Armed with concealed knives taken quietly from one of the kitchens, the men made their advance. They were watchful of others, but no one seemed to pay much attention to them. The ship never truly went to sleep, and a few passengers were still in the lounges and food was being consumed in a couple of the restaurants. However, most of the stewards, cooks, and others of the ship's staff were still in bed. There was very little movement in the hallways.

Torben gripped the knife handle more tightly in his palm and positioned several of the officers in strategic locations near the captain's outer office where they could watch for and hopefully intercept anyone who might approach the office. Then he and Hild dropped to their knees and approached the door. The one advantage that they had was that the Jackmans apparently didn't know that Eko and his men had been captured and placed in the brig. But even that thought didn't ease the churning in Torben's stomach. He knew that Hild was a brave man and very capable, but he'd never experienced anything quite like this.

Torben caught Hild's eye and gave him a thumbs up. They had to act quickly, for time was running out. The attack from the sea could happen soon. And it was imperative that they free the captain and first officer before it did.

Torben peeked cautiously through the small window beside the door while Hild knelt just beyond the door, a long carving knife in one hand. Captain Newkirk and the first officer were tied together, back to back, on the floor on the far side of the room. A man and a woman, unmistakably the Jackmans, had their backs to the door. They were carrying handguns.

Torben ducked back down and whispered what he had seen to Hild. Then he reached up and tried to silently open the door, but it was locked. There was only one other thing to do. Clearly, the onboard phones were still functioning since the captain had called him earlier, and so Torben opened Eko's cell phone and entered the office number. Then he peeked inside again as the phone started to ring. The woman picked up the phone, said something sternly to the captain, then put the phone to his ear.

Torben spoke quickly. "Give the phone back to her. Tell her it's Eko. We're here to help you, Captain."

The captain's expression didn't change, but Torben saw his lips move and watched as Leah Jackman put the phone back up to her ear.

Torben did his best to disguise his voice with Eko's accent. "Open the door quickly. I've run into a big problem," he said then ducked and scrambled to the other side of the door next to Hild and rose to his feet. To Hild he said quickly, "I'll take out the one who opens the door. Then I'll try to get to the other one. When you come in, come in low in case they start shooting. And move rapidly. Don't be afraid to use that knife."

Before he could whisper more instructions, the door opened, and Torben saw Chad Jackman standing there. Chad's eyes opened wide with surprise when Torben grabbed for the pirate's pistol as he simultaneously delivered a quick, hard thrust to his throat. But Chad was fast and skilled, and Torben missed the gun. Even worse, his blow to the throat did not connect with the force needed to disable Chad. The pirate fell backward but immediately bounded back to his feet. Then Torben was on him, and he managed to kick the gun before he could pull the trigger. The gun slid across floor.

Chad delivered a blow to Torben's face that stunned him, but he was able to keep his feet under him and, keeping the pirate's body between himself and Leah, he delivered a kick to his adversary's knee. Chad buckled, but not before his fist connected with Torben's stomach, driving the air from him. Both men hit the floor. Gasping, Torben dove forward and grabbed Chad's arm and brought it down over his knee. There was a loud crack as the bone broke, and Chad screamed in pain.

Torben was aware of Leah trying to get in a position where she could shoot at Torben without hitting her husband. He also saw Hild charging in, low and fast. She raised her gun and pulled the trigger, but Hild had dived to the floor and the bullet whizzed past him. Desperately, Torben threw a hard blow to Chad's throat, finally disabling him. Then, still trying to catch his breath, he sprang toward Leah, who was already firing again in the direction of Hild as he swiftly came at her again in a low crouch.

Torben let out a cry as a bullet struck his friend, but at the same instant, Hild drove his knife deep into her thigh.

Torben reached her and swiftly knocked the gun away. Leah tried to kick him, but her injured leg gave way, and as she fell sideways, Torben managed to render her unconscious with two rapid blows. Still gasping for breath, he turned on his knees to see Lieutenant DeHaven writhing on the floor, holding his side as blood seeped through his hands. His face was ashen.

"Hild," Torben gasped in fear. "I'll help you." Tears streamed down his face as the captain and first mate cried out to him as well, trying to find out what had happened.

The other officers, having heard the fight, came to their aid. They charged through the door and two of them, at Torben's wheezing directions, grabbed the Jackmans' guns and positioned themselves just outside the captain's door to make sure that no confederates of the captured pirates could catch them unawares. Another officer began to cut the captain and first officer loose while the last one began to secure the unconscious pirates. Torben tended to the badly injured lieutenant, praying that his life could be saved. "Get the doctor," he called to the first officer, who, along with the captain, was now free from his ropes. As he did so, the captain attempted to radio an SOS, calling for outside assistance.

"The radios are disabled," Torben cried. "Where's your cell phone?"

The captain motioned toward the floor. His cell phone was in pieces, having been destroyed by the Jackmans. Torben felt a bubble of panic. "Here," he said, handing the captain Eko's cell phone. "Get in contact with the FBI; the attack is going to take place anytime now."

As the captain grimly took the phone, Torben could only pray that their situation was being monitored closely and that the captain would be able to get through to his contact. The number had been stored in the cell phone that now lay destroyed on the floor, and without the radios, it would take time to connect with someone who could offer them the immediate assistance they needed.

"Help is on the way," Torben told Hild, whose eyes were closed as he lay on the floor, his head in Torben's lap. A few minutes later, the doctor, with the aid of two others, moved the unconscious lieutenant to the infirmary. They would do their best to stabilize him there until it could be arranged for an emergency helicopter to evacuate him to a hospital in Helsinki.

Torben hurriedly moved the Jackmans to the brig after the doctor bandaged Leah Jackman's leg just enough to stop the bleeding. Hers was a bad wound and would need more attention, but they couldn't take chances allowing her to remain free at the moment. Torben himself had miraculously sustained only a small cut near his left eye, which was swollen but minor.

With the captain's permission, Torben moved Stone to an unoccupied staff cabin until further notice, keeping a guard with him, though he was sorely tempted to enlist the guard's help in more pressing matters. As he ran back to the office, he desperately wished he could know that Aubree, Vanessa, and the twins were safe in their cabin. Nothing led him to believe that they were in danger—yet—but still, he knew that the knot in his stomach wouldn't begin to unravel until the attack had been averted and he could see them standing safely in front of him.

As the captain continued to make calls attempting to get in contact with those who could aid them in their peril, Torben got on the ship's intercom and asked for the attention of everyone on the ship. "There is an emergency," he said. "There is no need for panic, but we are requesting that all passengers in exterior suites move without delay from your rooms and go into the interior of the ship. The rest of you please stay in your rooms. And, please, no moving about the ship until you are given further notice." Then he dropped the bombshell he hoped would bring compliance but not cause panic. "We have taken a number of men and women into custody who were planning to take control of this ship. There are more pirates on the sea who are intending to intercept us shortly." He paused, hoping that his next words weren't a lie. "Know that there are ships and jet fighters coming to our aid. We will be safe, but we must evacuate the exterior areas of the ship in case gunfire is directed at us by the pirates' vessels."

*Please move quickly,* he thought as his mind went to Aubree and her family. *Please stay safe.* He looked over at the officers who were struggling to bring the radio back into operation without success and then, signing off the intercom, he hurried to check on Hild and join the captain once more to see if he could be of further assistance.

Torben saw them standing near the edge of the deck, the captain with his phone to his ear, staring off into the water. There was a stiff breeze blowing, causing whitecaps to cover the sea below.

"How is Hild?" the captain asked, clearly waiting for someone on the other end of the line to respond.

"I'm afraid he's hurt badly," Torben said somberly. "The doctor doesn't know if he'll make it." The thought made him tremble. He was about to express how bad he felt to the captain when a he saw the man's eyes change, widening in surprise and then fear.

"Get back from the deck," Captain Newkirk shouted, grabbing the first mate's arm but still holding the phone to his ear. "Hurry," he cried, snapping the phone shut.

Before Torben turned to flee, he saw the outline of two vessels approaching at a distance, quickly closing in on the ship. His heart sank, but he didn't stop to dwell on the scene before turning to follow the captain and first mate.

"Where are the warships? Where are the fighter jets?" Torben gasped as he ran.

"They should be here soon, I hope," the captain said. "That was my contact with the FBI on the phone just now. None of the warships are close enough yet to be of help. But if we can just hold on until the fighter—"

Gunfire blasted the air, and the sound of breaking glass filled Torben's ears. The ship had been hit.

Torben dropped to the deck as a barrage of bullets continued striking the *Stargazer,* and he murmured an urgent plea for help, praying that the passengers were all safely away from the outer rooms. When he hazarded a glance out to sea, he could see that the pirates were continuing their approach but had turned a little and sped past on the starboard side of the ship, firing repeatedly.

Torben squeezed his eyes shut, thinking of Aubree and her family. They were the ones these men with guns had come for—and in a few minutes, if nothing changed, their innocent lives would be at the pirates' mercy.

Then, suddenly, there was a roar from somewhere out to sea, and a fighter jet streaked into view. Torben's heart soared as the first pirate vessel, which was just a hundred yards or so from the *Stargazer,* was struck by a streak of light from the fighter jet. A split second later the little craft disappeared in a blinding flash of flame. Torben watched in fascination as a ball of fire burned brightly on the water for a moment and then died down. He could see nothing left of the pirates' vessel from where he was.

The second pirate vessel again opened fire on the *Stargazer* with automatic weapons, but only a smattering of bullets struck the cruise ship before the second vessel was likewise blown apart by another shell fired by a second fighter jet. Then there was silence.

After a minute had passed without further incident, the three men lifted themselves up to gain a better vantage point. When they looked about them with no sign of anything but the jets overhead and a clear ocean, save an approaching warship in the distance, they celebrated briefly.

Captain Newkirk now had Hild's cell phone, his own having been destroyed. When it suddenly began to ring, he answered and then briefly spoke to the person on the other end, indicating that he had not been able to assess the damage but would call back shortly. He then turned to the first mate with a serious look on his face. "We've got to check the ship for damage and see if anyone was injured by the bullets fired from the pirate vessels." To Torben, he said, "Start checking on the passengers. I'll get on the intercom and tell them to return to their cabins, but I need you to hurry and check on them. I'll send more of my officers to help as soon as I can make contact with them."

\* \* \*

Fifteen minutes later, a preliminary damage assessment had been completed, and the passengers had all been accounted for. Although the ship had sustained some damage, it was minor compared with what could have occurred, and although the passengers were badly frightened, no one had been injured.

Since Aubree and her family had been the objects of the attack, Torben felt it was well within his duties to seek them out. He knew they were safe, another officer having seen them, but he wanted to make personal contact with them. When he finally saw Aubree's long, dark, unmistakable hair amidst the crowd, he hurried to her side.

"Oh, Torben, we were so worried about you!" she cried as he pulled her into an embrace.

"You were worried about me?" He chuckled. "I was beside myself with worry about all of you."

"We were fine," Ryan said bravely and smiled proudly at him.

"How did it all happen?" Aubree asked. "Was there any warning? Is there still any threat?"

Torben briefly described what had happened. When he got to the part about the captain and first mate being held hostage, Vanessa drew a hand to her mouth involuntarily. "Who was it? Were they passengers?" she asked.

Torben nodded slowly. "I know you'll find this hard to believe, but it was the Jackmans."

Aubree gasped and grabbed Torben's arm for support. "It couldn't have been," she said, her eyes wide. "They . . . they . . ."

"I know what you're thinking; they tended the twins. They had us all fooled, Aubree." He shook his head and explained the rest of what had happened. "It was Leah who shot Hild," he added hollowly.

Aubree melted against Torben. He held her for a moment while watching Vanessa and the twins. Their mother was holding them. They were all in shock. Vanessa was shaking her head in disbelief. "Even people you think you can trust can be bad," she said softly. "I would never have suspected them."

Torben pulled back and Aubree reached up and tenderly touched his swollen eye. "I'm sorry about Hild," she said. "So what happened after that? We heard shooting and some explosions."

Torben had just started to explain when one of the confiscated phones in his pocket began to vibrate. He jerked it out. It was Eko's phone. Taking a deep breath, he opened it and said hello.

"Eko, what's going on?" It was Nadif's voice, and he sounded rattled. Torben said nothing, and in a moment Nadif went on. "I haven't been able to raise the attack boats. What is going on there?"

When Torben finally spoke, he made no effort to disguise his voice. "I am not Eko," he said. "Eko is in the *Stargazer's* brig, along with several others of your gang. He made some serious mistakes."

"Who are you?" Nadif demanded.

"It doesn't matter who I am," Torben said. "Just know that you have failed. But I would like to know one thing, Nadif. Who contracted with you to kidnap the three American young people?"

The phone went dead. But as Torben slipped it into his pocket and began to relay to Aubree and Vanessa what he'd just heard, the other phone in Torben's pocket began to vibrate. He answered in German, attempting to disguise his voice, just in case it was Nadif again. "Cord." It *was* Nadif. "Do you have any idea what is going on with the *Stargazer?*"

"What are you talking about?" Torben asked. "Is something wrong?"

Nadif cursed and then said, "Yes, something is wrong. Eko has been arrested."

"Who told you that?" Torben asked, hoping that maybe he would learn something on this call.

"I don't know, but it wasn't Eko. It was someone on his phone." He made an angry noise. "If you knew about any trouble, you should have reported it to me."

"I haven't heard anything," Torben said. "I don't know what you're talking about."

"You better not be lying," Nadif spat.

"Why would I lie?" Torben asked, trying to sound puzzled. "I need the money you promised me."

"You get paid only if we succeed, and it looks like we might have lost our boats on the sea. And something happened to Eko. Someone else has his phone," Nadif said. "Call his phone yourself. See what you can learn from whoever has it. Then let me know."

"I'll do that," Torben said, smiling now at Aubree and her family, who didn't understand a word that he was saying since none of them knew any German. "I'll call you back," he said, and the conversation was over.

"That was interesting," he said, and he quickly explained what had just happened. "I have to go take care of some other matters," he said, locking eyes with Aubree for a moment longer than necessary, "including your father." He saw something change in her eyes at the mention of her father, but to his amazement, there was no longer any fear.

# CHAPTER TWENTY-TWO

IT WAS LATE THAT EVENING when Kevin received a call from Aubree Lansing. He had only barely said hello when she burst into the story of the pirate attack on the *Stargazer*.

Kevin could tell Aubree was excited, but she also sounded rattled. "Are you and the twins all right?" he asked when he could get a word in.

"We're fine. So is Mom. My father is all right too," she said. "Torben and Hild saved us. Have you found anything out on your end?"

"We're making progress," he said. "Francesca Bruno came to talk to me earlier."

"Francesca? Why?"

"It seems that she saw someone running in front of your house on the day Olin was killed—just like your father said. It was never brought up in court, and she hadn't realized it was significant—until she spoke to your mother." He paused then added, "There's more. I don't know for certain what will come of this, but I've located a man named Leroy Sanders. He seems to be the person Stone saw Reginald arguing with on the day he went to his office. I don't know yet if there's a link there or not, but I plan to find out as soon as I can bring Mr. Sanders in for questioning."

"Will you tell my father that?" she asked, sounding hesitant yet excited by the news.

"How do I get in touch with him?" Kevin asked.

"He's right here," she said to Kevin's amazement. "After the attack, Mom and I went down to talk to him some more for a little while." Then Aubree got off the phone, and a moment later Stone's voice came on the line.

"Lieutenant, this is Stone Lansing. My daughter tells me you have some news."

Kevin took a deep breath and then told him some of what he and his officers had discovered.

"And you're bringing this Leroy Sanders in for questioning?" Stone asked quietly.

"I plan to do so first thing in the morning." Although Kevin knew he needed to remain objective on this matter, he had to admit that Stone's story was lending itself to more credibility than he'd originally expected. "I don't have any evidence yet that Mr. Sanders is in any way connected to the murder of Olin Gentry, but I'll find out."

"I appreciate that," Stone said somberly. "Have you made contact with Reginald yet?"

"Not yet," Kevin noted, irritated that he had still been unable to contact the man. "But I'm working on that as well."

Kevin hung up the phone and rubbed his eyes. He had been working too long without any sleep and so, despite the fact that there was still much to be done, he hurried home and got a few hours of shut-eye. However, when the alarm clock buzzed, letting him know it was six in the morning, he popped out of bed and was soon back to work.

To his relief, his efforts paid off. An hour later, Kevin was standing on the doorstep of a man by the name of Leroy Sanders. Leroy peered at him through the chained door, and when Kevin announced that he was an officer working with LA homicide, the skinny, balding man looked as if he might shut the door.

"I just have a few questions I need to ask you, Mr. Sanders. May I come in?"

"I don't feel like talking," the thin man muttered, shifting his eyes to look behind where Kevin was standing.

"Mr. Sanders, we can do this the easy way by talking right now, or I can bring you in to the station. I'm afraid this isn't a social call, and it's important that we talk."

The man stared at him for a full thirty seconds and then said, "You can bring me wherever you want, but I'm not talking to you until I've spoken to my attorney."

Disappointed, Kevin made arrangements to meet with Leroy Sanders another time, at the station, with an attorney present. He then left the man's house and returned to his office, thinking that he'd hit a dead end for the time being. However, he got lucky again a short while later. Two of his men believed they had identified the man known as Rambler. They were bringing him in to the station for Kevin to interrogate.

* * *

The American received the bad news from Nadif himself. "We failed, and it is your fault," Nadif told him angrily.

"How is it my fault?" the American asked warily.

"You let the woman go to the Baltic."

"How did you expect me to keep her here?" the American asked with annoyance. "Anyway, that only complicates my getting her money. Her leaving here could not in any way have compromised your failed operation."

"I choose not to believe that," Nadif said darkly.

"You're looking for excuses for your own incompetence," the American said as anger crept over him. "I met my obligations. I obtained the weapons as I said I would. And it shouldn't matter whether the woman was on the ship or not."

"You aren't listening to me," Nadif said, his voice low and threatening. "Someone tipped off your government that my men were going to take over the ship. It wasn't from my end—I'm certain of that. So it came from your end."

"There's no way you can know that," the American fired back, then said calmly, "I'm afraid that you have failed me. Our arrangement is over. You will, of course, not be receiving the weapons."

"You will send me the weapons," Nadif said, his voice rising in pitch.

"That will not happen," the American told him angrily. "I took some big risks to get those weapons. You may buy them at a price that I will name, but I will not give them to you."

"I will send you the information on shipping them," Nadif said as if he hadn't heard what the American had just told him.

"Those arms will be sold to whoever will give me the best price for them. You are not the only one who has need of weapons. We have nothing further to discuss." He slammed his phone shut.

The phone rang a minute later. When the American realized that it was Nadif calling back, it enraged him. He was not one who lightly accepted the incompetence of others. He shouted into the phone. "You don't know who you are messing with! The matter is over. Do not call me again," he said.

"I think you misunderstand me," Nadif said, his voice so calm it was chilling. "The choice is not yours. Ship me the guns as we had previously arranged."

"And if I don't?" the American challenged him.

"Then the U.S. Army will get a tip about who stole their weapons," Nadif said, and he abruptly ended the call, leaving the threat ringing in the American's ears.

* * *

Rambler appeared highly agitated when Kevin walked into the small interrogation room where the detectives were holding him. He was a smelly, unkempt little man of about forty who actually looked much older. He was missing several teeth, and what few he had left were yellow and chipped. He fit Stone's description exactly. Kevin introduced himself and then said, "Rambler, I would appreciate it if you would show me some identification."

"My name's Rambler. I don't use no other name," the man said.

"I suppose that since my men found you beneath an overpass that you are homeless," Kevin said. "Or do you have an address?"

"I got no address. People that know me can always find me," he said.

"So you have no ID on you?"

"I got none and I don't need none."

"Who paid you to deliver forged materials to Stone Lansing?" Kevin asked abruptly.

Rambler's face went white. Kevin had clearly caught him off guard. He stammered for a moment, and then he said, "Don't know what you're talking about, Lieutenant."

Kevin leaned across the table toward him, tapped his pen on the surface, and said, "Let me make one thing very clear to you, Rambler. I already know that you met with Stone Lansing on two successive evenings. And I also know that you brought him forged documents—a driver's license, a visa, and a passport. The picture on that forged passport was taken by you, and don't tell me it wasn't. I even know where these things occurred. Stone Lansing is prepared to testify, if he needs to, about what I just told you. So the ignorance tack won't work. Now, who did you do this for?"

Rambler was looking around and nervously rubbing his whiskered face. Without making eye contact, he said, "I can't tell you."

"Why can't you tell me?"

"Because I don't know the guy," Rambler said, seeming to settle down a little. Kevin took that as a sign that he thought his lie would get him out of trouble.

Kevin sat back and glared at the man for a moment. Then he decided to take a calculated risk. He didn't know for certain yet if Stone was telling the truth, but he was beginning to believe that he was. Rambler's reaction to the question he was about to ask would tell him a lot. "Maybe I could ask a different question." He paused and let Rambler squirm for a moment, and then, leaning toward Rambler, he asked, "How much did your friend Reginald Kern pay you for running this errand for him?"

The reaction Kevin got to this question confirmed his worst suspicions. To his amazement, Rambler gasped, and then he began to sweat. His face went pale again, and his hands shook. He looked around like he was trying to find a way to escape from the interrogation room. But when he saw that he was hopelessly trapped by Kevin and the other two detectives standing near the door, his mouth began to work nervously, like he was trying to speak but couldn't. Kevin waited for a couple of minutes while Rambler squirmed.

Finally he asked very sternly, "How much did he pay you?"

"I can't tell you that," he whined.

"That's okay. It doesn't matter anyway. I'll just let Kern know that you talked to me when I question him," Kevin said slyly.

Ramblers bulging eyes looked like they were about to pop from their sockets. He wiped sweat from his face. "No, you can't do that. He'll have somebody kill me!"

"Looks to me like you've got yourself in a bit of a bind," Kevin said, not letting his face register the shock he felt at Rambler's statement. "Mr. Kern must have paid you quite a bundle."

"He didn't pay me anything," Rambler said. "He made me do it."

"He *made* you do it?" Kevin pressed him.

"You don't understand," Rambler said.

"Then why don't you help me understand?" Kevin insisted. "You can start by telling me why you ran this errand for Mr. Kern, an errand that could land you in prison."

"I didn't know what else to do," Rambler insisted, his eyes darting back and forth. "Mr. Kern made me take them. He said I owed him."

"Did you owe him?" Kevin asked.

"I guess so, 'cause he had some dirt on me that he promised not to tell if I'd just do a little something for him once in a while."

Kevin had what he needed. Reginald Kern was definitely involved in this mess. And the fact that he hadn't been able to make contact with Reginald at all despite his repeated efforts in the past two days began to make some sense. "I'll need a statement written up and signed by you, and then you'll be free to go," he told Rambler.

"You can't let me go," Rambler said, trembling. "I swear I'll get killed—or worse."

"What's worse than getting killed?" Kevin asked. There was no mistaking the fear the repugnant little man was experiencing.

"You don't know Mr. Kern. He can be a very dangerous person," Rambler said. "Please, Lieutenant, I broke the law. Lock me up."

"I can do that," Kevin said.

Rambler nodded, but then his expression changed abruptly. "No, that won't work either. He can get to me in jail. He has lots of guys in there that owe him favors like I do. You gotta keep me safe."

"Why don't you just leave the area?" Kevin asked. "You have no job, no home. What keeps you here?"

"I know a few guys here. I get a little money from time to time."

"Like Reginald Kern gave you a little money? Is that what you mean?"

"Yeah, that's it, but Kern, he didn't give me much, just enough to buy some smokes and feed me for a few days."

Kevin shook his head, then he turned to his detectives and said, "Write up the statement and let me see it before he signs it. I'll be in my office. Then let him go."

"No, put me in jail," Rambler said.

"But you just told me that—" Kevin began.

Rambler cut him off. "Put me in jail. Just tell them to keep me safe. Put me in solitary if you have to, but don't let them let nobody hurt me."

Kevin gave the officers some instructions on what charges he thought ought to be filed. Then he said, "That should hold him until we can get to a prosecutor on Monday."

"Thank you, Lieutenant. I owe you, Lieutenant," Rambler groveled.

"You don't owe me. Just sign that statement when these officers get it typed up." Kevin turned away, disgusted by what he had just learned and more intent than ever on bringing Reginald Kern in.

\* \* \*

As evening approached, the ship was still abuzz with talk of their narrow escape. Bullets had penetrated some of the suites. Windows were broken, and the paint was scarred. But there was no damage serious enough to keep the ship from continuing on. To some of the passengers it was a horror beyond anything they could have imagined. Those passengers were demanding that they be returned to shore somewhere safe, that flight arrangements be made to get them home, and that the cost of the trip be reimbursed.

To others, it was an adventure of the highest order. They couldn't wait to tell their friends at home about the way they'd been attacked, shot at and nearly killed, or taken hostage by wild, lawless pirates.

Torben, however, still felt numb. By the time a helicopter arrived to take Hild to a hospital in Finland, he was in grave condition, and the medics weren't sure if he would survive the flight.

As he stood on the balcony, phone in hand as he waited for news, he saw Captain Newkirk approach from the left.

"How're you holding up?"

Torben shook his head. "It's my fault. I should have planned better."

"You didn't have time," the captain reminded him.

"I should have assumed they were highly skilled," he argued, his throat tightening. "I should have gone in alone. After all, I'm the security officer."

"That was not a job for one man, and you know it; so did Hild. If it hadn't been for Hild, you would have been dead and so would the first officer and I," the captain reminded him. "It was a job for two men, and you and Hild were the right two. Either or both of you could have died. It was the kind of situation that only men of uncommon courage would have attempted."

Nothing the captain could say made him feel better. Finally, he said, his head hanging, "I . . . I've been thinking that after this voyage I'll resign. I've failed in my duties."

That was when Captain Newkirk got firm with him. He pointed a finger in his face and shook it. "Torben, if not for you, this ship would have been taken over by pirates. Who knows how many would have died before the ship was returned to the owners, and who knows what it could have cost the cruise line financially. You must quit blaming yourself, and that's an order. And here's another order. Go get some rest. You'll feel better later. As for resigning, save your breath—I won't let you. In fact, I'm going to recommend a big raise for you."

Torben looked at him, shocked. "Thank you, but I don't deserve it." He was silent for a moment, staring out at the sun sinking in the horizon. Then he asked, "What will happen to the Jackmans?"

"They will be gone by tomorrow. They will be taken back to Holland to stand trial. And with the injuries Lieutenant DeHaven sustained, it means they'll be tried for attempted murder as well as piracy."

It turned out that both of the Jackmans, though Americans by birth, had criminal records in several countries under a number of aliases. And it appeared that they would probably spend the rest of their lives in prison. That gave Torben some satisfaction, although it didn't alleviate the hurt he felt as the minutes dragged slowly by without word of his friend Hild.

Knowing that there was really only one person he wanted to see right now, Torben turned and went to find Aubree. He knew they had no future, and he felt weak for allowing their friendship to grow ever closer, but somehow he couldn't help himself.

# CHAPTER TWENTY-THREE

KEVIN JENSEN GOT BACK IN his car, shaking his head, deeply disturbed over the information he had just learned. He had gone to Reginald Kern's office once more with the intent of bringing him in for questioning based on what he'd learned from Rambler. He had been unable as of yet to prove that Rambler's information was sound, but he intended to find out. However, when he arrived at the law office he had been told, as usual, that Reginald was unavailable.

However, this time he had gotten firm with the receptionist, telling her that if she didn't tell him where Reginald was, she would likely be charged with obstructing justice. Pale faced, she had finally given him the information he was after: Reginald had asked her to cover for him. He hadn't been busy with meetings, in court, or out of the office. It turned out that he had assigned his cases to a junior partner so he could take care of some business out of state, according to the reluctant secretary. A red flag went up in Kevin's mind. Not only had Kern asked his receptionist to lie for him, he'd lied to his wife: Vanessa too had been led to believe that he was in court hearings in Malibu while working on an important case.

He had pressed the receptionist further, but she refused to give him any more information, claiming she didn't know where Reginald had gone, what he was doing, or how long he would be away. Kevin left a final message with the secretary, informing Reginald in no uncertain terms that if he did not respond to Kevin's call within the next twenty-four hours, he would regret it. Then, despite that fact that Reginald had become perhaps the most important figure in the case, Kevin and his men concentrated on other avenues of investigation.

Kevin's next item of business was to spend some time at the hospital where Stone's original attorney, George Sedwig, had died. He went through the records and found the names of all the nurses who had worked at the hospital during the final days of George's life. He and his detectives began searching out every single one of the nurses on the list. They finally hit pay dirt.

Just two days before George had succumbed, an older nurse by the name of Carmen Trapp had worked a twelve-hour shift, and one of her patients had been George. She had retired five years earlier, and it didn't take long before he located her living at the home of one of her daughters in Monterey. She was now seventy and in poor health, but it seemed to Kevin, from his brief conversation on the phone with her, that her mind was still as sharp as ever.

Kevin apologized for the late notice but asked if he might visit her, and to his relief, she agreed. When he arrived, she was waiting in a chair by the window, and a few seconds later a younger woman who was introduced as Carmen's daughter opened the door. Carmen's gray hair was cut short and neatly curled. She wore a bright yellow robe with matching slippers. She was short and slender, and her fingernails were painted a pale shade of pink. She had a ready smile, and if it were not for the pain that showed in her eyes, Kevin would not have known she was truly ill.

Carmen never left her chair, and her daughter invited him to be seated on a hard-backed chair directly in front of her. "How can I help you, Lieutenant?" she asked.

"I understand you were the nurse for a man by the name of George Sedwig about ten years ago," Kevin said. "I know it's asking a lot, but I was hoping that you could remember him and some things about him."

Carmen smiled for a moment and then sat silently, clearly in deep thought. "An attorney," she said after a minute or so.

"Yes, he was an attorney, a very successful one," Kevin said.

Again she was thoughtful, and then she said, "I think I know who you're talking about. Was he a prominent lawyer?"

"Yes, and he'd been in the news a lot just before he fell ill," Kevin said, trying to help her recall.

"As a nurse, I always remembered important people or very pathetic people or people who simply won my heart over." She smiled placidly.

"Do you remember him, then?" Kevin asked. "Shortly before his illness he'd finished unsuccessfully defending a man by the name of Stone Lansing, an advertising executive."

"Was it a murder case?" the nurse asked, scrunching her eyebrows.

"Yes, Stone Lansing was convicted of killing a man in his home. His daughter, a young girl, was a witness during the trial," Kevin said, hoping that she would remember and be able to help him.

Carmen's brow furrowed, and she closed her eyes as she thought. Finally she said, "His wife was Vanessa Lansing, the model. Am I thinking about the right people?"

"Yes, Vanessa Lansing was Stone's wife," Kevin confirmed.

"She has the most gorgeous red hair. I know you can't tell anymore, but I was a redhead myself once. So I guess I'm partial to people blessed with beautiful hair like hers. I've always admired her."

"You have a very good memory," Kevin encouraged her in an attempt to keep her thinking.

"Thank you. I do, actually," she said. "Oh, her name isn't Lansing now—it's, let's see, it's Kern. Yes, that's it. Vanessa Kern." Her face brightened and her pain-filled eyes seemed to brighten as well. "Stone Lansing. Yes, I remember his name. I'm homebound now, and I don't get around much, but I do watch the TV a lot. Didn't I recently hear that he got out of prison?"

"Yes, he did," Kevin said.

Carmen nodded and suddenly her face brightened. "Yes, now I remember his attorney well. What was his name again?"

"George Sedwig," Kevin answered.

"He was very sick those last few days, and I spent quite a bit of time with him, trying to comfort him the best I could."

Remembering his interview with Stone, Kevin asked. "Did he ever mention his client, Stone Lansing, that you recall?"

"Yes, of course. He and I talked about Mr. Lansing several times. Mr. Sedwig believed he was innocent. It seems like he told me that several times in our talks. Mr. Sedwig was a nice man to talk to, even though I remember that he had a reputation for being a real bear in court. I never saw that side of him. He seemed to genuinely like Mr. Lansing. And he told me how sorry he was that his client had gone to prison. He said that Mr. Lansing was worried about his daughter and what a terrible position she had been placed in. Mr. Sedwig told me that Stone Lansing loved his little girl." She looked thoughtful and then added, "She's been in some photos with her mother the past year or two," she said.

Kevin nodded.

"Black hair. Gorgeous girl. Yes, Mr. Sedwig felt bad about her. And he said his client was proud of her even though her testimony helped convict him."

"He told you all that?" Kevin asked.

"Oh yes," the retired nurse responded.

"I wonder if you might be able to tell me anything about Reginald Kern, George's partner," Kevin inquired. "Did he ever come to visit that you recall?"

"Oh yes," Carmen said, nodding vigorously. "It's not easy to forget someone so unkind. I recall him arguing with George Sedwig about Stone," she said.

Kevin was listening intently. But Carmen grew silent, thinking, and he finally asked, "What was it about Stone that sparked their disagreement?"

"It was about Stone's guilt or innocence. Kern believed he was guilty, and George, as I just said, believed him innocent. There was more than that, though," she said. Kevin found himself almost holding his breath. "One day, shortly before he died, George told Reginald that Reginald wouldn't be in charge of Stone's appeals since Stone would be retaining another lawyer after George's death. I had just approached the door, and they didn't know I was there. I guess I was eavesdropping, but I *was* George's nurse. Anyway, I stood there quietly and listened. George told Reginald that Stone did not deserve to be in prison and that he was glad Stone would have a lawyer who believed in his innocence.

"That seemed to make Reginald very angry. He said that Stone was where he deserved to be," she said.

"Did that bother you?" Kevin asked when she was silent again for a moment.

"Yes, it bothered me a lot. But it got worse," she said.

"In what way?" Kevin asked.

"George talked about the little girl, Stone's daughter. As I think about this now, it's coming back to me very clearly," Carmen said.

"What about her?" Kevin asked.

"George told Mr. Kern what he had told me. He said that Stone loved that little girl and that he'd rather go to prison than ever hurt her."

Kevin nodded for her to continue, and Carmen went on.

"Reginald then reminded George of how hard he'd been on the child and how Stone had not attempted to stop the cross examination," Carmen said. "But George told him that Stone had gotten after him about that and had told him to tone it down. I think those were the exact words that George used. *Tone it down.* Yes, that's what he said. And George said to him that he did what Mr. Lansing asked since he didn't want to offend his client. He told Reginald that if it hadn't been for Stone asking him to do that, the trial might have had a different outcome."

"Are you sure you're remembering all these details correctly?" Kevin asked, not wanting to offend her but wanting to be certain.

"Oh yes, I know that's what was said. Mr. Kern left right after that, and he was angry. I pretended that I was just approaching the room when he came storming out. He nearly knocked me over," she said, narrowing her eyes angrily at the memory.

"I still can't imagine how that gorgeous Vanessa could have married him. He must be just awful to live with," she added with a frown. "But I digress. When I walked in the room, George was visibly upset. I asked him if he was in pain. And he said something about his partner *being* a pain. Then he told me again that he was certain Stone Lansing was innocent. He talked about it for a minute or two before he calmed down and let me take his vital signs. Needless to say, his blood pressure was quite high."

\* \* \*

Aubree received the news from Lieutenant Jensen with a mixture of shock and enthusiasm. The news was twofold. First, it was about Reginald apparently being responsible for the forged documents given to Stone. It was also about the elderly nurse, Carmen Trapp, who had heard George Sedwig tell Reginald that her father loved her and would go to prison before he hurt her. The words brought fresh tears to her eyes, and the lingering doubts she had about her father wanting to harm her were nearly wiped away.

She also felt a growing disgust toward Reginald. It was shocking to hear that he had done such horrible, hurtful things. It seemed he had started the rumors about Stone wanting revenge. She found herself pitying Ryan and Brandi. She had always thought she had such a terrible father while theirs, though busy, was a decent man. But now it appeared that those sweet children probably hadn't gotten a break after all. It broke her heart for them. She handed the phone to Vanessa so that Kevin could tell her the news and then sat quietly with her mother as she sobbed, her head in her hands. "I'm sorry, Mom," she said.

Vanessa waved a feeble hand. "Go on down and tell your dad. I just didn't want to believe that Reginald could be involved in this. I can't believe that he was being so treacherous. It really hurts."

Stone's anger at Reginald when she told him what Kevin had discovered was obvious in his dark eyes, but he spoke mildly. "I'm sorry that he caused you and your mother such worry by his lies," he said and then fixed her with a serious gaze. "Aubree, I want you to know that I do love you. I've always loved you. I don't know why Reginald wanted me on this ship, but if anything I've done has helped to keep you and your mother safe, I don't care." But Aubree suspected as she watched his clouded face that he had some ideas about why Reginald had done what he did. She was pretty sure it had something to do with what Torben had learned in his phone call with Nadif about the supposed Mr. Faulk. She shuddered, beginning to realize how blind she had been and how it had almost cost her father his life.

"Dad, I'm so sorry I believed what he said," Aubree said to him. "Maybe now the police can clear your name."

"I hope so," he said. "But I'm not counting on too much. Just because Reginald lied about what George Sedwig said, and the fact that he forged documents, it doesn't prove that I didn't kill Olin. They still need to find the real killer. Did the lieutenant mention if he was making any progress on that?"

"He says he is, but he didn't say exactly what he meant by that," she said then paused. "He also said that his detectives all believe now that you got a rotten deal and that they're determined to find the real killer and clear your name."

"That's great," Stone said with a sigh of relief. "It's nice to feel like the cops are on my side this time around." He shook his head, remembering.

"All those years ago, I was so disillusioned with the police investigation of the case . . . Once the cops had their sights on me, they were like bulldogs. It didn't matter what I said, they turned a blind eye." He took a breath, reining his anger back in. "Did Lieutenant Jensen say if he's been able to locate Reginald yet?"

"He can't find him," Aubree revealed. "But he finally got the receptionist to reveal that Reginald's actually been out of town for the past few days. He'd asked his receptionist to cover for him. He lied to Mom about it, too."

Aubree watched as the cloud again crossed her father's face. "Sweetheart," he began again, concern evident in his voice and his eyes, "I don't know what Reginald's intentions are, but I worry about you and about your mother. Tell her she needs to be watchful whenever she's off the ship. All four of you need to be."

"We'll be careful," she promised as the old fear and twisting in her stomach began all over again, only this time it was fear of her stepfather.

Stone looked down for a moment, and when his eyes found hers again, he changed the subject. "How is Torben doing? I know he's had a difficult time after that other officer was hurt. Have they heard if his condition has improved?"

"I don't know. I haven't seen Torben. I think he's been really busy," she said. "Or else he doesn't want to see me." She sighed and looked away.

"That I doubt, Aubree. Why don't you look him up and just talk to him? What he needs now is support. He's been through a terrible ordeal," her father said firmly. "Go see Torben. He's a fine young man."

\* \* \*

A light knocking on the door brought Torben to his feet. He opened it, and Aubree stared at him, looking at his tousled hair, wrinkled uniform, and sagging shoulders. He tried to smile, but he couldn't quite achieve it.

"Hi, come in," he said.

"I haven't seen you for a while," she said. "Are you okay?"

"I've been better," he admitted, his eyes dropping. "It's been a rough couple of days."

"From what I understand, you saved the ship, not to mention my family and me," she said.

"Because of me a good man is on the verge of death," Torben said with a bite in his voice.

"No, Torben," she protested. "Hild is going to make it. Have you heard any news?"

Torben shook his head. "Nothing but that he's still in critical condition. They're not very optimistic."

"You've got to quit blaming yourself," she said softly. Aubree took a tentative step closer to him, her eyes pleading. Torben watched her for a moment. His eyes slowly scanned her face. "Thanks," he said with a small smile. "I'll try."

She wrapped her arms around him and buried her head against his chest. Torben awkwardly returned the hug, and they stood together that way, each lost in their own thoughts. Eventually, Torben relaxed a little, and, after a few minutes, Aubree pulled back and said, "Why don't you come with me and get something to eat."

Torben nodded and then smiled. This time the smile reached his eyes. A few minutes later, they were seated at a table next to a window overlooking the sea. They were now churning toward Germany, having already docked for a short time in Helsinki, where the brig had been emptied of the pirates.

His mind drifted back again to the attack as he thought of the pirates and all the problems they had caused. But then Aubree spoke to him, her voice tender and her eyes once again pleading. "Torben, you're doing it again. You've got to quit blaming yourself. What happened is over with. You didn't cause it. The pirates did. You were trying to save lives, and you did! Hild was trying to save lives too, and he probably did, perhaps even yours. It's not your fault. And I really think Hild will make it. I've been praying for him, and each time I do, I feel peaceful about it."

Despite himself, Torben felt tears begin to wet his eyes. He reached out and covered Aubree's hand with his own as he gazed deeply into her eyes. Finally, he smiled. "Thank you for telling me that," he told her. "Tell me what's been happening with you."

As they ate, Aubree brought Torben up to date on what she knew about the investigation in Los Angeles. When she mentioned that Reginald Kern was missing, that he'd left LA, Torben tensed again and Aubree sensed that his attention had shifted from his own feelings of guilt to the safety of her and her family.

"It sounds to me like Reginald is a dangerous man," he said to her. "You've got to be really careful. He could be coming to meet the ship."

"That's what my father thinks too. He's worried that Reginald might be trying to cause more trouble. I don't know why he can't just leave people alone," she said with a touch of anger in her voice. "I actually thought Reginald cared about us when he was talking about how my father was after us and how he'd protect us. But now I don't know what to think. All the worry that I've done over my father was Reginald's fault, and now we learn that he made it all up, that he lied." She grimaced as she spoke, her eyes full of pain.

She looked like she had more to say, but her cell phone rang. She pulled it from her purse and answered. "Hi, Mom."

Torben studied her face as she talked to her mother. Her eyes were expressive as she spoke, and her hair, when it fell over the smooth skin of her face, cast an air of mystery about her. She unconsciously flipped it out of her eyes, but when it dropped back a moment later, she let it stay, and she stared at him as if looking through a veil.

When she closed the phone, she asked, "Do you still have Cord's phone?"

"Yes, why do you ask?"

"That was Mom. She just had a call from Lieutenant Jensen. He wanted to get Reginald's cell phone number. He was planning on calling it himself, but while they were talking, he thought about something else," she said hesitantly. "He wonders if you could use Cord's phone and call him pretending to be Cord."

"Do you think he knows it's really me?" Torben asked.

"I have no idea. But there's one way to find out," she said. "Let's talk to Mom again then call Kevin and see what he has to say. According to Mom, he said to call whenever we can."

"If you're okay with it, I am too," he said, standing when she did and taking her hand in his. Then the two of them hurried to find Vanessa.

* * *

After speaking with Vanessa, Kevin Jensen hurried to make his appointment with Leroy Sanders. However, after ten minutes, Kevin knew this was going to be a waste of time if something didn't change. Leroy was as ornery and tight-lipped as he had been earlier, and Kevin wasn't getting any information. His attorney was making it especially difficult.

Finally, Kevin pulled out his ace—insinuating that he had spoken with Reginald and that Reginald was ready to talk. As the words left his mouth, he knew he had succeeded. Leroy's face went first pale and then bright red.

Glancing at his lawyer, who hesitantly nodded, Leroy said, "I'm not the person you need to be talking to. You leave me alone, and I'll point you in the right direction. Okay?"

"I can't make you any promises, but if the information you give me really does point me in the right direction, I won't need to bother you anymore, will I?"

"Her name's Angel Vaughn," he said. "And that's all you'll get. And don't tell her I told you nothin'."

# CHAPTER TWENTY-FOUR

As the evening wore on and the other officers went home, Kevin still found himself in his office—there was simply too much to get done. And there was a chance that he would be there the rest of the night. He had sent out some preliminary feelers on Angel Vaughn but had so far turned up nothing. And so, as he searched, he had been reading files he had obtained from Internal Affairs.

Once again his persistence had paid off. He'd found something significant. The lead investigator on the Olin Gentry murder case no longer worked for the Los Angeles Police Department, having been fired for accepting bribes six years ago. He had also spent time in prison and had not been released until about a year ago. The bribes had nothing to do with Stone Lansing's conviction, but the similarities on the case that he'd been busted for and Stone Lansing's were too many to ignore. Further reading revealed that two more of the detectives on the Gentry case had later been busted by Internal Affairs for bribery as well. It wasn't proof, but Kevin was convinced that Stone Lansing had directed him in the right direction. Someone with the right motives may well have paid off some officers to make certain that Stone went to prison. And that someone was looking more and more like Reginald Kern.

This called for further follow up, but it would have to wait until morning when he would turn that part of his investigation back over to Internal Affairs. Kevin was just putting the case files away when his cell phone rang. A moment later he was told that two of his officers had learned where Angel Vaughn was living and that, with a little luck, they would be bringing her in to the station first thing in the morning.

Kevin sighed with relief, grateful for his officers' hard work. Moments later, his cell phone buzzed again. The call was coming from Torben.

The first words from Torben's mouth were, "I'm sorry to be calling at such an awful hour for you, but Vanessa said that you insisted."

"Yes, I did. I'm still in my office. I'm afraid this is one of those times in the life of a homicide detective when the family gets the short end of it," he said. "But I sure appreciate your taking time to call me. I know you've been through a rough time there."

"Things are better now. The ship took some damage from the pirates' gunfire, but nothing serious enough to stop the trip. The crew has made what repairs they can until the ship can be taken in for more extensive work following the cruise." He sighed. "A few passengers were so frightened that they left the cruise in Finland, but I think the rest of the people are okay," Torben said. "I am worried about the situation with Reginald Kern. What do you think he's up to?"

"I'm worried about the same thing, and I wish I knew the answer to that question," Kevin said. "I'm afraid Reginald might be planning to meet the *Stargazer*. If that's the case, and if he's involved in the pirate attack gone bad, he could cause some real problems. We also have no idea what alias he's traveling under. As we so recently learned, forged passports and other types of ID seem to be one of his specialties."

"What do you want me to do?" Torben asked.

"If you still have access to the German pirate's phone, I'd like you to try to call Reginald. With your accent you might be able to make him believe you're Cord. Vanessa has Reginald's cell phone number, and we can only hope he answers it."

"I can try that, but what do I say to him?" Torben asked.

"I've been thinking about that," Kevin said. "Perhaps you can act like you know who Nadif is. The FBI agents I'm working with want to know if Reginald is involved with the pirates. So do I. It seems remote, but we believe that someone from here in the Los Angeles area is involved."

"Okay, but what else do I say?" Torben asked.

"Just say whatever comes to mind. Maybe you could make him think that Nadif has identified him to some his men. If Reginald is involved, we hope to rattle him. Then, Torben, if you are able to learn that Reginald is part of this operation, we want you to call Nadif again. But wait to do that until you have some help at your side."

"What kind of help?"

"An FBI agent. One is headed for the ship as we speak. He is flying by helicopter from Sweden. Your captain knows he's coming already, but he doesn't know why. Again, we may be way off track here, but we have to consider this possibility. Anyway, if Reginald falls for our little ruse, you can let the captain know."

"Wow, you don't ask much of a guy, do you?" Torben said. "I hope I don't let you down."

"Torben," Kevin said seriously, "you've already proven you're up to the task. I admire what you've done. And I'm confident that you can pull this off. But let's make sure before you go into this that you know everything I do about both the case here in California and the piracy." He then spent several minutes filling in the latest details for Torben, including what he'd learned about several of the officers who had investigated the Olin Gentry case and how they had later been discovered accepting bribes in other cases. Then he said, "That's all I can think to tell you. Call me back whether you reach Reginald or not and let me know what happens."

"Okay," he agreed then said in a low voice, "but I've got one more question before I hang up. Do I gather from what you've told me that Reginald not only may have been involved in bribery, but that he is also now a suspect in the murder Stone was convicted of?"

Kevin hesitated, unsure whether he should be revealing this information. Finally he said, "Yes, but don't let him know about that. I don't want him to know that the police are looking at him in relation to the murder. So if you reach him, limit your conversation to the piracy. But let me explain so you will understand. Reginald didn't pull the trigger—he couldn't have. But I'm definitely not ruling him out as having orchestrated it. So listen carefully to what he says if you get ahold of him. It could be helpful to me in the murder case."

\* \* \*

Aubree was watching Torben as he ended the call. She smiled encouragingly at him, showing her support and faith. Torben reached for her hand and squeezed it gently, his eyes never leaving hers as he did so. Finally, with a look of determination, he turned and, using Cord's phone, punched in what Vanessa had written down as the number for Reginald Kern's private cell phone.

It rang several times, but finally, just as Torben was about to give up, the call was answered. "Who is this?" a suspicious male voice on the other end asked.

"My name is Cord, Mr. Kern. I work with Nadif," Torben said, trying to make his Danish accent sound more German.

"I don't know what you're talking about. How did you get my number?" the voice asked.

Torben now knew that he had Reginald on the phone. But he had not anticipated this question from him. He remembered what Kevin had just told him—to say whatever came to mind. Something did come to mind. "A pretty redheaded woman by the name of Vanessa gave it to me," Torben said truthfully. "I am holding her for Nadif."

"What!" Reginald shouted. "Why are you doing that?"

"Because Nadif told me to. I caught her trying to board the *Stargazer* in St. Petersburg, Russia. She is very angry with you," Torben said. "But so is Nadif. He thinks you sabotaged his plan." Torben didn't know where that came from, but it sounded good.

"He's still trying to get the guns," Reginald muttered. "He knows I'm already in contact with another buyer."

Torben was reeling. *The guns.* It had to be the guns that were stolen from the army in California. This was astonishing information. He took a deep breath as he tried to make sure he didn't let the shock he was feeling affect the way he spoke to Reginald. He hoped he didn't blow it. He was thinking rapidly as he spoke again. "He expects to receive them. Make no mistake about that, Mr. Kern. If you want to see your wife alive again, you will do as he has told you." Again, Torben didn't know where that came from. He met Aubree's steady gaze and then he knew. That girl had faith. She was pulling for the Lord to help him.

"You are lying, Mr. Cord," Reginald said. "I want to talk to her—then I'll believe you."

"Get your mother," Torben whispered frantically to Aubree as he momentarily covered the phone with his hand. "And fill her in." Aubree didn't hesitate but pulled her phone out of her pocket as she hurried toward her suite. Then Torben said to Reginald, "It isn't *Mr.* Cord. It's just Cord."

"I don't care what your name is; I want to talk to my wife."

"You will want to remember this name," Torben said, trying to stall while Aubree called and then escorted her mother to his cabin. "If you don't do exactly what I say, you will be meeting me, and it will not be a pleasant experience for you."

Torben thought about the words he'd just spoken and couldn't help but smile at the irony. Cord would be hard to meet at this point.

"Get her on the phone, Cord!" Reginald thundered.

"She's not with me right at the moment. I have her in a secure place. Remember, she and I are in St. Petersburg. Give me a couple of minutes, and I'll get to her. Then you will see that I am not bluffing."

"Is someone else with you?" Reginald asked suspiciously.

"We are an international group," Torben said, hoping that Reginald would believe he was referring to the pirates. "There are several brave Russians helping me keep the red-haired one secure. I am German, but I speak Russian as well. Just a moment while I give my friend some instructions—he speaks no English or German." Then in an effort to prove his point, he pretended to speak to a Russian. He fired off a couple of sentences in rapid Russian before speaking to Reginald again. "You will speak to her shortly."

When Reginald spoke again, he didn't sound so confident. Torben thought he actually might have rattled him. "Tell Nadif I will need more than my wife back to secure the guns for him. He will need to send me the money. He knows how much."

"Mr. Kern, I don't think you appreciate Nadif's temper. He feels you betrayed him and he is very angry," Torben said. "We lost two of our ships and several brave men when the fighter jets attacked. The United States government knew they were coming, and only you could have told them."

"But I didn't," Reginald said. "I swear that's the truth. I was to get a lot of money when the ransom was paid, just like I'm sure you were. I had no reason to sabotage the operation." He cursed under his breath then added, "Just hurry and put my wife on the phone. I'll set things right—you just wait and see. I think we can pull off this ransom thing yet."

"I certainly hope so, Mr. Kern," Torben said, wondering what Reginald was planning. "Your treachery has cost me a lot of money. I don't like you, Mr. Kern," Torben said on an impulse.

There was a knock on the door, and Torben pulled it open, putting his finger to his lips. The two women came in and he shut the door. They were both breathing hard. He needed to buy a little more time while Vanessa caught her breath. So he said, "Just a moment, these Russians can be stupid sometimes." Then he again spoke in Russian. He kept it up for a minute or more while Vanessa got her breathing under control. When he again spoke in English, he said to Reginald, "She is here now. Be careful what you say to her. I will be listening."

Vanessa and Aubree both crowded next to him. He punched a button to put the phone on speaker, then held the it toward Vanessa and said, "This is your husband. He wants to make sure my Russian friends and I are taking good care of you."

Vanessa, looking just a little white but squaring her shoulders, said, "Reginald, is that you, honey?"

"Of course it's me," he said. "Are you all right?"

"I'm managing, despite what's happened to me."

"It is your own fault, you know that?" Reginald said coldly. "How could you let this happen?"

Vanessa's expression was stricken. "They won't let me see my children," she said, beginning to sound hysterical, but her eyes met Torben's, and he was reassured that she was acting, and doing quite well at that.

"You've only made things worse, stumbling into their trap like you did," he said. "They now have not only you, but the three of them," he lied. "They are demanding two hundred million dollars ransom for the return of the four of you."

Torben glanced at Aubree's face to gauge her reaction to Reginald's blatant lie. Vanessa looked totally stunned. But she continued to play her part well. She gritted her teeth, squared her shoulders again, and said, "Then you'll have to give them the money."

"You know that I don't have that kind of money, not in our joint accounts. You'll need to give me the information on how to access your foreign accounts so I can get it for them," he said.

Torben watched as the stricken look on Vanessa's face turned to anger. Clearly Reginald was after money she had hidden from him. Despite the shock of what she was hearing, Vanessa managed to keep up her façade. However, her anger came through when she asked, "How did you know I had money in other countries? It is none of your business." A tear slid silently down Vanessa's cheek, and as Torben watched her, he realized she wasn't just acting. She was genuinely hurt.

"It *is* my business, Vanessa. You're my wife. And I'm not as much of an idiot as you seem to think I am. Give me access to those accounts and I will pay the ransom so that my family can come home safe and sound."

"I don't have that information with me. I'm a hostage, remember?"

"Cord?" Reginald barked into the phone. "I trust you'll make sure she gets the information she needs." Then, softening his voice, he added, "Vanessa, I love you. You are the most important thing in my life. We may have to give up a lot of money, but to get all of you back will make it worth it. I—"

Torben picked up the phone and pushed the button to take it off speaker. "That's enough talk. As you can see, your wife is alive and well. You would do well to do what you are told."

"I will," Reginald said, his tone of voice much more pleased than it had been earlier. "Nadif will get his guns and money. Let her make some calls and then have her call me back."

Torben cleared his throat. "My men are escorting her out of the room." He waited a moment, keeping eye contact with a seething Vanessa, then said, "Now I may speak freely again. I'll do that, but remember one thing, Mr. Kern. We only have your wife. We would have had your children as well had you not tipped the Americans off to our little plan."

"I didn't tip anybody off!" Reginald shouted into the phone. "I don't know how that happened, but I want my wife back," he added, sounding like he meant it, but Torben didn't believe him.

"Enough," Torben said. "Get the guns shipped. I'll see about your wife making those calls. Expect to hear from me again," Torben said. Then, as an afterthought, he added, "Our men in California say you can't be found. Where are you?"

"That's none of your business," Reginald said. The call ended on that note.

"That horrible man!" Vanessa exclaimed as she wiped at her tears in sharp, angry strokes. "He cares about nothing but my money. I mean nothing to him."

Aubree shook her head in dismay. Torben and Vanessa looked at her and Vanessa asked, "What is it, Aubree?"

"He actually thinks he will get your money. This is unbelievable. He thinks you're a hostage."

"He seems to, all right. I can't believe he betrayed me like that. I knew what Stone was saying about him, but somehow it just didn't seem like the man I knew was the same person he was talking about. It seemed too terrible to be true. I kept hoping there was another explanation," she said, rubbing her eyes and wringing her hands. "He's been using me all these years." Tears kept coming, and she kept swiping them away.

"What about Brandi and Ryan? He's their father," Aubree said, choking back a sob. Torben looked at her; her fondness for the twins was evident on her face.

"They hardly know him," Vanessa said softly, shaking her head. "He's so busy with his work, they hardly ever see him."

"I guess that makes it even sadder. I know how they feel, but I'm lucky. I got my father back," she said in a choked voice, rubbing her eyes. Then she looked at Torben. "Actually, I take that back. I'm not lucky, I'm blessed."

* * *

"That didn't take long," Kevin said. "Did you talk to him?"

"Did I ever, and so did Vanessa," Torben told him. "You'll never believe what we learned."

"Tell me," Kevin said.

"We're with the captain and Stone down in the infirmary now," Torben told them. "We don't want to have to tell this unbelievable story more than once."

Ten minutes later, Kevin said, "The FBI agent I told you about will be there within a few hours. Call Nadif after you've had time to talk things over with the agent. And call me back when you know more. I won't lie to you. I am very tired, so I might try to catch a few winks here in the office before anyone gets here. And first thing in the morning, a couple hours from now here, I'll be meeting with Angel, the woman I told you about. So if you can't get ahold of me beforehand, call as soon as you've talked to Nadif if you reach him."

Hanging up the call, Kevin laid his head down on his arm in the quiet office, hoping sleep would come to him, at least for a short time, so that he could make it through the rapidly approaching day. A few short minutes later, he drifted off.

After what seemed like only a few minutes, he was awakened by his cell phone. The office was still quiet, but he realized that a couple of hours had gone past and that it was now morning. He answered his phone and was informed that the two detectives were here with Angel Vaughn in tow. A few moments later he entered the interrogation room.

"Angel Vaughn," he said as he sat across from her at the small table, "My name is Lieutenant Kevin Jensen." He looked at her closely, studying her face, unable to pinpoint why she looked so familiar to him. He continued to puzzle on the strange feeling as he added, "I'm investigating a case and believe you may have some information for me." He then advised her of her rights.

"What case," she said, looking at him nervously, her eyes darting back and forth. "I don't know what you want from me or why you brought me here. I don't have any information about anything. You have the wrong person."

"Hold on," Kevin said, still struck by a nagging feeling at the back of his mind that he knew this woman. "I understand that you're confused, but if we can just chat for a few minutes . . ."

"What is this about?" she interrupted in a high-pitched voice.

At that moment, a quiet knocking came at the door of the interrogation room, and one of Kevin's detectives poked his head in the door. "Uh, Lieutenant," he said, his eyes darting between Angel Vaughn and Kevin. "Could you come outside for a sec?"

Kevin quickly stepped outside, wondering what could be wrong. But a few seconds later, he knew. He also knew why the woman, this Angel Vaughn, seemed so familiar to him.

Stepping back into the room and locking eyes with her, he spoke once more. "It seems we've been introduced improperly. Let's start over again. My name is Lieutenant Kevin Jensen. And you are?"

"Angel Vaughn," the woman squeaked out after a short silence.

"Bridget Summer," Kevin countered, and then, in a calculated move, he said, "Identities provided for people by Reginald Kern mean nothing to the LAPD."

Bridget's face gave her away at the mention of her name. Her eyes grew wide and her jaw dropped. "How did you know that?" she asked.

"Let's just say that Reginald Kern cares only about Reginald Kern," he said, having no idea how she would react to that.

He soon learned, however, for she signed a form saying that she understood her rights and agreed to answer Kevin's questions without an attorney present. She was livid with Reginald Kern, she was tired of the lies, and she spilled her guts to Kevin. Every word was recorded. There was still more work to do, some facts to check, but as far as Lieutenant Kevin Jensen was concerned, he had just solved the eleven-year-old cold case in the violent death of Olin Gentry.

He smiled to himself. She had looked familiar because her picture had been included in the police file he had studied so diligently—Stone's file.

\* \* \*

Aubree was given the privilege of breaking the good news to her father that afternoon. "Dad," she said excitedly as she opened the door to the infirmary and stepped past the guard, "your name has been cleared!" She grabbed the hand of his uninjured arm, her eyes shining excitedly. "Tomorrow, Kevin will be approaching a prosecutor about presenting the facts to a judge and asking that your conviction be overturned." She paused, smiling, and continued. "The captain says that when that happens, you'll be released from custody, too, and you won't have to stay down here in the infirmary anymore."

Stone looked at her in shock at the announcement, then closed his eyes and he buried his face in his hands. When he looked up at Aubree, his cheeks were wet and his body was shaking, but he smiled through his tears. Aubree's heart broke as the full impact of what he'd been forced to suffer the past eleven years slammed into her. He reached for her, and she hugged him fiercely. "Oh, Daddy, I'm so sorry."

After they cried together, mourning the loss of all those years, they finally pulled themselves together and wiped away their tears. Stone took his daughter's face in his hands, and looking into her eyes, said, "At least now we have a future to look forward to." He hugged her again.

Aubree and Torben then repeated the details of what they had learned from Lieutenant Jensen minutes earlier. Then Aubree hurried back to her suite to check on Vanessa, who had seemed dazed and withdrawn ever since the disturbing conversation on the phone with Reginald. She'd waited for a little while to break the news about Reginald to the twins, but Aubree knew she had likely just told them.

Brandi and Ryan were outside on the balcony and Vanessa lay on the bed with her back turned toward the door. Aubree waited a moment, and then she joined the twins on the balcony. They were sitting on the deck chairs, their little shoulders slumped, staring into the distance. Aubree knelt between them and put her arms around their little shoulders. The moment she touched them, she felt them begin to tremble. "I'm so sorry," she said.

She was aware of them wiping tears away after a minute or two of quiet sobbing. She finally stood up and moved to the railing. Almost in unison, they followed her. She turned toward them, and they melted into her arms. She held them for a long time. "Are you going to be okay?" she asked.

Brandi nodded as Ryan said, "Yeah, we'll be okay," and took her hand in his.

Together they went back inside. Aubree rubbed her eyes as she noticed the way her mom was quietly watching her and the twins from the bed. A tentative smile touched her lips, and a look of understanding passed between them as the twins went to their mother, hugging her. There was a lot of hurt and deep wounds that would have to be healed, but somehow she knew that everything was going to be all right.

\* \* \*

Special Agent Burke Spiker entered Captain Newkirk's office late that afternoon, having just been dropped off by helicopter. He was a stocky man who stood about five-foot-ten, with neatly trimmed brown hair and intelligent green eyes. At forty-six, he was a veteran agent. He introduced himself to all in the room, which included the captain, his first officer, Stone—who had been brought from the infirmary for this meeting—Vanessa, Aubree, Brandi, Ryan, and Torben. To Torben he said in flawless German, "I hear good things about you, young man. I'm stationed in Germany. I flew by jet to Stockholm and from there to this ship on a helicopter."

Then he turned to the others. "Sorry about that. I just wanted Torben to know that I speak German." He grinned and added, "I don't know that there's much more briefing you need from me before you make this call. So let's make some plans and some notes, and then we'll see if Captain Hook—I mean, Nadif—will speak to you." He chuckled.

An hour later, Torben's palms sweated and he could feel perspiration on his face. He told himself that he shouldn't be nervous, that he'd gained a lot of experience with this type of thing lately. He tried to calm himself as his call went through. Nadif answered in a language Torben didn't understand, but he spoke in German as he once again imitated the late German pirate. "This is Cord. You'll need to speak either German or English," he said.

"Cord, you were not to call me! What are you doing?" Nadif asked angrily in English.

"There has been a major development," Torben said. "You need to know about it."

"Where are you?" Nadif demanded.

"I'm in Berlin."

"At least you followed that order. This had better be good."

"Do two hundred million American dollars sound okay?" Torben asked.

"What are you talking about?" Nadif said. "Come to the point."

"An American by the name of Reginald Kern called me and—" Torben began, but he was interrupted by an enraged Nadif.

"Where did you hear that name?" the pirate demanded.

"I don't know how he got this number, but he has it. And he called me," Torben tried again. This time Nadif did not interrupt, so Torben went on, following the script he and Special Agent Spiker had drafted. "Reginald is prepared to send you the automatic weapons and me the money—the two hundred million—when we return his wife to him."

"You fool. We don't have his wife. She is dead. You know that. You killed her," Nadif said angrily.

"I know that, but Kern doesn't. He says he can deliver the money to me in Berlin tomorrow."

"You better not be trying to pull something, Cord, or you're a dead man."

Nadif was right about Cord being dead, but he didn't know it. "I'm not trying to pull anything," the fake Cord said.

"I'll be there," Nadif said before Torben could make that suggestion himself. "You name the location and time. But I want one thing very clear. Reginald Kern had better be there or I'll have your head."

"He'll be there," Torben promised. "And when he has delivered the money and is given his cut, he will arrange for the delivery of the weapons." He paused for a moment then said, "Nadif, Kern told me he doesn't trust you, so you can't tell him you will be there too. He needs to think he is meeting only me. And he specifically told me that you are not to call him until the money is exchanged."

"Then that's how it will be," Nadif said in a dangerous tone. "Now, when and where will the exchange take place? And what do we do about the fact that we don't actually have his wife?"

"I've told Kern that his wife is in St. Petersburg. He has agreed to have a Russian associate of his there to meet her. She won't be there, but he thinks she will be, and you'll have your money and guns long before he figures out that we've duped him," Torben said. "Now, he insists that we meet in a public place, a place filled with people. There is a location here in Berlin called the Sony Center. And in the Sony Center is a giant yellow giraffe made of Legos. He will meet us right in front of the giraffe. We'll meet you there at noon, Berlin time."

"I will be there, Cord. And it had all better go as you say."

"It will," Torben told him. "But remember, Kern doesn't know you will be there."

After the call was over, Special Agent Spiker said, "I hope he comes through. I'll head there now. And I'll have some men with me who resemble both your late friend Cord and Mr. Kern. With any luck at all, the German authorities and I will have him in custody by noon tomorrow."

"If I can talk Reginald Kern into it, he'll be there too, and you won't need your look-alike officer. It's still doubtful whether I'll be able to convince him," Torben said, "but I can try. It would be nice if you could get both men at once."

# CHAPTER TWENTY-FIVE

Torben and Agent Spiker had only just arrived at Aubree's suite to check on the family when Torben received a call from Reginald Kern. It had been half an hour since they had first spoken, and he quickly picked up the phone. "Do you have the information I requested?" he asked abruptly.

"Not all of it." He glanced at Vanessa, who had a disgusted look on her face. "Your wife is having a difficult time getting the information she needs. She says she keeps the documents she needs in her office at her studio," Torben said.

It was true that Vanessa kept the information in a small safe in her studio, but she had informed Torben that she kept the same information in a safety deposit box at a bank in San Diego that Reginald knew nothing about. Reginald said, "I can send one of my law partners there without him knowing what he's after. Then, after he gets the documents, he can give me the information. I assume it's in a safe. All I need is the combination and for her to call the studio and tell them that one of my associates will be coming."

"You will need the money in cash by noon tomorrow," Torben responded. "And you must be in Berlin to deliver the money at that time. I will be there, and your wife will be in St. Petersburg." He forced an edge into his voice. "I get the money and you get your wife back. Meet us at noon in front of the giant Lego giraffe at the Sony Center. And have your man in St. Petersburg in front of the fountains in the gardens at Peterhof. And don't be late in either place."

"Two hundred million is a lot of money to get in cash in such a short time," Reginald hedged, and for a moment Torben worried he was going to back out. But then he added, "Don't worry, I'll get it. And I do have associates in Russia. I'll have someone in St. Petersburg so you can deliver her to him"

"I'll see you in Berlin," Torben said and terminated the call. "You're sure he can't get the money out quicker than that?" he asked Vanessa.

"I know he can't. I can't either."

"Do you think he'll show up at your studio, or will he send someone else?" Special Agent Spiker asked.

"He'll send someone, just like he said." She shook her head. "If he can make it to Berlin by tomorrow at noon, he must be close by, at least somewhere in the Baltic," she said. "I'm sure he wanted to track us down. I just hope he's in Berlin tomorrow." She wrapped her arms tightly around herself. "I'm frightened of what he might do to any of us. I won't feel like we're safe until he's in custody." She shook her head sadly. "I still can't believe he's doing this to me. He's my husband!" The anguish on her face was almost too much for Torben to bear.

"If his partner takes the information from your safe, how will you be able to move your money before he gets it?" Burke Spiker asked.

Vanessa gave a fleeting smile. "I have the information in more than one place. And my accountant, one that Reginald knows nothing about, also has the information. I'll call him with some instructions. My money will be secure."

* * *

Later that morning in California, one of the lawyers from Kern's firm came to the studio. Kevin and his men stayed out of sight and let the man get the information he was after from the safe. When he left, Kevin's forces left as well. Kevin had hoped that Reginald would show up himself, despite the odds against it, and after the other man left, he shook his head in disappointment. After what he'd learned the past few days, he honestly believed that Reginald was capable of stooping to whatever depths it took for him to get what he wanted. He couldn't imagine that he would turn up in Berlin, but if he did, the warrants were in place, and the German authorities had agreed to arrest him.

Knowing what he knew now, Kevin was sure of one thing: Reginald had reason to believe that Stone could do him great damage in the courts. And for that reason, he believed Stone was in more danger than the others.

The Gentry case was almost wrapped up. Kevin had the answers, but he didn't have all the arrests made that needed to take place. When Reginald Kern was netted, Kevin would relax, but not until then.

However, there was one important step Kevin had achieved; a superior court judge had formally thrown out the murder conviction for which Stone had spent ten years of his life in prison. He had called the captain as soon as the ruling had been made to let him know that Stone would no longer need to be guarded. When the call had been transferred to Stone and Kevin personally told him the good news, he didn't sound bitter, just grateful. There was no longer a parole, and no charges were pending against him. Even though he was abroad on a forged passport, Kevin chose not to pursue that. The man had suffered more than enough already. He needed to be left in peace for now.

\* \* \*

On the ship, Vanessa and her three children stayed busy and enjoyed one another's company. Stone spent much of his time with them. And although Brandi and Ryan were fearful at first, and Vanessa seemed a bit withdrawn at times, Stone showed a gentleness with all of them that Aubree hadn't remembered seeing as a child. He teased Brandi and Ryan, getting them to laugh, and asked them about their interests, showing them that he truly wanted to get to know them. Aubree watched it all with a growing hope in her heart. The only pall cast over the scene was not knowing where Reginald was or what his intentions were. Because of that, when the ship docked in Stockholm, they all stayed on board.

Aubree didn't see Torben all that morning, though she wasn't surprised, considering how busy the ship was when it docked at a port. She kept hoping that he would contact her and tell her that her stepfather had been arrested in Berlin. She glanced at her watch more and more frequently as noon came. She was becoming increasingly worried.

Torben finally called her cell phone while she was having lunch with her mother and the twins. She picked up the call as quickly as she could but could instantly hear the disappointment in his voice when he spoke of the operation in Germany. "Reginald wasn't there. Nadif either. It was a total bust."

"What are we going to do now?" she asked, her heart sinking.

"Special Agent Spiker wants me to try to call Nadif again. I guess I will, but I'm not so sure it'll work."

"When are you calling him?" she asked.

"Soon," Torben said. "Agent Spiker said not to wait for him to come back, that he was going to wait in Berlin just in case something turns up there."

"I'd like to be with you when you call Nadif," Aubree ventured.

"I'd appreciate the moral support," he agreed. Then his tone brightened as he added. "But Aubree, there is a little good news. I got a call right before Agent Spiker and his men went to the Sony Center. It was from the hospital in Helsinki. Hild's going to make it. It will take time, but they expect him to make a complete recovery."

Aubree broke into a grin. "That's wonderful news, Torben! I'm so glad he's going to be okay."

"Me too," Torben said seriously. "I feel like a weight's been taken off my shoulders. Hey, one second." The phone went silent for a moment and when he came back on the line he said, "I have to see to a couple passengers, but I'll meet you in your suite in ten minutes, okay?"

Aubree agreed, and soon she and Torben were sitting beside each other on the sofa as Torben raised the phone to make the call. She scooted closer to him, partially so she could hear the conversation and partially just to enjoy being right next to the man she had come to care so much about.

Nadif answered after several rings. "You didn't come," Torben said.

"I couldn't, whoever you are," Nadif said with a bite to his voice.

"What are you talking about?" Torben protested.

"I have contacts in Russia," Nadif said coldly. "I finally learned that Cord is dead. Your game is up. And so is that of your friend, Reginald Kern."

The call was abruptly terminated. "He's on to us," he said, fear in his voice. "I need to try to call Reginald. He's done some bad things, but I feel like I need to warn him that Nadif could be a danger to him."

Aubree hesitated, but then said, "You're right. See if you can reach him."

Torben tried to call him on Cord's phone. But he got no answer. "Try mine," Aubree said. "Maybe he's avoiding Cord's number."

Again there was no answer. "We'll try again later," Torben said. "But right now, I think I need to go check with the captain and see if anyone is scheduled to join the cruise here. And if there is, I'll personally watch for Reginald until everyone is on the ship this evening. We can't have him slipping on board."

"And I'll watch with you," Aubree said firmly. "But I need to let my family know what has happened first."

\* \* \*

Kevin was disappointed but not surprised that neither Nadif nor Reginald had been captured in Berlin. But back in California, things were happening. At the moment, Kevin was on his way to Long Beach. The stolen weapons from the Presidio in Monterey had been found, and three men were in custody. He already knew that Reginald was behind the theft, but he wanted to confirm it with further evidence if he could.

However, after two hours of grilling the three suspects, Kevin and the federal authorities involved in the interrogations were all convinced that none of the men knew who they were working for. It would take more time to tie Reginald to the theft with enough evidence to convict him.

Later, talking to Vanessa's accountant, Kevin discovered that the money in Vanessa's overseas accounts had not been touched. In fact, as near as anyone had been able to determine, there had not even been an attempt made. Kevin made a stop at Reginald's law firm on his way back home to question the attorney who had accessed the safe at Vanessa's studio. And although the man admitted that he was doing a favor for Reginald, he denied knowing where Reginald Kern had called him from.

\* \* \*

The ensuing days seemed like an eternity as Aubree constantly wondered where Reginald was and what he was doing. However, she enjoyed the cruise, especially her time with Torben. But the dreaded day finally arrived. Stone, Vanessa, Aubree, and the twins had returned to Copenhagen on the *Stargazer,* and they were leaving the ship there. It was hard to believe that she and her family would be back in California the next day.

Aubree's heart was breaking as she kept a sharp lookout and finally saw Torben approaching on the dock. His eyes seemed to hold conflicting emotions. When he reached her, he took one of her hands in both of his and looked into her eyes. "Come here for a moment," he said. Aubree was grateful for the privacy as he led her to the other end of the dock where they could talk without being overheard.

Torben turned her gently until she was facing him. They each looked deeply into the other's eyes as if trying to read what the other was thinking.

It was Aubree who broke the silence. "I've decided to have the missionaries teach me after I get home."

Torben smiled at her. They had spent many hours talking about the Church when he was off duty the past few days. "I'm glad," he said.

Then Torben took her face gently in his hands and pulled her closer. After a slight hesitation, his lips found hers. It was a sweet and tender kiss, and Aubree wished it would never end. But when Torben finally pulled back, there was turmoil in his eyes.

"I'm sorry, Aubree, I hadn't intended to do that."

Aubree bit her bottom lip and looked down, trying to hide her hurt from him. Torben sighed and took her in his arms. "Aubree, we come from very different worlds. We have very little in common. You come from wealth and social standing. I am from a very poor family and a town with practically no social life. You're used to the good things of the world. I'm used to very little." Torben paused and cleared his throat before continuing. "I never expected to meet someone like you on the ship. I've resisted my feelings, and I've tried to hold back because I didn't want to hurt you. You've suffered too much already." He lifted a hand to stroke her cheek gently. "But you've had a bigger impact on me than I could have ever dreamed." He looked away.

"Do you think it's possible that we might see each other again?" she asked, even as she felt like he was slipping away from her.

"I don't know. I just don't know. I need time to sort things through, and so do you."

Aubree's heart sank, but she leaned her head against his chest and tried to soak in all of him before she had to let him go. Torben tightened his hold on her and held her close. She put her arms around his waist and clung to him until it was time to say good-bye. After rejoining her family again, Torben gazed at her longingly, his blue eyes reflecting the anguish he felt. Then he said softly, "Please keep in touch."

Aubree couldn't speak, so she simply nodded, even as she wondered what the future could possibly hold for the two of them.

* * *

News awaited them when the Kerns and the Lansings landed at the Los Angeles International Airport seventeen days after Aubree and the twins had left for the cruise. Kevin was waiting at the baggage claim area to meet them. Aubree hugged him unashamedly. Ryan and Brandi hugged him too, and as Aubree watched them clinging to him, she saw pain in his caring face. She wondered what could possibly be wrong now. Her stomach began to roll.

Kevin looked at Vanessa as he spoke, his expression somber. "Reginald won't be standing trial," he said after they had collected their bags and moved to a quiet area a few yards up the terminal.

"Why not?" Stone asked with a frown on his face.

"He was found dead in Berlin several hours ago," he said. "He had been shot in the back and was dumped in the Spree River. Some children playing along the riverbank at the edge of Tiergarten Park found his body washed up on the shore. The police there say that he had been dead for several days."

A gasp escaped Vanessa and she searched for a chair and sank into it, burying her face in her hands.

Stone looked at Vanessa with sympathy in his eyes, and then he asked Kevin, "Did it happen before he was supposed to meet with Nadif?"

"Special Agent Burke Spiker was with the police when they recovered his body. He thinks so. We'll never know who did it, but, of course, Nadif is probably the one, either him or one of his surviving gang," Kevin told them. "Mrs. Kern, I'm so sorry."

Aubree looked at her mother, whose shoulders were shaking now as she cried into her hands. Aubree sat next to her and handed her a tissue she'd pulled from her purse. Then she put an arm around her. "Oh, Mom," she said as her own voice filled with emotion. The two hugged for a long time, until Vanessa's tears finally slowed.

The twins had been standing off to the side. They were both softly crying. Vanessa saw them and reached for them. They came into her arms, and for a few minutes they simply cried together. Eventually, the three of them gained control and the twins stepped away from their mother, hand in hand, their little blond heads close together. Vanessa watched them for a moment, and then she again put her face in her hands.

Stone walked over and placed a hand on Vanessa's shoulder. Startled, she looked up at him. Their eyes held for a moment, and then he said, "I'm sorry too."

Aubree looked at both her mother and father with respect. She loved them. And she looked forward to spending a lot of time with them in the coming weeks and months. As she watched them look at each other at that moment, she couldn't help but hope that they would someday be a family and that the twins would have a father who loved them.

\* \* \*

As they were leaving the baggage area later, Vanessa's agent came striding in, his face like granite and his bald head shining under the airport's fluorescent lights. Vanessa frowned when she saw him, but he continued until he was standing right in front of her, his arms folded and his legs set wide apart. He acknowledged Stone with a mere nod of his head, and then he said, "Vanessa, I know you're angry with me, but I need to explain."

She shot daggers with her eyes and said, "I've been telling myself that the next time I saw you I'd fire you," she said.

"Please don't. I'm sorry for giving you so much trouble," he said, his confident exterior beginning to crack. "You need to understand something."

"What I understand is that you were a huge pain to work with and put up major obstacles in an attempt to keep me from getting to my family," she said sharply. "And I further understand that you tried to threaten my standing with clients when I didn't agree with your priorities. I don't need that kind of person working for me."

"I understand," he said, looking a bit contrite. "But I didn't do any of it maliciously. Reginald called me to tell me that you were under so much stress with your ex-husband being released from prison that you needed to stay at home with him, and that the only way that would happen was if I convinced you. He told me to make sure you stayed, for your own good."

Understanding dawned. Aubree knew exactly what Reginald had been up to. Vanessa knew too. She said, "That doesn't surprise me, but you didn't work for Reginald, you work for me. I need some time."

"I want to keep working with you," Miles said, his face finally showing some real emotion. "I'll make sure that Reginald doesn't interfere again."

Stone took hold of Vanessa's hand and said, "He won't, Miles. Someone else took care of that. He's dead."

\* \* \*

One of the first things Vanessa did after they got home that afternoon was to call Francesca Bruno, who was staying with her son while the family was on their cruise. Francesca was overjoyed and told Vanessa she'd be over as soon as possible. "I've been worried sick about all of you." Then she abruptly asked, "What are you having for dinner tonight?"

Vanessa chuckled. "We don't have any idea, but we'll—"

"I'll be there in fifteen minutes and stir something up," she said.

Francesca's face lit up like the sunrise when she entered the mansion. She hugged Aubree and the twins, exclaiming over each of them. Her face lit up when she saw Stone sitting in an easy chair on the far side of the room. "Guess who's visiting us for dinner," Vanessa said with a smile.

"Mr. Lansing!" she squealed, then reigned in her emotions, clearly embarrassed. "I mean, it is a pleasure to see you, sir." She glanced at Vanessa, her eyes full of questions she would never be so bold to ask. Then she apologetically added, "I'll go get dinner started."

"Not yet," Vanessa said. "Wouldn't you like to know what happened on our trip? And more importantly, what happened in our house that horrible day of the murder?"

"I haven't heard a word. And I would like to know, but I know my place. I couldn't ask, now could I? I was just hoping and praying that the nice detective, Lieutenant Jensen, would figure it out. I am so glad it wasn't Mr. Lansing. But I've been at my son's house, and I haven't watched the news or read a paper or anything like that," she explained.

"Then sit down and we'll tell you," Vanessa invited. She turned to the twins. "You kids can go play if you'd like to. You don't have to stay and listen to this." Still very somber, the two of them walked side by side from the room and into the hallway.

"Mr. Kern had something to do with it, didn't he?" Francesca asked hesitantly after she was seated and the twins were gone.

Vanessa nodded slowly, glancing at Stone. "It was his fault that Stone was convicted, but he didn't kill Olin Gentry himself," Vanessa said.

"That's just as bad," the cook said with a scowl as she looked toward Stone. "You lost eleven good years of your life and your wife and your daughter because of him."

"But I got them back," Stone said and then paused. "Or at least I hope I have." His voice was husky, and his eyes met Vanessa's from across the room. Something seemed to pass between the two of them, and it was almost as if no one else were present.

After a long moment, Vanessa reluctantly broke the tender connection and turned to Francesca. "Reginald is dead. He was murdered in Berlin."

"What was he doing there?" Francesca asked, her eyes wide with shock.

"That's part of what we have to tell you," Stone said.

"Then tell me. But start with who shot the nanny's boyfriend. It had to have been the guy Mr. Lansing and I saw that day."

"No, it wasn't him," Vanessa said. "It wasn't even a murder. Bridget Summer killed him herself, but it was in a struggle. Olin Gentry had gone back into the bedroom after Stone left the house. But Stone had forgotten the papers he'd come to get, so he went back in. Meanwhile, Olin had thought he was gone, so he decided to steal some of my jewelry. He already knew where I kept it. He went back into the bedroom, but Bridget ran after him and begged him not to steal from me. Olin had found Stone's pistol where he kept it hidden in the dresser. He had even taken it out and loaded it. He'd intended to steal that, too. When Bridget came back in to stop him from stealing the jewelry, he was holding the gun."

Francesca interrupted. "What about the skinny guy running outside the house?" she asked.

"His name is Leroy Sanders," Vanessa told her. "He's Bridget's half-brother—although according to Lieutenant Jensen, they've been estranged for some time. Stone didn't see Leroy in the house because he was in the study where he'd been begging Bridget for some money when her boyfriend came in. They'd argued there, but when Olin headed for the bedroom to get 'something worthwhile,' as he put it, Bridget followed but her brother stayed in the study. Stone and Bridget and Olin had the argument that Aubree heard first. Stone told him to leave, and he did, but he went right back in there when Stone left the house." She shook her head, clearly still in disbelief. "That second time, he and Bridget were arguing, and then they started fighting. Leroy came in too and started shouting at Olin. The gun, which Olin had threatened Bridget with when she came into the room and saw him stealing, was in both their hands as they wrestled for it. Bridget had gotten ahold of the trigger, and the gun went off. It killed Olin. Bridget and her brother got scared. He ran out of the house. That was when you saw him from one angle and Stone saw him from another. Bridget didn't know what to do, but she was so scared that she finally just ran."

"It was self-defense," Francesca said slowly as reality sank in. "She should have stayed instead of running off and letting Mr. Lansing take the blame."

"She realized that later, so she went to an attorney for advice—the same attorney who had represented her brother in an auto theft case and gotten him off. Leroy told her he was real good," Vanessa said.

"Let me guess. Reginald?" the cook asked.

"It was Reginald, all right," Vanessa said. "She went to him and told him what had happened—that she had shot him in a struggle over the gun. She asked him to help her know what to say when she talked to the police because she wanted to turn herself in rather than let Stone take the fall for it."

"So why didn't she go to the police?" Francesca asked.

"Because Reginald told her not to. He even gave her a lot of money, got her a new ID, something we've since learned he was very good at, and sent her out of the country," Vanessa explained.

"He not only gave her money and an ID," Stone added, "but he also told her that she'd get life in prison at the very least if she turned herself in. She believed him and it scared her to death. He also told her that he and his partner, George Sedwig, were going to defend me and that they would get me off without implicating her. She took the money and went to England, believing that I would never be convicted. She stayed there, living under the alias Angel Vaughn until just a year or two ago."

"But Mr. Kern and the other lawyer didn't do a very good job," Francesca stated emphatically.

"Sedwig did his best," Stone said, unable to mask the frustration in his voice. "But it turned out that Reginald wanted my money and my wife. He worked against me behind Mr. Sedwig's back. We think he even bribed the cops."

"That awful man," Francesca said with venom in her voice. "But what about her brother? What did he do?"

"He took a different route than his sister. In fact, when I became certain that something was very wrong and that Reginald was dirty was when I saw Leroy talking to Reginald and then recognized Leroy as the man I'd seen the day of the murder," Stone said, his expression twisting as he remembered. "Leroy was after money, just like his sister got. In other words, he was trying to blackmail Reginald," he said.

"I see," Francesca mused. "Did he give him money?"

"He did, because Leroy threatened to go to the police with what he knew if he didn't," Vanessa told her.

Francesca turned to Stone and said, "Mr. Lansing, can you ever forgive me? I should have gone to the police a long time ago. Maybe I could have helped you if I had."

"And maybe not," he said bitterly. "They had me in their sights, and they weren't interested in even looking for anyone else. And, as I just said, Reginald very likely bribed the police. I was sunk." He lifted his gaze then. "But I do want to thank you for going to Lieutenant Jensen when you did. It was what you told him that started his investigation in the right direction. Because of what you did, my conviction has been vacated."

"I'm still so sorry that you spent those terrible years in prison for something you didn't do. Now tell me what happened to Mr. Kern," she said, her expression sober.

They told Francesca about how Reginald had somehow become involved with pirates and had lied about what Stone said about Aubree. They explained how he'd arranged the cruise and that he had planned all along to make an excuse at the last minute so he wouldn't be going.

They also told her how he had used Vanessa's manager, Miles Jordan, to attempt to keep her from going on the trip.

His plan all along had been for Aubree and the twins to be kidnapped by pirates and demand a huge ransom from Vanessa's private bank accounts to get them back. Meanwhile, a large portion of her money would end up in Reginald's hand without her knowing he was ever involved. Francesca could hardly believe her ears when she learned that Reginald had arranged for the theft of a large shipment of firearms to go to the pirates and that he had planned to use Vanessa's fortune to pay the ransom. In return, Stone explained to her, that same money would have been paid back to him in exchange for the stolen firearms.

"Had it not been for Stone deciding to risk breaking his parole and coming to watch out for us, I would have been killed, murdered by one of the pirates," Vanessa said, looking at Stone with tears brimming in her eyes. And they went on to explain what happened that day in St. Petersburg.

"I guess the pirates thought that if Vanessa was dead, Reginald would inherit her estate and still be able to get to her money," Stone explained, his eyes cold and angry.

After telling her about the pirate attack, Stone said, "Reginald disappeared from Los Angeles. His office claimed he was out of state on business. But we believe he was coming to find me since he had failed to get rid of me when the pirates' plans were foiled. The man, Nadif, who was to get the guns, was angry with Reginald. I'm sure it'll never be proven, but after his body turned up in a river in Berlin with a bullet in it, the authorities believe that he was killed by Nadif or someone working for him."

Francesca looked from Vanessa to Stone, overwhelmed by the tale she heard, and said, "I don't know what else to say besides you need the best meal I can prepare. Will you give me two hours?"

"Whatever you need," Vanessa said gratefully as the cook rose to her feet.

"Then dinner will be at seven," she said and hustled off to the kitchen to resume her job.

# EPILOGUE

*Three months later*

October 30th was a big day for Aubree—it was both her baptism day and her nineteenth birthday. To Aubree's great joy, Ryan and Brandi, with Vanessa's permission, were also being baptized. They were scheduled to be at the chapel shortly before five that evening. Both of her parents were planning to be there, as well as lots of new friends from the ward and stake. Kevin and Rosanne Jensen and their children were also coming. At her request, Kevin was going to perform the baptisms.

Aubree smiled, feeling butterflies in her stomach as she combed her hair, tying it into a loose ponytail. She thought about the two missionaries who had taught her the discussions and had become such good friends. She recalled how surprised she'd been when they had shown up at the mansion and introduced themselves as Sister Elwood and Sister Gonzales. She had expected young men, like Torben. But the sisters had been excellent missionaries. The twins adored them, and even Vanessa had listened in on many of the discussions.

Francesca, although a devout Catholic, had also been invited to the baptism. Since their return from the Baltic, she had become even closer to the three children and Vanessa. She seemed like part of the family now. She had even been invited to move into the mansion, something Reginald had strictly forbidden any of the servants from doing. She had promised to prepare a delicious meal for everyone who wanted to come to the mansion after the baptismal ceremony. It was to be a combined celebration for both the baptisms and Aubree's birthday.

By four thirty, everyone was ready to go to the church. Even Stone had arrived, having driven over from his apartment. Without further ado, everyone, including Francesca and two other servants, piled into two limousines. As they rode to the church, everyone chattered excitedly about what was going to happen that evening. Aubree listened to them speak without adding much to the conversation, feeling very excited herself—but also a bit sad. Everything was perfect it seemed, except for one thing. She missed Torben more than she thought possible. His being so far away on some foreign sea aboard the *Stargazer* left an empty place deep in her heart.

She and Torben had corresponded by e-mail quite regularly, and they were even able to speak occasionally by phone. He knew of her impending baptism, and in his last e-mail he told her how he wished he could be there, but he would be at sea on a cruise. He seemed sincere, but Aubree wasn't sure where she stood with him. She often recalled his last words to her—that he cared for her but that they were from very different worlds. She struggled to keep the painful thought from dampening her mood, determined to simply be grateful for the time she had shared with him. Nothing could take that away.

Aubree had made friends with many of the young single adults from the ward and stake she was about to become affiliated with. She had even gone on a couple of dates with young men. And the twins had made friends as well. As they entered the church building, several young adults passed them in the hallway speaking words of congratulations to Aubree and the twins.

After they were dressed in white and seated on the front row of the Relief Society room with Kevin Jensen, the seats behind Aubree began to fill. She looked back a couple of times. Many of her new friends were there, and a lot of adults had come as well. Ryan and Brandi were also excited at all the Primary children who had come and waved excitedly to their new friends.

Aubree looked at the clock on the wall and realized with a tingle up her spine that it was finally time to begin. Aubree and the twins faced forward. They paid close attention to the bishop and his counselors, who were seated at the front. The bishop conducted, welcoming all who were present. There was a song and prayer, then each of the sister missionaries who had taught Aubree gave a short talk. Then, before Aubree knew it, it was time for the baptism.

The bishop announced that the twins would be baptized by Brother Jensen, the man who had first introduced them to the Church. Then a smile spread across his features and he said, "A young man who was also very influential in their conversion will baptize Aubree. Brother Torben Davidsen will baptize Aubree first, and then Brother Jensen will baptize the twins."

Aubree's heart began to pound. It couldn't be. Torben was thousands of miles away. His family needed the money he earned—he couldn't afford such a trip. She stood up and looked around, hoping beyond hope that she hadn't imagined the bishop's words. But there he stood—the most wonderful sight she had ever seen. Torben had apparently slipped into a seat in the back corner. He was dressed all in white, and his bright red hair shone like polished copper.

Her heart nearly bursting with joy, she proceeded toward the font, and he met her at the door there. He looked deep into her eyes and whispered, "I couldn't miss this day."

"Thank you for coming. You don't know how much this means to me," she whispered in return, her eyes filling with tears.

Torben then took her by the hand and led her into the font. As she held his hand tightly and gently closed her eyes, he solemnly said the baptismal prayer and lowered her into the water. Aubree felt a lightness within her heart as he carefully helped her stand once more, and then they both stood in their wet clothes and watched as Kevin baptized the twins—Ryan first, and then Brandi.

After the ceremony, there was a grand procession to the mansion where Francesca, assisted by two of the other servants, served an exquisite meal to nearly one hundred people.

As they waited for dessert to be served, Stone tapped his glass with a spoon and asked for everyone's attention. He said, "Vanessa and I have an announcement. And we need her cook and the others in here for this."

As Francesca and her helpers entered, Torben and Aubree looked at each other. Aubree's eyes were wide, and she realized she was holding her breath.

Stone took Vanessa's hand, and she slowly rose to her feet, her eyes shining like a girl's. "To say the least, it's been a rough few years for us," he said, drawing a few quiet chuckles from the assembly. "But I never stopped loving this wonderful woman. And, thank goodness, she still loves me." His voice grew husky with emotion. "We plan to be married again. Most of you here don't know us, but we thank you for accepting our children and making them a part of your church. Who knows, maybe someday you'll get us as well."

He looked directly at Kevin. "We owe a special thanks to four important people today," he said. "If it were not for Lieutenant Jensen, I shudder to think what might have happened. He did what other officers before him had failed to do. He investigated until he arrived at the truth. And he, along with his family, reached out in love to Aubree, Ryan, and Brandi."

Kevin nodded modestly. Then Stone said, "And to Francesca, we owe our deepest gratitude. She courageously came forward and gave information to Lieutenant Jensen that put events in motion that would end up in my exoneration."

Francesca wiped her eyes with a tissue as those in the large dining room looked her way.

"And finally, my deepest thanks to my wonderful daughter, Aubree, and her very good friend Torben Davidsen. They are heroes in every sense of the word. My family—myself included—would not have survived our ordeal at sea had it not been for him," he said. He looked straight at Torben and added, "We're indebted to you, Torben. Thank you for teaching our daughter to pray. I truly believe that her prayers brought the blessings of God to all of us. I've never been much of a God-fearing man, but I am now, and it's because of you two young people."

To Aubree's amazement, through tear-blurred eyes, she saw her father cry in front of everyone, most of whom were strangers. And her mother did the same. Her father wiped his eyes and said, "I need to say one more thing. Ryan and Brandi, I would like to be your father. If you'll have me, I'll try to be the father I wasn't to Aubree when she was little. I already love you like you are my own."

The two little towheads flew from their chairs and threw their arms around Stone's waist. His offer had been accepted.

As dessert was served, Aubree sighed in happiness. The day truly had been one of the most perfect she had ever experienced. And yet one mystery hadn't been solved for her. How could Torben afford to come to her baptism? After dessert, the guests slowly filtered out, and she looked toward Torben, who still sat chasing a few crumbs around his plate. He seemed troubled somehow, and she couldn't imagine what the problem was. She took his arm and led him outside where they wandered far from the house on the huge estate.

"This is unbelievable," he said as they walked past a fountain making gentle bubbling noises as it crossed through a stone garden. "It's beautiful."

He stopped to run his fingers over the stones, taking a deep breath as he did so. "All of this is just for you and your family?" he asked.

She nodded, worried about the tone of his voice as he spoke. When they passed the tennis court he said nothing, but he still seemed distant. At the stables, he again stopped. "Who do the horses belong to?" he asked, avoiding her eyes.

She couldn't keep the quivering from her voice when she said, "Some are ours, some belong to friends. We stable them all here."

"Who takes care of them?" he asked.

"We have a couple of stable hands who do that," she said.

"I see," he responded, sounding increasingly troubled.

Aubree watched him. He kept shaking his head, and when he finally met her gaze, there was something in his eyes she couldn't quite define.

They eventually came to a small canyon situated at the edge of the property. There was a bench there that Aubree had always loved to sit on, where she could gaze across the canyon at the beautiful homes on the other side.

Torben seemed to have turned inward, she realized, as they sat down together. The silence still stretched between them. She had imagined them sitting here peacefully and talking about everything under the sun, but that somehow felt impossible. Something was very wrong, and she hoped that this wasn't about to be a disastrous ending to a perfect day. Torben was holding her hand, but he released it and got to his feet. She sat and watched him. Finally, he turned to her. Nervously, she rose to her feet as well.

"You probably wonder how I was able to come today," he said.

"Yes, that crossed my mind a few times," she said, trying to sound lighthearted while feeling anything but.

"Two people made it possible," he said.

"Who?" she asked.

"Captain Newkirk said he would just have to sail the ship without a security officer for a few days. He told me to come. He told me that I had earned the right to some paid vacation. He's been very good to me. I even got a large raise."

"He is a good man, but you did save his life and his ship," she reminded him with an attempt at humor.

Torben nodded seriously. "I helped. Others were involved too. Like Lieutenant Jensen, who got the attention of important people, people who could send ships and fighter jets to help us."

"But you played the most important role," she persisted. "And a lot of us will always be grateful to you for that. You said two people. Who was the other one?"

"Your mother paid for my ticket. She insisted that I come. I didn't feel right accepting her help, but I finally decided that being here for you on this special occasion was important enough that I could swallow my pride," he said.

"Torben, I'm just so glad that you could come," she said, reaching out to him once more.

"And so am I, but it's not right that your mother spent so much on me," he insisted, his blue eyes troubled.

"Maybe she spent it on me," Aubree suggested.

He thought a moment. "I suppose you could look at it that way," he agreed.

"My mother is a different person than she used to be. Every day I see differences in her. And it makes me so happy. She wants to give instead of just accumulate more money."

"I'm glad she's such a good mother," he said.

"She is that. And Dad is the father I always wanted but never had—even when he was in our lives before."

He made no response, and she watched as he turned and looked out over the canyon. She hadn't known that one person could care so much for another. She literally ached with love for this young Danish man. But something was still troubling him, and she had to find out what it was.

"Torben," she said softly as she laid her hand on his arm. "Something's wrong. What is it?"

Slowly he turned and faced her. She looked up into those perfect blue eyes of his, and he began to slowly move his head back and forth.

Then, at last, he spoke again. "Aubree," he said, "when I knew that I was coming to see you on your baptism day, I was excited. But now that I'm here and have spent time in your home, I realize more than ever what different worlds we come from."

Her heart nearly stopped beating. She didn't want to hear this. But she said nothing, trying very hard to keep any emotion from showing on her face.

"Your home is amazing, and it must be worth millions and millions of dollars," he said in a strained voice. "I knew your family was rich, but I guess I didn't really understand how rich. Twenty or thirty homes in my town would fit on your property. My father's house would fit in a small section of yours. Even the servants' house is much larger than our place. Everything is so beautiful that I wonder if I dare touch anything. Your house is a mansion. Mine is a little home with a thatched roof."

He stopped and looked at her, his eyes pleading for understanding. Aubree's heart was breaking. She couldn't hold it in any longer. She turned from Torben so he wouldn't see her sadness as tears escaped from her eyes. She had tried to prepare herself for this, but she had failed miserably. She couldn't understand how he had worked his way so deeply into her heart in such a short time. Frustrated, she wiped at her cheeks, but more tears rushed down to replace the ones she'd wiped away.

Torben reached out and placed his big hands gently on her shoulder. He turned her so she was facing him. She still couldn't meet his eyes, so she buried her face in his chest, and his arms went around her, pulling her close.

Aubree took a few deep breaths to calm herself, and then she spoke in a quiet voice, without looking at him. "Torben, I love you, and I want you to be happy. And if that means that you and I can't be together—"

Before she could say anything else, Torben's mouth had closed on hers, leaving her suddenly breathless. When the kiss ended, Torben looked at her seriously and said, "I can't imagine anyone but you. I love you too, Aubree."

Aubree looked at him in wonder and confusion as she tried to steady her beating heart. "I guess I don't understand what's wrong, then."

Torben took her hands in his, tenderly kissed her fingers, and then said, "I realized more than ever today how very different our lives are. I can't ask you to leave everything you know behind. I don't have wealth and station in Denmark like you are used to here. I'll never make much more than what is needed to live on. And," he continued with a chuckle, "you don't speak Danish." He grew serious again when she didn't respond to his humor. "Aubree, what are you thinking?"

Aubree clearly surprised him when she answered. "Why can't you ask that of me, Torben? Why can't you let me choose whether or not I'm willing to leave everything behind, as you say? Money isn't what makes someone happy. Love is. Until a few months ago, I was lonely and unhappy. Money was there, and some love, but not the kind of love I needed. Then I found love, both from my family and from you and from members of the Church. I've been truly happy for the first time in my life. And," she said, her eyes narrowing, "do you really think that I couldn't learn Danish?"

Torben's eyes were wide as he took in all of her words. Then, stroking her hands, which he'd continued to hold, he swallowed, looking nervous. He studied her intently, wrestling with his thoughts. Finally, with a newfound resolution, he swallowed, his eyes locked on hers, and asked, "Aubree, will you marry me?"

Aubree froze as she took in his words.

"I'm sorry," Torben stammered, his face reddening quickly, "I know we don't know each other as well as we could if we hadn't been separated these last few months—"

"Yes!" Aubree cried out, throwing her arms tightly around his neck.

"Yes?" repeated Torben, suddenly perplexed.

"Yes, I will marry you," Aubree cried again, her eyes shining.

Torben stared at her and then burst out in exhilarated laughter as he hugged her so close her feet left the ground. He spun her around several times before he gently set her back down. He looked deep into her dark brown eyes as he tenderly brushed her hair out of her face. "Aubree Lansing, I love you." Then, ever so gently, he pressed his lips against hers as they shared a kiss filled with the promise of a happy future.

"Aubree," he said hesitantly a few minutes later, "you know that we won't be able to be married for a year."

"Why a year?" she asked, surprised.

"Because new members of the Church can't go to the temple until they've been in the Church for a year," he explained. "I'd like to marry you in the temple in Denmark."

Aubree relaxed, her face glowing. "I'd like to be married in the temple too. It sounds like we've set a date. And by then, I will have learned Danish," she added as she winked at him.

Laughing, he scooped her up into his arms, and the two made their way back to the house to share their happy news.

# ABOUT THE AUTHOR

 Clair M. Poulson retired after twenty years in law enforcement. During his career he served in the U.S. Military Police Corps, the Utah Highway Patrol, and the Duchesne County Sheriff's Department, where he was first a deputy and then the county sheriff. He currently serves as a justice court judge for Duchesne County, a position he has held for nineteen years. His nearly forty-year career working in the criminal justice system has provided a wealth of material from which he draws in writing his books.

Clair has served on numerous boards and committees over the years. Among them are the Utah Judicial Council, an FBI advisory board, the Peace Officer Standards and Training Council, the Utah Justice Court Board of Directors, and the Utah Commission on Criminal and Juvenile Justice.

Other interests include activity in the LDS Church, assisting his oldest son in operating their grocery store, ranching with his oldest son and other family members, and raising registered Missouri Fox Trotter horses.

With this latest book, Clair has published seventeen novels, many of them bestsellers.

Clair and his wife, Ruth, live in Duchesne and are the parents of five married children. They have twenty-one grandchildren.